andry tried to remember all the
asons why ~~this woman was diff-~~
nits, but he ...

e.

rything about J... ...s
sual appetite. The pale glittering skin, full lips
unusually dark eyes framed by black hair were
lifferent from any other woman he'd known.

crackled with energy and a directness that cut
ough his usual barriers and ...anded sole
us on her own unique qualities.

leaned closer, a glint of desire sparkling like
pixie dust in her enlarged pupils, and Landry's jaw
ensed at his body's immediate tug to draw closer.

e touched his chest with one hand, and even
rough his thick cotton shirt, the heat of her skin
veled downward, and his stomach tightened.

...He had to feel her, taste her, claim

SIREN'S TREASURE

DEBBIE HERBERT

Published in Great Britain 2014
by Mills & Boon, an imprint of Harlequin (UK) Limited,
Eton House, 18-24 Paradise Road, Richmond, Surrey, TW9 1SR

© 2014 Debbie Herbert

ISBN: 978-0-263-91412-2

89-1114

Harlequin (UK) Limited's policy is to use papers that are natural, renewable and recyclable products and made from wood grown in sustainable forests. The logging and manufacturing processes conform to the legal environmental regulations of the country of origin.

Printed and bound in Spain
by CPI, Barcelona

Debbie Herbert writes paranormal romance novels reflecting her belief that love, like magic, casts its own spell of enchantment. She's always been fascinated by magic, romance and gothic stories. Married and living in Alabama, she roots for the Crimson Tide football team. Her oldest son, like many of her characters, has autism. Her youngest son is in the US army. A past Maggie Award finalist in both young-adult and paranormal romance, she's a member of the Georgia Romance Writers of America. Debbie has a degree in English (Berry College, Georgia) and a master's in library studies (University of Alabama).

As always, to my husband and parents for their support.

To my agent, Victoria Lea, Aponte Literary Agency, for her faith in my writing, and to Harlequin Nocturne editor Ann Leslie Tuttle, who gave me a publishing opportunity.

I also want to thank the amazing copy editors and proofreaders at Harlequin who whip my manuscripts into shape and make them shine.

Away down deep in the 'Bama bayou,
You'll find a mysterious Gothic brew
Where Spanish moss drapes ancient oaks,
And sea-slithery lizards and gators croak.
The swampy water creeps ever in,
And lured down many a man has been
By magical, whispering, haunting sounds
Where not another soul is found.
Stay out of the water, whatever you do,
Ain't no telling what will become of you
If you can't resist a quick little dip.
Let me give you a tiny tip:
Should you feel a tug at your feet,
It mightn't be the tide pulling underneath.
Be wary, human, you must beware—
For some say mermaids lurk down there.

"Siren's Song," old folk tune, Bayou La Siryna,
Alabama

Prologue

Placing second or third? Not good enough.

She *had* to win the Undines' Challenge this year at the Poseidon Games, had to discover the reason other merfolk shunned her.

Jet whipped her tail fin and surged forward through the turquoise water—pushing, pushing—speeding through the sea like a rocket, streams of bubbles in her wake. Only one goal consumed her.

Winning.

The adrenaline rush, combined with Jet's superior strength and determination, propelled her ahead of the other merfolk within the first minute. She took a quick peek over her left shoulder and found Orpheous mere feet behind and rapidly closing in.

Her nemesis was gaining.

Jet sped past the Dismals, a barnacle-ridden limestone outcropping, and toward the next hurdle of the race. At the entrance of the honeycombs she cast a quick glance backward. Orpheous grinned, displaying jagged, pointy teeth. His long cobalt hair and teal tail fin distinctly marked him as one of the rare full-blooded members of the notorious Blue Mermen Clan. Ruthlessly aggressive and muscular, his kind usually won most sporting events.

Jet slowed as she slid through the first opening of a large coral with a series of slender gaps. Although beautiful, the hot-pink coral was razor sharp and could gash exposed flesh and scales, causing painful injuries. Each contestant had to maneuver through the marked portals without any part of their body touching the coral. If they did touch, one of the judges on the sidelines would blow a conch shell, signaling the contestant must start over.

Halfway through the coral maze, the muted bellow of conch blasted. Jet's heart tripped. She hadn't touched, had she? She looked at the judges perched on a rock ledge twelve feet away, but they pointed to Orpheous and signaled him to exit and start over.

"Liars!" he screamed, ignoring the stream of blood spiraling upward from a gash on his arm. "I did not touch. You are prejudiced against my clan."

Jet resumed swimming through the narrow twists and turns. She would win and take her place among the strongest and most skilled. Surely then they would respect her.

A quarter mile ahead, the Wrath of Mer loomed. Already, her breath grew shallower in the methane-laced water and her gills flared, struggling to suck in more of the declining oxygen. A methane vent disturbed the water's buoyancy under the mile-long towering rock ledge.

The bubbling fields let Jet know what to expect. As her body hit the area, she propelled forward, as if powered by jet fuel. What a rush! Better than any runner's high she'd experienced on land in human form. She luxuriated a moment in the sensation of near weightlessness.

A mass of black stone was suddenly three feet ahead. She'd miscalculated.

Jet abruptly swished her tail fin to turn but it was too late. She slammed into the rock with her right shoulder and tail fin taking the brunt of the blow. Searing pain radiated from her shoulder down to her fingertips and she drifted downward, fighting unconsciousness. The metallic scent of blood prickled her nose. Jet surveyed her body but didn't see any open wound.

Orpheous is near.

He shot through the swirl of bubbles, almost slapping her face with his tail fin. He leered at her briefly, his hair a storm of blue, before shooting away.

Jet clenched her jaw and thrust both arms forward. Her shoulder pain transformed to a numbing sensation. *Keep going. Don't stop.* She swam out of the methane trap and came to the roofed cavern, selected for its strong crosscurrents.

Piece of salmon cake.

Orpheous entered the cavern and purposely whacked his tail fin against its walls before racing out. The wall appeared to disintegrate as dozens of disturbed gulper eels oozed out of its crevices, their long snaky bodies slithering into the churning water.

Great. She would have to swim through a mass of pissed-off eels.

She made it through without slowing. With her speed, she could overtake him en route to the Devil's Well, an ancient, dormant volcano. But once inside, he would have an advantage.

Jet kept up the rhythmic pattern of swimming that best suited her—extending her arms forward first, then crunching her abs and thrusting out her tail fin. At the volcano's tip, she dived into the narrow passage with Orpheous close by. The light quickly dissipated and Jet extended an arm along the side wall to keep her bearings. Each contestant had to swim the five hundred feet to its bottom and collect a piece of lava rock.

Halfway down, she realized something was wrong. Orpheous had stopped swimming and was moving upward. "Chickening out?" she asked. She swam closer to his vibration until she could make out the blue-white of his teeth.

He exposed his jagged molars in a grin that was half snarl, half glee and held up something in his hand.

Jet fumbled in the darkness until she found his fist, which was closed over a smooth, flat piece of lava rock.

"I've got my token."

Jet's mouth dropped open. "But how? We haven't reached bottom yet."

"I brought it with me. Rules are for losers. Better luck next year." He turned his back, dismissing her.

Anger shot up from the tip of her tail fin to the top of her scalp like an electrical burn. Jet surged forward, bent her body in two and whammed her tail fin into the back of his scalp. A bubbling *argh* sound filtered down. The lava rock loosened from his grip and fell.

"I won't let you cheat me again," she shouted, racing down with Orpheous hot on her tail.

His voice vibrated close behind. "Ever ask yourself why winning means so much to you?"

She frowned. "It just does."

"Look at you." His tone was amused, condescending. "Hair so black it shines blue in the sun. So strong, so competitive. You're nothing like Lily."

"Leave my sister out of it." She hated hearing Lily's

name on his foul blue lips. "You're trying to delay me with stupid chatter.".

"True." His voice was closer. "But the two of you look nothing alike. Ever suspect you are one of us?"

One of the Blue Clan? Impossible. "Never," Jet hissed. She swam faster, all the while expecting Orpheous to grab her tail fin and drag her down into the black abyss. At the volcano's craggy bottom, she extended her fingers until they scraped hardened lava and extracted a loose nugget. Jet surged upward, passing Orpheous moments before he touched bottom.

She pushed on, free of the volcano. Ahead, a crowd of merfolk perched on rocks, waiting for the winner to leap over Rainbow Rock and claim the golden trident.

Jet had envisioned this moment for years. She gathered speed, dived downward and then thrust upward, breaching water. As she crested the rock, she savored the moment—the drops of water coating her naked breasts, the dark blue and purple tail-fin scales glinting in the afternoon sun and her sleek, muscled torso poised in a perfect arc before diving under the sea.

She slowed and came to a halt at the winner's platform, a tall, flat boulder where the head judge sat upon a chair of abalone shell, trophy in hand.

She'd done it! Finally she'd won the grand prize.

Jet held out her hand. Firth, a Blue Merman and former winner, was the honorary head judge. He examined the rock and scowled, blue lips twisting over sharp, pointy teeth.

She looked past him and spotted her mother and cousins seated in the first row, smiling and waving.

Orpheous swam to her side and Firth scowled at his fellow clan member. "You dishonor us. Yet, I must perform my duties." He addressed the crowd. "Jet Bosarge is the winner," he said flatly, then thrust the golden trident into Jet's right hand.

Her arm was still numb from the injury but she managed to close her fist over the solid gold trident, which nearly matched her height. Jet stomped the base of the trident in the sand three times and chanted, "As descendant of Poseidon, I claim my reward."

Instead of the thundering cheer Jet expected, the whistling and applause was decidedly lukewarm. Large swarms of merfolk swam away, moving on to the highly anticipated Siren Song event. Even her mother's chair was now empty.

"You know how this works," Firth said, nodding at the trident. "On land, the trident will shrink to the size of a charm pendant. It contains a onetime wish, good for one year."

Jet bowed her head, eager to get away and watch Lily win the siren contest, but a strong hand closed over her arm. She frowned at the green talons and long fingers resembling seaweed.

"Not so fast," Orpheous said, rubbing her arm suggestively. "Come with me and meet others in your clan."

His breath smelled like fish guts and Jet tried not to visualize those jagged teeth ripping apart some tasty amberjack. "Go away, you thug fish."

Orpheous was seriously getting under her skin. Damn it, she was a Bosarge woman, descended from a long line of mermaids well-known for exceptional beauty and intelligence.

He shrugged. "Deny all you like, but I see Blue in you."

Jet smacked his midsection with her tail fin and he doubled over. She swam as fast as an eel and made her escape. At the crowded Siren Song competition, she saw her family had not saved a place for her at the front of the stage.

Jet regarded her mother and the rest of her family with new eyes. Every one of them was gorgeous, even by mermaid standards: petite, curvy bodies, pale, gleaming skin, lovely pastel hair tints and varying shades of blue eyes spanning from the lightest ultramarine to the deepest cobalt. All dripping with feminine allure and charm.

Not for the first time, Jet considered her own black hair, cut short to prevent drag in the races, and eyes so dark only a hint of brown radiated from the irises. Mom had even chosen the name "Jet" because of their color. No, she wasn't a precious gem like Ruby or Sapphire or Pearl. Jet was nothing more than fossilized wood that had fallen into stagnant waters; so common it could be found on most beaches.

Clearly, she was no delicate aquatic flower like Lily.

A hush swept over the crowd as Lily swam to the front of the rock and took her place. Lily raised a hand and the crowd hushed again.

It was hard to call what came out mere singing. It was a symphony of sound, the epitome of tone meeting strength. Judges swam a hundred yards away, measuring the distance of the sound vibrations.

Jet closed her eyes and let the notes wash over her. Even though Lily could charm humans above, her voice was at its purest undersea with the crystal notes melding in the currents.

Jet gave a little shake and studied the seascape. All the hard training had been for naught. No one cared that she'd won the Undines' Challenge. She scanned the crowd, all in awe of Lily.

At least she had the trident. She would return home, and when Mom arrived later, she would use the trident's onetime wish. Jet tried to catch her mother's eye to wave goodbye, but Adriana's gaze was locked on the fair Lily. Typical.

She pictured Orpheous's leering face. *You are one of us.*

Was this why most merfolk shunned her? Why she felt like an outcast even among her own family? Could it be that her bloodline was mixed with the shunned Blue Clan?

Soon, she would demand the answer.

Chapter 1

Perry's back. Two words that shook Jet's world, but not in a good way. She'd returned home from the Poseidon Games two nights ago, exhausted, when her cousin Shelly had broken the news.

Jet sighed as she scanned the bored, impatient crowd packed inside the government-services waiting room, its ambience a curious mixture of sterility and shabbiness. The old building was painted an institutional green and smelled faintly of disinfectant, mold and stale coffee. In the lobby, cheap metal folding chairs were set up in rows.

Outside, the morning rain beat down in gusting sheets. Jet eyed the few people roaming Main Street, searching for a certain build, that certain shock of brown hair and chiseled profile.

Stop it. You'll see Perry soon enough. And oh, how she'd make him pay. That rat would get on his knees, by

Poseidon, and beg her forgiveness before she sent him on his way.

Oh, no. Huge mistake. She shouldn't have pictured him in that position, those brown eyes staring up at her naked body with hunger. Jet squirmed. *Think of something else.* She closed her eyes, imagined swimming the warm waters of the Florida Keys and scooping up antique cuff links and coins sunk in ships hundreds of years ago, like a child picking up dropped marbles on a school playground.

It wasn't helping. Jet placed a hand over her stomach. Sexual need fierce as a knife wound seared and twisted her guts. Damn, she hated that part of her mermaid nature that intensified sexual hunger. It could be a hindrance if she saw Perry after this meeting as she'd planned. But she had to face him eventually and see what he wanted. She would have to keep her sexual need under control and send him away with the tongue-lashing of the century.

Ugh, tongues lashing. Now she could taste his lips and tongue in her mouth, his long, slow, languid kisses that made her frantic with desire in nanoseconds.

There she went again. She was the biggest fool on the planet to pine for Perry's kisses. He'd been out of prison for weeks. If he'd been languishing in a jail cell for the past three years, missing her and regretting his betrayal, he'd have shown up long before now. Forget him—he'd done the unforgivable.

"Jet Bosarge," the receptionist called out.

She grabbed her backpack, and the man seated across from her frowned. "I've been here longer than you," he grumbled.

She shrugged. "Take it up with them." Jet marched down the labyrinthine hallway until she found a door marked IRS. No one answered her knock, so she opened it and stuck her head in.

The office was tiny and contained an old wooden desk. A metal folding chair, identical to those in the waiting area, was positioned across from it. The IRS could have sprung for better accommodations; it collected enough money to do better than this bare cubbyhole. A cheap, utilitarian clock hung on the wall; its secondhand clicked inconsistently—slow, fast, fast, slow—as if it were spitting out Morse code. She paused, wondering if she were in the right place, until she spotted the nameplate that read Landry Fields.

She dropped her backpack by the chair and stood at the lone rectangular window. Quite a show played outside with the swirling rain pounding the parking-lot pavement.

Jet pressed her face against the cool, damp pane. She loved the rain. Loved every pore on her body drenched in raindrops. The only thing better than land-walking on days like this was swimming undersea during a thunderstorm. She'd swim close to the ocean surface, watching raindrops bounce on top of the water and meld into a white, bubbling cauldron of energy while underneath, the pull of the tide crested and heaved in response to the wind. And if a rain shower coincided with the night of a full moon, the energy was electric with intensity.

She closed her eyes and touched her palms to the glass, imagined swimming under the rain's onslaught right now. Her body came alive, prickling with sensation—

"It's a mess out there, isn't it?" came a voice, low, rumbling and way too close.

Jet jumped and spun around. Her eyes bored into a pin-striped suit covering a broad chest. Her gaze traveled upward, taking in a strong jaw and ice-blue eyes that pinned her as if she were a trapped butterfly the man wanted to dissect.

"Mr. Fields?" she guessed. Her voice came out a touch squeaky and she cleared her throat.

He extended a hand. "Miss Bosarge?"

His grip was firm and brief, but far from impersonal, at least on her end. Her palm tingled from the contact and she had a wild urge to curl her fingers over his hand and never let go.

Insane. Jet hastily withdrew her hand and crossed her arms over her stomach. Fields gestured to the folding chair, his face reflecting no sign that their contact had affected him at all. "Have a seat."

She sank into the chair, feeling underdressed. She usually sported black yoga pants, a T-shirt and sneakers, perfectly fine for helping Lily at the salon or working out at the gym. In honor of this visit, she had slightly altered her normal attire by wearing jeans, a purple long-sleeved top and a purple-and-red scarf. Jet wished she'd taken more time with her appearance and played with Lily's boxes of lotions and potions. At the very least, she could have styled her asymmetrical bob. Oh, well, she had remembered earrings. Maybe her five-carat diamond studs would deflect attention from her plain, unadorned face. Humans seemed to care inordinately about such things.

Under his probing gaze, Jet readjusted the scarf to ensure it completely covered her three-inch gills, which extended from the top of the collarbone to her windpipe on each side of her neck. Although the slotted marks in her flesh were faint, she was careful to keep them covered to avoid questions by any observant human. And this guy looked way too sharp. Jet mentally noted to grow her hair out a few more inches so it would be long enough to cover the gills by the time summer arrived, when scarves and turtlenecks would appear odd. Since her hair grew an inch a week, it should be plenty long enough at summer's advent.

Fields pulled out a single file from the front drawer and placed it on the desk's otherwise bare surface. He opened the file and glanced through it, as if refreshing his memory.

"Your letter stated you only found an irregularity in my tax records," Jet volunteered.

"Mmm-hmm." He kept reading, never looking up, even when the printer kicked up an odd whirring sound, as if a hive of angry hornets had swarmed to life. The noise ended as suddenly as it had started.

Jet stifled an exasperated sigh and started swinging one crossed leg. The small room was stifling. The man's mere presence completely engulfed her senses and she stared at his large hands with the clipped, clean nails. No wedding band, but he wore a ruby ring set in a gold band on his right hand. Some kind of class ring, probably from an elite college. His clothes looked tailored and his facial features bore a patrician vibe. The harsh planes of his face, strong jaw and chilly eyes made him appear stern.

The man certainly didn't fit in with the shabby surroundings. Jet admired his clean, crisp aura and sniffed discreetly, picking up a lingering scent of soap, as if he'd just showered and dressed. And didn't *that* make her squirm. Hell, what was wrong with her today? She didn't even know this man. News of Perry's arrival must have unsettled her more than she first suspected.

The silence got on her nerves. "Since when did our town warrant an IRS office?" she asked. "I don't remember ever seeing one here before."

His gaze stayed fixed on her file as he answered, "It's a temporary field office for tax season. We'll close by the end of May. It's all part of our agency's public service."

Public Service? More like a public nuisance. What was so interesting about her tax records? True, she had bucketloads of money in trust funds, but her inheritance was legit. Her ancestors had always been careful to hire the best attorneys to cover where the real money originated—from expensive undersea trinkets strategically sold in bits and pieces over decades.

He finally gave a small nod and faced her. "I remember viewing your file now. The first thing that caught my attention was the income fluctuation in two of your businesses. Four years ago, you claimed a net annual profit of over fifty thousand dollars with The Pirate's Chest. The business is still listed as open, yet no more profits have been claimed. Then three years ago, another business of yours, The Mermaid's Hair Lair, reported steady profits until it shut down last year. For the past six months, you've been earning an income solely from the interests and profits of various trust funds and stocks."

She couldn't help but notice the slight, contemptuous curve at the corners of his mouth. Jet bristled; it rankled when people assumed she must be some sort of privileged society girl. She'd worked hard to contribute to the Bosarge family fortune with years of physically exhausting and high-risk ventures, reclaiming sea treasure with the rat-bastard Perry Hammonds. Not that she could tell this numbers nerd *that* particular bit of information. "Is inheriting money against the law? It's not like I intend to live off the trust fund forever. I'm reopening The Pirate's Chest. I've already purchased a downtown building and I'm stocking inventory. A big shipment of antique furniture should arrive from Mobile tomorrow."

The auditor remained unruffled and silent while rain splattered the window, loud as a knocking at the door. The beating rain outside created a cozy sense of intimacy in the small room and Jet fantasized what it would be like to lean over the desk and kiss Mr. All-Business-Man until he lost that aloof self-control and had his way with her... Jet shook her head slightly and blinked. This had to stop.

Against her better judgment, she spoke up again, eager to get her mind back on track. "My sister, Lily, and I jointly owned the salon. She's taken an extended leave of absence to travel. We might open it again one day, though." Jet bit the inside of her lip at the white lie. Not likely the beauty shop would reopen; Lily seemed happiest living undersea and using her siren talent to attract mermen.

Fields wasn't interested. "Okay, moving on. In reviewing your inventory and sales at the antiques store, I noted you sold maritime artifacts, some quite rare. Are the manifests for these items on file?"

Jet swallowed. As far as she was concerned, once a ship sank, whatever cargo sank with it became the property of the merfolk. What good was all that treasure sitting at the bottom of the ocean? The sea belonged to the merfolk, not humans, and they could keep it or sell it to dirt dwellers as they chose. But she could hardly tell him that, either. "Of course, I have paperwork," she said coolly. "I also have an excellent accountant who filed my taxes. Perhaps I should have brought either him or my attorney with me. However, your letter phrased this meeting as discussing an irregularity and not a full-blown audit."

"You're always welcome to bring an attorney or accountant. That's perfectly within your rights as a citizen." He studied her, no emotion showing in those frozen eyes.

His face was stern, his manner stiff and formal. "Moving on to your stock portfolio," he said, as if she hadn't voiced a concern. "Over twenty percent of your stock is invested in one company, Gulf Coast Treasures and Salvage, LLC."

Damn. She and Perry had sold, without papers, plenty of shipwrecked, illegal items to that very company. In return, they were given cash, which they used, in part, to purchase stock in the salvage company. Jet kept her mouth shut and merely raised an eyebrow.

The silence between them stretched, but she refused to be the one to break it this time.

"These types of ocean recovery companies are very risky," Fields continued. "Even if they do find treasure, they must have a profitable way to recover items and bring them up to land using approved archaeological methods. And if all *that* is accomplished, there's the thorny issue of who gets a share of the profits—the state, foreign governments, the originating ship's company, distant heirs of the original property—"

So maybe all this wasn't about her, she decided with an internal whoosh of relief. It was about the government clamping down on these industries, making sure they got their own profit cuts. A treasure-salvage company in Tampa had been in the news recently when it recovered over five hundred million dollars worth of silver and gold coins from a colonial-era wreck near Portugal. Naturally, the Spanish government filed an immediate claim of ownership and refused to pay the company any salvage fee.

Jet hated worrying about pesky ownership issues. The mermaid philosophy of finders keepers seemed fairer. She was relieved to be out of business with Perry and leave that aspect of her life in the past where it belonged.

"So call me a risk-taker," she replied with a shrug. "I think it's a good investment. There are over three million known shipwrecks. It's a potential billion-dollar industry." She couldn't resist showing off a little and letting him know why she suspected the IRS had a sudden interest in the maritime salvage industry. "Especially since an American salvage company found three billion dollars worth of platinum on a World War II merchant vessel."

He ignored her mention of the platinum discovery. "But of those millions of shipwrecks, only thirty thousand of them are believed to have valuable lost cargo."

Jet shrugged again. "Your point?"

"We're taking a closer look at these companies. You have a huge amount of money invested in Gulf Coast Salvage, a disproportional amount of your assets."

She surmised it must be difficult for a stodgy man like him to understand people willing to take risky ventures, and suspected the auditor was about to go down a path she didn't want to follow. Jet stood. "Thanks so much for your concern about my portfolio. Warning taken."

He rose also and frowned. "Sit down, Miss Bosarge." This time his voice had an edge as sharp as a stingray's barbed stinger. "Only a couple more questions."

She reluctantly planted her butt back in the cheap chair.

"Are you acquainted with any of the officers of this company?"

"No."

Perry had handled all aspects of their treasure sales to Gulf Coast Salvage. She'd checked the company out on the internet and they'd seemed legit. Her accountant had warned her not to put so many eggs in one basket, but he'd also found the company aboveboard. But if it was being investigated and about to go under, she'd better pull out quick.

"How did you hear of them to start with?"

Jet again stood. "They're large and well-known. I live on the coast and have always been fascinated by treasure. Why wouldn't I pursue my interest? I haven't done anything wrong. I may be an incompetent judge in picking stocks—" *damn you, Perry* "—but that's it. If you have any more questions, I'd prefer to exercise my right to have an attorney or my accountant present."

He nodded and rose. "No need to be on the defensive. If I need more information, I'll get in touch."

Easy for him not to be upset—he wasn't the one being drilled. Why did they always have to go after the little guy anyway? Plenty of hedge fund investors and private equity firms, with tons more money than she'd ever see, had been flocking to invest in increasingly specialized treasure ventures.

Fields walked with her toward the door. "Much success on reopening your antiques store. You already have employees hired?" he asked. His previously intense manner, combined with his sharp, wintry eyes, mellowed to a casualness that she suspected was false.

"No. Not yet," she admitted.

"I see. Well, I wish you much success."

His body was close to hers. Too close. The soapy, clean smell was strong. Jet swallowed and licked her dry lips. "Thanks."

She swept around him and into the hallway, inhaling the stale air deeply, ridding her lungs of the auditor's masculine, clean scent.

"Miss Bosarge?"

Jet whipped around.

"I'll need to take a look at the manifests for all the

items you and your business partner sold to Gulf Coast Savage."

"All of them?"

His mouth curved upward, but those arctic eyes gleamed with sardonic amusement. "Every last one."

She frowned. The gleaming teeth made her think of a shark. Perhaps Landry Fields was as lethal on land as a shark was at sea. Only the faintest curling at the ends of his light brown hair ruined the predatory image. "I'll have my accountant call you and make arrangements to send the paperwork."

"No need for all that. I'll drop by your store to collect them, or your home if you prefer." His smile widened, but she wasn't fooled by the offhand manner with which he requested the paperwork or by the way he casually leaned against the doorframe, arms crossed.

Jet scowled back. She most certainly *didn't* prefer Landry Fields inside her house. The whole thing reeked of unprofessionalism and an interest that went beyond the norm of an IRS audit. What was his real game? "Give me a couple days and come by the store. I'll have them."

"Thank you so much for your coop—"

Jet turned and scrambled away before he could finish the insincere thank-you. As if she had a damned choice, as if he wasn't issuing an order.

The rain outside felt wonderfully fresh and she didn't bother with an umbrella, unlike the few humans venturing outdoor in the storm. The contact of water on skin somewhat calmed her agitation and Jet smiled ruefully. How desperate was she that a number cruncher like Landry Fields could affect her body so deeply during an IRS audit? The man was probably as passionate as cold pudding and would laugh his ass off if he guessed her errant thoughts.

She lifted her face to the rain one last time before getting in the truck, absorbing moisture as if it were sustenance. The water fortified her. At least Mr. Conservative-Government-Man provided a convenient excuse to confront Perry today. Her pride no longer demanded she sit and wait for him to show up again.

Perry was the one with the contacts at Gulf Coast Salvage and had insisted the company provided a perfect cover for selling their stuff without bothering with legal hoopla. Did he personally know the company owners or major stockholders? Did it have a reputation for playing fast and loose with maritime-reclamation laws? She had never asked him.

That was what you got for trusting someone. It always came back to bite you in the ass.

What an unusual woman.

Landry Fields stood at the window, watching Jet Bosarge in the parking lot as she lifted her face skyward, closed her eyes and smiled. Rain ran down dark eyelashes onto an elegantly sculpted nose, lush lips and then down her long, pale neck before disappearing in cleavage. The wet purple cotton shirt molded to the curve of her breasts. Abandoning his usual professional detachment and gentlemanly manners, Landry leaned forward against the windowpane, curious if there might be an outline of nipples.

Damn, she was too far away to tell. He ran a hand through his hair, which annoyingly curled at the ends, despite his best efforts to comb it down straight. Bosarge wasn't easy to peg, and he liked to classify people he interviewed into categories within minutes of meeting them: Con Man, Bad Guy with Attitude, Psychopath, Injured Wife, Slutty Girlfriend, or—more rarely—the Innocent or Unknowing. All part of his job as an FBI agent.

Too soon to know what type of woman he was dealing with. And the sexual tension crackling between them played havoc with his normal analytical observations. It made no sense. He'd never before had chemistry with someone he interviewed and Bosarge was unlike any other woman he found physically attractive. She was dark-haired, tall and athletic, deep-voiced and a bit edgy. His usual type was a petite, curvy blonde with a soft voice and an easy, uncomplicated smile.

The woman jumped into a battered red pickup truck and pulled out much too fast, tires squealing on the wet pavement. The corners of his lips involuntarily tugged upward. What kind of woman wore diamond earrings and drove a beater jalopy? She could easily afford a Rolls-Royce.

Everything about Jet Bosarge was a contradiction. Dark hair and eyes contrasted with pale skin and deep red lips. She dressed casually, as if she'd thrown together an outfit with no thought, but the choppy haircut and diamonds gave an air of natural, feminine elegance. At first, she gave one the impression of an overgrown tomboy with her lean, muscular body, short hair and direct mannerisms. Yet, her long legs and low, throaty voice had distracted him so much, only his considerable willpower had allowed him to remain professional during the interview.

He'd studied photographs of the woman, but those cold prints didn't do her justice. Something about Bosarge in the flesh was vibrant and pulsing with energy. It was as if the rainy day had been nothing but gloomy shades of gray until she'd walked into the office. The effect was akin to when Dorothy in *The Wizard of Oz* tumbled out of the ruined Kansas farmhouse and stepped into an explosively Technicolor alternate universe.

Landry shook his head at the direction of his thoughts. The woman most likely was a thief and a liar. Getting personally involved with her would be inappropriate and potentially damaging to his career. He was here to do a job and at last things were moving. He'd spent a whole week in the bayou doing nothing but watching Perry Hammonds and reviewing, yet again, the case files with which he'd grown sickeningly familiar. Evidently, the suspect had been in a holding pattern like him. Hammonds did nothing but bum around his rental cottage drinking beer and watching television.

If there was one thing he despised more than deceit, it was sloth. Laziness should be one of the top sins; there was no excuse for sloppy living. You might fail, but at least you got up every morning and made your own way in the world. That belief had helped him rise above a childhood of poverty and emotional chaos.

He'd been about to approach Hammonds directly when Bosarge had returned from out of town. Past experience taught him it was always easier to get to the girlfriend, or ex-girlfriend—whatever the status of their relationship happened to be—and dig around for preliminary information.

Bosarge's records were most unusual. She possessed a staggering family trust fund. The interest alone provided a comfortable living without her ever having to dip into the fund's capital. And almost every dime she'd earned from selling maritime artifacts with Hammonds had been donated to various ocean-related charities: Save the Dolphins, Save the Whales, Save the Oceans, Save the Manatees.

Could be she was a spoiled princess who got involved

with Bad Boy Hammonds for excitement. The philan-
thropy could be a smoke screen or a means of assuaging
her guilt over stealing. Because it *was* theft if the collection site was close to shore. That salvage technically
belonged to the government and the taxpayers. And Hammonds and Bosarge hadn't owned an expensive vessel
with all the bells and whistles needed for deep-sea ex-
tractions.

Landry picked up the fake tax file and shoved it into
a drawer. She'd bought his accountant act hook, line
and sinker. The important files were locked in his desk
at home. He turned off the printer before opening and
checking it for jammed papers. Nothing appeared wrong,
as usual. With a sigh, Landry turned his attention to the
clock and reset it to the correct time. He held it to his
ear and picked up the slight hum of the battery he'd in-
stalled yesterday.

Finished with his afternoon ritual, Landry retrieved a
jacket and umbrella. No need to hurry; he knew exactly
where she was heading.

Sure enough, ten minutes later he drove past Hammonds's cottage and spotted her red truck pulling into
the driveway, splashing mud like an angry beast. Landry
gripped the steering wheel tightly until the cottage was
out of sight. He flipped on public radio, trying to lose
himself in a news story, but it was no good. He couldn't
help wondering how the post-prison reunion was unfold-
ing between them. No doubt they had once been lovers
and not merely business partners. He'd been privy to
many pictures of them embracing or kissing on board the
boat they sailed in search of maritime artifacts.

Forget her. He had an investigation and he would concentrate on doing his job. His real focus was on Hammonds. Their past crimes, if they were guilty, were fairly

small in the grand scheme of things—he had coworkers covering billion-dollar drug-smuggling rings, after all— but the FBI took notice when Hammonds was released early from a South American prison. That early payoff had been financed by one Sylvester Vargas, a known crime figure with a reputation for dabbling in foreign intrigue. Hammonds had wandered aimlessly for weeks until Vargas's men collected him and put him on a one- way flight back to Alabama. Now Hammonds was back in the States, and the coupling of maritime salvage with foreign investors and criminal activity was a red flag.

The woods grew denser as Landry passed into a less populous area of Bayou La Siryna until he reached home. He climbed the wooden staircase to the humble cottage set up on stilts like many others in the remote bayou.

The plain door gave way with its customary squeak of rusty hinges. Most things eventually corroded in the salt air. If he took up permanent residence, his sleek BMW would have to be traded in for the ubiquitous pickup truck. Seemed Bosarge was onto something after all with her rusted truck.

The smell of lemon and ammonia mixed with brine meant the maid had come by today. He'd used the same one for years. The first time Landry returned to the cot- tage after Mimi's death, the scent of musty decay had been depressing, so he had his real-estate agent hire someone to clean and air out the rooms before his vis- its. Now that he'd moved in for the next few weeks, he'd been able to keep the same cleaner.

His grandmother had taken great pride in maintain- ing the tiny place. The scarred pine floors were always waxed, the air-dried bedsheets were crisp and smelled of the ocean, and the cheap linoleum-tiled kitchen had smelled of corn bread, pecan pies, roasts or shrimp boils.

Mimi had spoiled him every summer, as if compensating for his shitty life with a careless mom and her string of increasingly sorry boyfriends. His mother's house was filled with half siblings from stepfathers that came and went, and constant drama from financial pressures. Every new romantic relationship of his mother's had created new sets of problems and complications.

Landry placed the car keys on a table in the den and surveyed the interior with satisfaction. Most of the furniture he'd replaced over the years. Mimi's sofa had been upgraded to a modern leather sectional. He'd kept what he could. The leather couch was draped with one of her crocheted afghan throws, a patchwork of rainbow colors against a sleek sea of black. Her old wicker rocking chair remained in the same spot. The bathroom, however, had no sentimental value and he'd gutted and expanded it the first year after Mimi's death.

He hung his suit jacket in the bedroom closet and stepped out of the black leather loafers. Back in the den, he adjusted a glass cat figurine on the battered sideboard. The cleaning company knew his peculiarity for detail and sameness, but they weren't perfect. His fingers accidentally brushed against a red sequined coin purse and he recoiled, as if the haunting memories associated with it could transfer into his heart. It had been one of Mimi's treasured possessions but he had never liked the purse openly displayed. After Mimi's death, he'd taken it off the sideboard but then wandered about the cottage, unsure of an appropriate resting place for the ghostly memento mori. In the end, Landry had returned it to just where Mimi had left it.

After a few more minor tweaks to the figurines display, he slipped open the glass doors and stepped onto the wooden deck.

The scent of salty brine swirled in the early-April wind. He inhaled deeply and leaned over the wooden railing. Mimi's house could best be described as quaint—or ramshackle to be more precise. But here lay its secret charm—the million-dollar view. Located at the bend of one of the bayou's fingers, Landry could look over the pine and cypress trees hugging the shoreline and see the vast expanse of the Gulf of Mexico.

A tiny flash of orange darted at the base of a tree.

"I'll be damned," Landry muttered. He hurried inside and found the binoculars in the sideboard drawer, rushed back out, then focused in on the orange patch. A ginger tabby nestled in a bed of pine needles. Closer examination revealed a swollen belly. Landry set the binoculars on the rail with a sigh. The feral cat population was alive and thriving. It was a losing battle, but he'd try to entice the mama cat into a trap and do what he could to find the kittens a home.

His eyes scanned the ocean. The waters were calm, a blue-gray sheen with a few scatterings of tame whitecaps.

But despite its calm facade, Landry secretly suspected that beneath its placid surface lay a foreign world teeming with mystery and creatures beyond most humans' imaginations.

He knew. He'd witnessed it with his own eyes.

No, don't go there. Landry ran a hand through his hair and dismissed the foolish memories. He'd been a kid. A scared, ridiculous kid with a huge imagination. Nothing more to it. He reentered the cottage and made his way to the kitchen, determined to change the direction of his thoughts. He opened the fridge for a drink. His hand drew back abruptly at the sight of the porcelain cat figurine sitting on the shelf by the soda cans.

The same figurine he'd straightened on the sideboard less than ten minutes ago.

Damn. It was getting worse.

Chapter 2

*S*tay strong.

Jet repeated the phrase like a mantra as she sped through the rain-sloshed streets. Although it was not yet night, dark storm clouds blanketed the bayou. The town square was a jumble of small shops clustered around an old courthouse, much like any small Southern town.

But the life-size mermaid statue in the middle of the square was a departure from the norm. Rainwater streamed off the mermaid's stone-and-steel form, giving the impression that the siren had just emerged, dripping, from the nearby gulf waters. The etched half smile on her face bespoke secrets buried deep within the mysterious body that was part sea creature, part human.

Bayou La Siryna's founding fathers might have bought into the mermaid myth—old newspaper articles recorded local sightings—but nowadays, the natives scoffed at such nonsense. Most didn't even recollect that the town's name was given in recognition of the sea sirens.

Which suited Jet fine. With modern science, if humans suspected the old tales were true, mermaids would be hunted down and subjected to who-knew-what kind of experiments.

Her heart quickened as she rounded the curve on Shell Line Road with its row of rental bungalows nestled in thick pine and cypress. Lights glowed on porches and behind curtained windows like a promise, beacons of love and comfort that pierced her with longing. At one time she'd dreamed of fitting into this human world, since the merfolk didn't have much use for her.

There it was. Third cottage on the left, where Perry had once lived. Light glimmered inside and a red Mustang was parked in the driveway, the kind of flashy car Perry would drive.

Three years. Three freaking years with no phone call, no letters, no nothing. She'd waited for an apology or any expression of remorse, had hoped incarceration would lead to introspection and recognition that he needed to change and beg her forgiveness. Stupid, stupid and more stupid. The memory of the last time she saw him replayed in her mind. During an expedition, Chilean marine police had caught them unawares. If only she had still been underwater, she would have heard the boat engine miles away. But after hours of bringing up the day's catch, they'd taken a nap.

At their capture, Perry had pointed a finger at her, declaring it was her boat and her stuff. He'd even told them she was a freaking mermaid, a claim they laughingly dismissed. She'd had no choice but to jump overboard to protect her kind from possible exposure. The bleat of the horn and the shouting above had given way to the silence of the sea. But the usual numbing cocoon of the deep fathoms had failed to silence her despair.

In many ways, it still haunted her thoughts.

I've never gotten over it. All the pain of that betrayal churned inside her like a giant tidal wave as she pulled in behind the Mustang. Perry probably thought they would get back in business together. Hell, why wouldn't he think she'd run back to him? In the past, she'd always done so, had overlooked his faults and dalliances.

She'd thought they really had something, until Shelly and her fiancé, Tillman, became a couple. Their trust and acceptance of one another had been a revelation. Jet realized that all along she'd wanted something Perry was incapable of giving—love.

She got out of her truck, hardly noticing the rain pelting her body as she strode to the door and rapped loudly. Deep inside came the muffled sound of a television. The volume lowered and footsteps approached. The door creaked open and there Perry stood.

White teeth flashed as he gave an easy grin, leaned his tall, sculpted body against the doorframe and crossed his arms. Jet reluctantly drank in the familiar image. Being near her former lover, with all their physical history, churned up memories and feelings she'd rather forget.

Don't even think about it. Jet lifted her chin and met his amused smile. *Conceited ass.* Perry's shoulder-length brown hair curled in waves, while a faint bit of stubble lined his jaw.

He gave a slow, knowing wink. "You are as beautiful as ever."

"Prison seems to have suited you," Jet snapped.

Perry's smile didn't falter. "Direct as always."

"Aren't you going to ask me in? I'm getting soaked out here, in case you haven't noticed."

"Since when has water ever bothered you? I remember you love rain." He stepped aside and waved an arm. "But do come in," he added, as if offering the keys to the palace.

She swept past, careful not to brush against him. Still, she caught a whiff of his designer aftershave, which smelled of male skin warmed by the sun. Unable to pronounce the Italian product's name, Jet had dubbed it Aqua de Sexy. It tugged at memories of them together, her face pressed against his chest.

But the memory didn't devastate her as she expected. Instead, Jet recalled Landry Fields's soapy after-shower scent: simple, unpretentious and casually masculine. No use dwelling on *that*. Fields was not potential boyfriend material. Besides, getting seriously involved with anyone would mean again confiding that she was a mermaid, which compounded the risk of their secret race being exposed to scrutiny.

Jet drew a deep breath. "I've just come from the IRS office. The auditor asked all kinds of questions about my investments with Gulf Coast Treasures and Salvage."

Perry shrugged.

"Has anyone from the IRS contacted you?"

"Nope. The only good thing about prison is that there's no paperwork to file. I haven't had an income to report in years, so there's nothing they could question me about."

"You were sentenced to ten years. Why did you get released early?"

"Good behavior." He lowered his chin and waggled his eyebrows. "You know how good I can be."

He crossed the distance between them, but Jet turned away and walked to the window. She was too unnerved to handle the closeness. "How well do you know the owners of that company?"

He scowled. "Who said I knew them?"

"*You* did. When we first started selling stuff we pulled from the ocean, you claimed to know a company willing to accept our merchandise with no questions asked."

"I heard about them from other divers and met up with a couple of them a time or two." Perry laid his hands on her shoulders and guided her toward him.

Jet clenched her jaw, willed her body not to respond to the steady pressure of his palms.

"We have far more interesting things—" he gave a smoldering once-over gaze from the top of her body to the bottom "—to discuss."

"Like how you tried to screw me over three years ago?"

He ran a hand through his long brown locks. "Yeah, that."

Jet shook off his hands and paced. The cottage was sparsely furnished, like most rentals, but clean despite a dirty dish on the kitchen table and a newspaper spread out on a coffee table.

"I only told the police you were a mermaid to protect you."

Jet stopped in her tracks. Somehow, he always managed to catch her off guard, like he had since they met five years ago. He'd reeled her in like a dumb, hungry fish. She'd been so lonely, so damned grateful he accepted her shape-shifting body. And when Perry went away, Jet was left gasping and flailing on land, like the same stupid fish she'd been all along.

Her jaw dropped and she snorted in disbelief. "You did it to *protect* me?"

Perry clasped her arms in one swift movement, his eyes a mask of concern. "I knew if I didn't piss you off, you'd stay with me out of stubbornness. No sense both of us going to jail."

She found herself drawn into an embrace. "Stop it." She pulled away and inhaled deeply. "If I'd been captured and interrogated, my fate would have been far worse than your jail time."

"Nobody would have believed me."

"Not at first. No. But if they probed enough, saw holes in our story of how we accidentally found treasure, ran background checks on our enterprises…"

"I wouldn't have told them anything else," Perry insisted.

"And what if I'd gotten sick and they had a doctor find freaky things in my medical tests? Or what if the police had thrown me into the sea to test if I changed? You didn't put only me in jeopardy. You put my entire race at risk of exposure."

He gave a disarming grin. "Ah, come on, sweetie. Don't get melodramatic on me now."

Of all the nerve. "You really are a son of a bitch, you know that? You knew about my nightmare."

His brow crinkled, then cleared. "The aquarium thing?"

Jet dug her nails into her fists, concentrated on the painful half-moon indentations in her fleshy palm, recalling one of the few times she'd shown her vulnerability to Perry. She'd awakened one night from that recurring nightmare, gasping for air, and spilled all about it. "Yeah, that thing," she snapped.

"Never going to happen. But if it does—" he flashed a grin "—I'll rescue you like a knight in shining armor."

Right. Perry would be a hero only if it suited his own purposes. Jet sucked in the pheromone-filled air of the tiny room. The man grinned so confidently, as if the past three years had never happened. As if he'd been some noble person when he'd ratted her out.

"Why are you here?" she asked.

"Why wouldn't I come back?" He ran a hand down her hair and neck, pausing slightly as his fingers brushed the trace of her gills. "I missed you." His lips brushed her forehead. "Missed this." His lips dropped to her mouth.

Jet gasped as Perry's hands cupped her ass and drew her against his body. It would be so easy to surrender, enjoy the moment before—

"No." Jet tore away and drew in a few ragged breaths, unexpectedly grateful for the IRS meeting earlier. Landry Fields's questions served to make her more wary of Perry's lies and manipulation. "I need to set you straight on a few things."

Perry scowled and flung himself onto the sofa. "I explained why I told the police you were a mermaid. What else do you expect me to say?"

"For starters, how come I didn't hear from you the whole time you were locked up?"

"They wouldn't let me post mail."

"Bull. And you've been out for weeks before showing up here."

Perry narrowed his eyes. "How do you know when I was released?"

"You don't know?" No reason not to tell him. "The deputy sheriff, Carl Dismukes, told me. You remember him."

Perry slapped his palm to his forehead. "Of course, the crooked cop. But how did he know I got out?"

"I'm not sure. Maybe because your last driver's license listed you as living here in the bayou and they notify law enforcement when an ex-felon is released."

"Well, we aren't paying him shit anymore. He had a

lot of nerve, blackmailing us for his silence. I don't know how he figured out what we were doing."

Jet bit her tongue. Dismukes might be despicable, but distant merblood ran in his veins, and she wouldn't betray his secret to a human. The deputy knew everything that happened on land and guessed a great deal about what happened undersea.

Perry narrowed his eyes. "Do you hear me? Dismukes gets nothing."

"Obviously. There won't be anything to split. You and I are history."

"Come on, baby." His voice grew husky. "Let's do one more job together. Give me a chance to prove I love you."

Her stomach clenched in response to Perry's gruff, low tone and his familiar declaration of love. *Stay strong.* "After what you've pulled, I'd be crazy to do it."

"I told you, babe! I honestly thought it was the only way to get you to jump ship and save yourself."

Liar. Could he learn to love someone other than himself? Her thoughts shifted from Perry's dark brown eyes to the ice-blue eyes of the IRS agent. Those penetrating, no-bullshit eyes that cut through her defenses. Landry Fields would burn through Perry's charming facade like dry ice on tender skin. Too bad her eyes didn't have a similar effect on Perry.

And why was she thinking of Landry Fields anyway?

"Please, Jet," Perry wheedled in that tone he used when he wanted something. "One last big haul to help me get back on my feet."

Her mouth widened in surprise. "What do you mean? You should have plenty of money socked away from all we've collected."

He hung his head. "I, um, had lots of lawyer bills and stuff."

"What about your fancy Mercedes-Benz? Your jewelry?"

"Gone." His face tightened. "I bought everything on credit and when I got thrown in the slammer, everything went to shit with my finances. All that stuff got repossessed."

Jet gave a low whistle. This was the real reason Perry had returned, of course. The guy was broke and needed her. Angry as she was, Jet couldn't help feeling a little sorry for him. "Maybe there is some way I can help," she answered evasively. Perhaps she could buy him off and get him to leave her alone. "What did you have in mind?"

He brightened and Jet tried to ignore the gleam of triumph in his chocolate-brown eyes.

"There's a site with a huge potential profit at Tybee Island, Georgia," he answered promptly.

"Never heard of any shipwreck there."

"It's an old Spanish ship supposedly loaded with gold and silver colonial coins."

Jet frowned. "Seems I would have heard about it. What's the ship's name? Do you have the cargo manifest?" It always amazed her that Perry got such great tips on treasure sites.

Perry waved a hand dismissively. "Leave all the research and details with me."

"I'll think about it." Jet bolted for the door. She had to get out quick, before he suckered her into a commitment. That would be colossal stupidity on her part.

Perry overtook her and laid a hand on the door. "Don't make me beg. All I'm asking for is one more job."

Jet swallowed hard and stiffened her spine. He'd left her hanging for years with no word. She could make him wait a day or two. Let him be the one to sweat it out. She had to get out of the cottage and think over everything rationally. Despite the years of silence, Jet knew Perry wasn't finished with her—she was much too valuable for him to completely abandon. Without her, he'd be back in the same boat he'd been in before they met, living a hand-to-mouth existence with the few treasures he could scavenge alone.

There must be some way to get Perry out of her life without agreeing to another treasure excavation. If she turned him down flat, there was no telling what he'd do for spite. "I said I'd think about it." She yanked the doorknob, sending Perry stumbling back a few steps. "See you around."

She stepped into the swirling rain and made her escape.

Jet was no fun anymore.

Perry kicked over the coffee table. She was playing a game. Trying to show who was boss, especially when he'd tried to stop her from leaving. Damn her abnormal mermaid strength.

But that freaky bitch still wanted him, would eventually cave in, and they could pick up where they'd left off.

Or maybe not. Sylvester Vargas claimed this Tybee Island thing was BIG. Enough money in it for all of them to live easy the rest of their lives. With enough dough, he'd move far away to someplace that didn't stink of bilge and shucked oysters like this bayou.

And then he wouldn't need Jet. At first, it had been fun, an ocean salvager's dream come true. She knew where the nearest, best stuff lay on the ocean floor. And once he got over his initial revulsion about touching a mermaid creature, the sex had been great. But slowly, Jet had changed, had begun to stifle him like any other woman he'd slept with more than a few times.

That woman-animal-sideshow-thing believed she had the upper hand. But he was the one with the contacts to sell the shit.

The sharp trill of his cell phone went off and he glanced at the screen: *Sylvester Vargas*.

Damn. The timing couldn't be worse.

"I see your girlfriend just left," said a heavily accented Spanish voice. "When can we set the date?"

Wow. Are they watching everything I do? Perry cleared his throat. "She's a little miffed at me right now. But she'll come around," he added quickly.

An ominous silence settled on the connection.

"I'm getting impatient."

"Yes, sir." He should have contacted Jet long before now but he'd had so much fun reacquainting himself with post-prison pleasures. The days had sped by with his indulgence of booze, women, gambling and partying.

"My company paid to get you out of that hellhole prison in South America. I'm beginning to think you're stringing us along with your wild tales."

"No, no. Not at all. Haven't you checked out what I told you?"

"That's the only reason I agreed to get you out of jail. I don't believe in that mermaid shit, but I can't deny how incredibly lucky you've been with sea finds. I contacted the managers of my salvage company you used as a front. They said you were their most reliable supplier."

"Told you so."

"No doubt something *fishy* is going on down there." Sylvester barked out a laugh at his own pun.

"And don't forget the police report."

"All it stated was that a female went missing during the arrest and is presumed dead."

"She jumped off the damn boat! That's why she went missing."

"From that I'm supposed to believe that your Jet grew a tail and swam hundreds of miles to some backwater Alabama bayou?"

Perry swallowed an angry retort. Sylvester was not a man to antagonize. He forced himself to speak with respect. "I need another week or so to convince Jet to go along with us."

"You have until the end of this week. If she doesn't agree by then, we'll have to use force."

Perry's mouth went dry. He wasn't sure if Sylvester was threatening *him* or Jet.

Or possibly both of them.

"Jet will come willingly. No need for force," he said with false confidence.

But the line was dead.

The library was quiet and musty-smelling with an antiquated vibe only punctuated by the sparse number of elderly people at reading tables with magazines. All eyes turned to him. Landry gave a rusty smile that he suspected looked more like a grimace. Where was that woman? She'd entered ahead of him just minutes ago. Surprisingly, she had not stayed long at Hammonds's rental.

"May I help you?" a middle-aged librarian asked, tilting her head slightly downward to examine him better with her bifocals.

"No, um…" He noticed the stairs to his right. She must have slipped up there. "I'm fine."

The carpeted steps muffled the noise of his entrance. Despite the room's small size, he couldn't see her. But she was there. Ripples of energy stirred his senses, just like in the office earlier. Landry walked to the rows of bookshelves and spotted her running a finger over the spines of several titles. Time to up the pressure on Jet today and ask more direct questions.

"Find what you're looking for?" His voice boomed like a firecracker in the muted space.

She jumped and nearly dropped a load of books cradled in one arm. "What are you doing here?" Dark eyes narrowed. "Are you following me?"

"Why would I do that?" He folded his arms and leaned against a shelf. "I mean, you're not a criminal or anything." Landry arched an eyebrow. "Are you?"

"Of course not." Red flushed her pale cheeks. "What do you want from me?"

He wanted... Unbidden, he imagined the woman in his bed, naked skin against naked skin. Something about her stirred him deeply, in ways he didn't understand. "Answers," he said. "I want answers."

"I'll get those stupid papers to you."

Landry leaned in close enough to read the book titles clutched against her like a shield—*Treasure Hunting in the Gulf, Shipwrecks in the Panhandle, History of Tybee Island* and— He snorted at the last title. "*Little Women?* Aren't you a little old for that one?"

Her chin lifted an inch. "Never. It's a wonderful book about family sticking together through hard times."

"A fairy tale."

"You're a cynical man, Mr. Fields. Got family issues, huh?"

To put it mildly. His family was a disaster, had been since The Incident when he was five years old. Not that home had ever been exactly harmonious, but at least it had been stable up until that time. Landry pushed down the bitter taste of those childhood memories. "Doesn't everyone have family issues?" he said with elaborate casualness. He didn't talk about that past with anybody. No sense rehashing something he was powerless to change. All he could do now was try to prevent it from happening to anyone else.

The tight set to her lips relaxed a fraction. "I suppose you're right, to some degree. But in the end, family's all we have."

Then I am so screwed. "I depend on myself and nobody else."

"Guess you're never disappointed, then." She lifted a shoulder. "But it sounds a bit lonely if you ask me."

"Hardly." Landry stiffened. He had his share of women, had a few male acquaintances from work that he got together with for the occasional beer and football-game parties. Sure, a family would be nice, but you could live a perfectly fine life without them. He was proof of that.

"If you say so," she said in a tone that conveyed she didn't believe it.

Landry shook his head. *Wait a minute.* This conversation had taken a turn into the unexpected. He was supposed to shake *her* up, rattle *her* composure, not the other way around. He pointed at the book on shipwrecks. "You said you were through with the salvage business. But it looks like you're still interested in treasure hunting."

"It's a hobby. You should get your head out of your ledgers and find one." She turned and stormed toward the end of the aisle.

"A hobby?" He overtook her, blocking the exit. "So you didn't meet with your ex-partner today after you left my office?"

She drew her breath in sharply. "How did you— You *are* following me."

The flash of fear in her eyes made him want to pull her to him, to kiss her until she couldn't even remember Perry Hammonds's name, to protect her from her own dangerous impulses.

What was wrong with him? She crackled with spirit and a unique beauty that was downright unnerving. He'd never felt such a strong pull to a complete stranger. Especially a woman clearly on the wrong side of the law. But just how far had she gone? And was all that truly in her past?

Her eyes hardened. "Not that I have to explain anything to you, but my ex-partner is just that. An ex. I'm done with him."

He wasn't used to hostile female suspects. Most fell over themselves to be cooperative and friendly in the hopes of being left alone. Then again, Bosarge thought he was an IRS accountant.

Those people sure got no respect.

"I hope that's the truth," he said, meaning it. Bugged the hell out of him that he couldn't pin Miss Jet Bosarge into his usual tidy categories of good or bad. He wanted to believe she had no involvement with a ruthless criminal like Vargas. But if she knew something, a cooperative informant in the investigation would be useful before the agency closed in.

"You don't believe me," she said flatly.

Landry shrugged. "Time will tell."

"Look, whatever you may think of my past business dealings—"

A clamor erupted behind her and they both stared at the pile of books that had fallen and lay helter-skelter on the floor.

"I must have accidently knocked them off the shelf," Jet said, forehead scrunching in confusion.

She bent down to pick them up at the same time he did, their hands touching as they picked up the fallen books. He glanced up, startled, and Jet's face was mere inches from his own. He didn't move—couldn't if he wanted to anyway. Their breath joined and he felt absorbed in her impossibly dark, wide eyes. If he believed in magic— which he most certainly did *not*—he'd swear she was a witch casting a spell.

She broke contact first, swooping up the books and piling them haphazardly on the shelf. He stood, resisting the impulse to reshelf them in the correct Dewey decimal order. Keeping his own world in tight order was work enough. No need to take on librarian duties.

"As I was saying," Jet said, standing with her arms crossed. "I've been out of that line of work for three years. Maritime salvage is a cutthroat business filled with lots of gray areas about what is and isn't legal. I'm done with it. I've dabbled in a few other ventures since quitting and now I'm reopening my shop."

Must be nice to *dabble* for years, courtesy of a wealthy family. He sure hadn't had that luxury. Landry shoved the thought aside. It wasn't her fault she'd been born into a family with advantages unimagined by his parents and siblings. Sometimes life just screwed you that way.

"Tell you what," he said, as if coming to a quick decision. "I've got some photographs I want you to look at."

Her brow wrinkled. "Right now?"

"Yes. While digging into your finances, my audit has broadened to other people and companies."

She followed him to the unused computer in the corner and watched as he logged in and uploaded a photo from his personal email account. It wasn't the greatest picture. Too bad he couldn't display the mug shot on the FBI site. Landry scrutinized the photo along with Jet.

Sylvester Vargas was standing with a group of men by
the docks and wore a hat, but the lower half of his face
was fairly visible. If she'd met him before, she'd recognize him in the photograph.

"This guy look familiar to you?"

She leaned in and he inhaled her scent—fresh and in-
vigorating like cooling rain after a long drought. Except
her closeness felt anything but cool. His gut clenched
at the fierce stab of longing that washed through him.

"No," she said, her breath sending tempting wisps of
desire by his ear. Her arm brushed against his shirt, and
even through the cotton fabric, heat spread over his entire body.

Landry fought not to squirm. If just being near her
and not touching got him this aroused, what would it be
like to have her in his arms? In his bed? He cleared his
throat. "Are you sure?" Damn, his voice sounded husky
and strained.

"I'm sure."

He glanced up in quick surprise. She sounded out of
breath.

Bosarge straightened and patted her black hair in place
about her long, slender neck. Must be a nervous habit,
because she did the same thing this morning when he
questioned her.

So much for getting anywhere with a photo identifi-
cation. Landry signed off the computer with a sigh and
stood. He hadn't gained a thing in this second meeting.
All it had done was reemphasize the strange attraction
to this woman. She met his gaze head-on, direct and un-
flinching.

"Your name matches your eye color," he blurted. Hell,
what a stupid remark.

"Really?" Her upper lip curled. "Thanks, I didn't know that."

Sarcastic witch. "Is that any way to talk to the man auditing your tax records?"

"It's about as appropriate as a government employee commenting on my personal appearance."

She had him there. "Touché." He nodded before delivering a parting shot. "I look forward to examining your complete records in excruciating detail."

Jet hadn't planned on visiting Dolly tonight, but evidently her subconscious was in charge. She'd driven on autopilot, consumed with the day's meetings with two very different men. One a stranger, the other a man who knew her secrets.

But Jet didn't think of loam-brown eyes so similar to her own; rather she recalled blue eyes sharp as barbed wire. She didn't think of the casually familiar bearing of an old boyfriend, but the tight, controlled precision of an auditor. Most surprising, she didn't continue mulling over the long distances and spaces that marked her past relationship. Instead, her mind and body focused on the unexpectedly cozy intimacy of a library's book stacks.

It was all very confusing.

She parked by the only other vehicle at the water park, Dusty's old Cadillac. Jet beeped the horn in three short blasts and grabbed a tote bag from the backseat.

"Glad you made it today," Dusty said as she approached. "Our girl is a bit down."

Although his merblood was distant, Dusty had inherited a special feel for sea life. Jet impatiently shifted the weight on her feet until at last his gnarled fingers released the gate's lock.

She swept past him to the restroom, changing into a

tank top and bikini bottoms. When she emerged, Dusty was mopping inside the office. He nodded before turning his back.

At the pool's edge, Jet bent down and slapped the water's surface. In seconds, over four hundred pounds of sleek silver-blue dolphin breached the water in a graceful arc before swimming like a torpedo toward her hand. Dolly playfully pushed against Jet's palm with her bottlenose beak and squeaked out a greeting.

Jet grinned. "I'm coming in for a swim." This was exactly what she needed. To hell with the complex human male species. She shed the bikini bottoms and slid into the water, legs instantly fusing into a long, shimmering tail fin.

A whiff of urine and feces assaulted her. Andrew Morgan, the park's owner, wasn't using the equipment properly. Damn, he had no business keeping a wild mammal from its natural habitat. The saltwater pool felt sterile, so unlike the ocean, which teemed with everything from gigantic blue whales to tiny microorganisms like plankton drifting in the ever-flowing currents.

She reigned in her distaste and anger. Dolly sensed emotions and Jet didn't want to add to her unhappiness. She ran a hand down her sleek side, fingers lightly tracing deep scars. Dolly was lucky that when she washed ashore on the bayou banks with severely lacerated flanks, a group of locals banded together to help save her.

Andrew, to give him credit, had provided a healing home as Dolly recovered. But instead of releasing her back to the sea, he discovered that Dolly's popularity brought in enough money to refurbish his formerly rundown park.

Dolly clicked and chattered, leading Jet to her favorite toy, a purple beach ball. Once she reached it, Dolly tossed it to Jet with her beak. Jet dived down in the water and flipped it back to Dolly with a flick of her tail fin. Back and forth it went for several minutes.

But something was off. Dolly didn't have her normal energy, her jumps weren't quite as high, and her turns and underwater maneuvers were a tad slower, too. Jet swam closer to Dolly for a better look. The dolphin tossed her head, pointing it toward the deep end of the pool, where Andrew kept the food buckets.

"Is that all? You hungry, girl?" Relief bubbled inside Jet. The dolphin couldn't be too depressed if her appetite was strong. Jet obligingly dumped a bucket of food for Dolly, who ate as if she were starving. Jet frowned. Time she had a talk with Andrew.

Dolly seemed energized after the meal and ready for play. She blew air from her blowhole, casting underwater rings. Jet gracefully swam through the bubbling circles, as eager as Dolly for companionship. She had precious little of it, since her family lived in near isolation. Oil spills had run off the few full-blooded mermaids who had lingered in the gulf. Lily had been at sea for months and Shelly was preoccupied with Tillman and their upcoming wedding later this summer.

Jet stifled a familiar pang of loneliness. She was happy for Shelly. It wasn't her cousin's fault that her relationship with Tillman was a constant reminder of what Jet lacked in her own life.

Yet again, Dolly tired quickly and floated, nuzzling her beak in Jet's palm with a slight clacking sound that could have been a sigh or a whimper. Despite the dolphin's appearance of a perpetually smiling mouth, something was definitely amiss.

Jet sang a lullaby, wishing Lily was here to soothe Dolly with her magical siren's voice. Dolly floated as Jet stroked the rubbery-smooth flanks, careful not to touch any old injuries.

A tiny wave of motion rippled the underside of Dolly's lower flank, so subtle Jet almost missed it. Her hand stilled on Dolly's thick skin, and there it was again. Something inside Dolly was alive and flipping. Awe and understanding dawned.

Dolly was with calf.

"No wonder you're so tired and hungry," Jet cooed, doing some quick calculations. Dolly had been here six months, so she was at least halfway through a dolphin's twelve-month gestation period. She laid a cheek against Dolly's warm-blooded body. Dolly should be with other females in her pod, who would aid her during labor and later share mothering duties.

"I'll get you out of here somehow," Jet whispered.

Dolly faced her sideways; one small black eye gazed into Jet's. Comprehension emanated like a wave of intelligent words. Dolly understood her heart's intent.

"I promise," Jet vowed.

Chapter 3

The crunch of gravel lifted Landry out of his musings on Jet Bosarge. He didn't know many people in Bayou La Siryna, preferring to keep to himself. Life was simpler that way, more predictable. Only a couple of old ladies at the humane shelter even gave him a casual nod of recognition. Landry went to the window and drew back the curtain.

Damn. He frowned at the battered Plymouth Duster. Only one person in the world owned that classic piece of shit. He rubbed his jaw, then stilled when two people got out of the car instead of one. And—oh, hell—they were unloading dozens of bags from the trunk.

He slipped a pair of sneakers on and walked outside. In the deepening twilight, Landry focused on the tall, lanky teenager. Which of his many half siblings was this one?

"Seth, say hello to your brother." His mother banged down the trunk, the sound echoing in the lonely gloom.

The kid regarded him sullenly.

This was the youngest of his mother's brood and the one he knew the least. She'd asked him if he could stay a few days this summer. Give Mom the tiniest opening and she'd bulldoze through it.

He eyed their cargo with mounting unease. "What's with all these bags?"

"Seth's here for a visit." She stuffed some into his arms. "Help us get this stuff inside."

"A *little* visit?" Between the three of them, there were over a dozen such crammed bags.

His mother stalked toward the porch before Seth found his voice. "You can't make me stay here," he complained. "This place looks like a shit hole and it stinks like one, too."

His mother whirled around as if the words were a knife launched into her spine. "You're staying. I've had all I can take of your stealing. And your mouth."

"Stealing?" Landry asked, looking back and forth between them.

Seth kicked at the gravel with a pair of frayed sneakers. "It's no big deal."

Landry suppressed a sigh. "What do you expect me to do?"

She crossed her arms. "You work for the FBI, don't you? Be a positive role model. He's got no father to speak of."

A flush of anger darkened the kid's neck. "I've got a dad," he said hotly.

His mother raised her hands and spun in a half circle, looking around the deserted stretch of bayou. "Really? Where is he?"

"He's oil rigging. Making money."

"Which we see precious little of," she snapped.

Sounded like old times. Five minutes with his family and his stomach was knotted. He'd been on his own for so many years he'd lost tolerance for the past drama of Life With Mom.

Landry gave a time-out signal. "Truce. Let's go inside and discuss this over dinner."

His mother stalked off again. "I'm not hungry," she called over her shoulder. "I need to get home real quick-like."

"Well, *I'm* hungry." Laundry motioned for Seth to follow them. At first it appeared the kid wasn't going to budge from his slouch against the old Plymouth, but with a sigh worthy of a Shakespearian actor, he dragged his feet forward, shoulders slumped and head down.

Inside, his mother threw her load of bags onto the couch. "Nice setup. This place used to be a real dump when your grandmother was alive."

Landry faced Seth and got his first good look at the kid. His chin-length brown hair hung in oily locks that partially shielded heavy-lidded dark eyes. He wore an olive camouflage jacket two sizes too large and a pair of faded jeans. "I'm grilling steaks. You hungry?"

"I'd rather have a hamburger. Can't we just go to Mc-Donald's?"

Landry suspected the fast-food preference was a ploy for Seth to get rid of their mother faster. That had to be one tense ride from Mobile to the bayou. Landry grabbed his car keys and tossed them to Seth. In two seconds, the kid was out the door.

"You're taking a mighty big risk with your expensive car," his mother chastised.

Landry rounded on her. "I can't believe you showed up like this."

She had the grace to appear somewhat sheepish. "You agreed to a visit this summer."

"It's early April, not summer. And I'm in the middle of an investigation," Landry growled. "For Christ's sake, isn't the kid still in school?"

Her hard eyes clouded with tears. "He was suspended for cutting classes. In fact, he missed so many he might as well stay out of school the rest of the year and make it all up in summer school. Please let him stay. You're my only hope," she sobbed.

The great big ole fake. He knew it, she knew he knew it, and yet it worked every time. Landry tried to remember her the way she was before their lives were destroyed. He'd lost more than a sibling that dark day; he'd lost his mother and father, too.

Landry groaned and threw up his hands. "Okay. *Okay.* He can stay a few days. I'll try to talk to him but there's no guarantee it'll do one bit of good."

Mom hugged him tight with a smug smile she couldn't entirely hide. "You're my anchor."

"Just this week," he reiterated.

Jet riffled through the stack of invoices and moaned. Paperwork sucked. Tomorrow would be much more fun when the delivery from Mobile came in.

A sharp rap at the front door startled her. The shop wouldn't open for a couple more weeks. The front windows were taped over, so she couldn't see who'd knocked. She stuffed her feet into a pair of flip-flops, went to the door and unlocked it.

Crap. If she'd known who it was, she wouldn't have bothered. "Sorry, we're not open for business yet," she said quickly and began shutting the door.

"Not looking to buy anything," Landry Fields said,

stepping inside before the door closed. His sharp eyes roamed the mostly empty space. "When do you anticipate opening?"

Jet inhaled the soapy-clean male scent she remembered from yesterday. "Not for a few more weeks. I've got a big shipment of furniture coming tomorrow. It'll take some time to get everything arranged." She resisted the urge to touch a curling tendril of light brown hair grazing the auditor's stiff white collar. His hair was slightly damp, as if he'd just showered or combed his hair down in a failed attempt to flatten the curly ends. Jet shook her head at the sight of his gray jacket and trousers. "You keep wearing suits like that and by next month the humidity will eat you alive."

"I'm from Mobile. I'm used to it." Landry didn't even give a polite smile, bearing an air as formal and reserved as his attire.

It only sent Jet's imagination into overdrive, fantasizing about what lay beneath the conservative clothing. She tried to convince herself Landry was probably pasty-white and about as fit as a dead June bug but as he walked away toward the front counter, something about the energy of his movements refuted that theory.

Landry stopped at the huge mahogany bar that served as a front counter and ran a hand down its gleaming, nicked surface. "Nice. You don't see these kinds of large pieces anymore."

Jet nodded, unexpectedly pleased at the compliment. "It's the reason I bought this space to begin with. Came with the property." She closed the door and walked to him. "I don't have the manifests yet that you requested."

Landry sat on one of the counter bar stools, as if settling in for a long chat. "How could you?" he asked with a wry smile. "I didn't specify how many years back I wanted you to go."

Jet scowled. "Years?"

"Correct. I want the documentation on all the salvage property you sold to Gulf Coast Salvage."

"I didn't think about it while I was in your office, but the company should have a record of that. Can't you get it from them?"

"You should have a copy, as well."

Landry didn't look at her, instead he riffled through the invoices she'd left lying on the counter. Nosy man. Her pleasure quickly turned sour. "What are you doing?" she asked tartly.

He laid down a paper and faced her. "Just curious. I find everything about you curious and fascinating."

A warm glow settled in the pit of her stomach at the words. No one had ever called her fascinating before.

"I want to satisfy my curiosity about you and your business associations." His eyes returned to the icy-blue she remembered from their first meeting. "Especially your association with one Perry Andrew Hammonds. The third, to be precise."

The warm glow died, replaced by a sharp chill up her spine. Damn. She knew it; Perry had somehow brought this fresh hell into her life. "What about him?"

"Now that Hammonds is out of prison, do you plan on resuming the treasure-hunting business with him?"

That was the million-dollar question. Jet opened her mouth, but no words came out. She'd had a sleepless night, debating whether to help Perry one last time. Maybe if she did he would make enough money to go away and leave her the hell alone. "I don't know," she answered truthfully.

"If you're serious about operating this store, you won't

have time for long excursions." His eyes honed in on the help-wanted sign by the door. "Hired any employees yet?"

So, he was trying to see if she was truly making a run at this venture or if it might be a front to shelter money. "No." Jet crossed her arms and changed the subject. "What about your plans? You said the IRS field office here would only be around for tax season. When do you go back to Mobile?"

The blue chips in his eyes thawed a bit. "Trying to get rid of me? I was actually thinking of staying in Bayou La Siryna permanently and commuting."

She almost laughed. "Why would you want to do that?" Mr. Sophisticated-Government-Man would die of boredom. Nobody visited their town and stayed. The bayou was an acquired taste—you were either born and raised in it, so that over the years the place settled into your blood and bone and brain like a fever, or you married a local. A disturbing thought hit her. "Are you seeing somebody in town?"

"No. But I have roots here."

Jet narrowed her eyes and scrutinized him. "What roots? I've never seen you before." She'd sure as hell remember if she had.

"I used to visit my grandmother most summers growing up, out by Murrell's Point."

"Hmm, thought I knew most everyone in these parts. What was her name?"

"Claudia Margaret Simpson."

Simpson, Simpson... Jet ran the name through her mind's inner database but came up blank. "How about her husband's or children's names?"

"What is it with people in small towns and the need to

identify someone's family history?" he grumbled. "Doubt you ever crossed paths. Mimi kept to herself a lot."

"A family trait?" Jet observed wryly.

Landry tipped his head slightly in assent. "Could say the same about your family. In spite of the fact that your kin is one of the wealthiest and oldest in Bayou La Siryna, the Bosarges have a reputation for being aloof and reserved."

"Can't deny that." Jet grinned, until it struck her that he was prying again for tidbits of information about her. "Are all IRS guys as nosy as you?"

"If they're any good—yes."

What was good for the goose... "All right, then, since you seem to know so much about me, what are your grandfather's name and your mom's name?"

"Edward Fields. He died before I was born. And Mom's name—get ready for this—is Clytie Sands-Fields-Riley-Johnston-Hogge-Riley-Grimes."

Jet raised a brow. "Two Rileys?"

"Married and divorced twice."

"Ouch." Jet snapped her fingers. "It's coming to me now. Did your grandmother live in that blue cottage on Adele Avenue and drive a yellow Continental?"

"That's the one. Impressive memory."

"We all knew her as the crazy cat lady." Jet clamped a hand over her mouth. She really needed to get a mouth filter one day. She quickly grabbed a bunch of scattered invoices and stuffed them into a folder. Normally, it took a lot to fluster her, but something about Landry Fields kept her off-kilter.

A warm, large hand lay over her right arm, near the elbow. "It's okay."

The touch, combined with his low, husky voice, made Jet quiver even more than she had at the library. Her eyes slowly traveled up his forearm, across lean muscle and a coating of light hair that was so…damned…sexy. How could a man's *arm* be sexy, for Poseidon's sake? She met his eyes—so blue, so deep. As deep as the ocean she swam on summer nights. Landry leaned closer and Jet shut her eyes, wanting nothing more than to smell his clean scent and feel his lips on hers.

The bells above the door jangled and a cool draft lifted the hairs at the back of her neck.

"Well, shit," Landry muttered. "It's Perry the Pirate."

"Huh?" Jet abruptly opened her eyes and blinked. She'd been so totally wrapped in Landry's spell that the worldly intrusion caught her off guard. In a nanosecond, Landry's eyes returned to their previous remote chill. She stepped back and faced Perry.

He sauntered in, smiling easily, dressed in a white shirt and white jeans, just as he had the day she first met him at Harbor Bay. The Greek-god look, she'd laughingly dubbed it. Only now it looked more like a poor imitation of Don Johnson in an old rerun of *Miami Vice*. And since everything Perry did was calculated for effect, Jet wondered at the significance of his attire. His dark hair was artfully, yet casually, combed back and he sported a day's growth of hair on his chin and jaw.

"That your BMW parked out front?" he asked Landry.

"It is," Landry said stiffly, not returning the breezy smile.

"Classy car. A little conservative for my taste, though. I drive a red Mustang."

Yeah, a rented one. The flashy clothes and cars gave a false impression of wealth, and Perry was dead broke. Or so he claimed.

"Sporty car. But a bit too lame on the engineering for my taste," Landry remarked drily.

Perry pulled Jet to his side in a propriety gesture that made her want to give him a good kick in the shins. His Aqua de Sexy cologne did nothing for her after being so close to Landry minutes earlier. Everything about Perry now struck her as synthetic and fake.

It could never work between them again after all that had happened and the years apart. Still, letting go was like a little death. For too long, she'd clung to the hope they could be a real, loving couple, and dreams like that didn't die easily.

"Perry, this is Landry Fields, the IRS auditor that I spoke with yesterday."

"Nice to meet you. I'm Perry Hammonds."

Perry held out a hand, and for a moment Jet wasn't sure Landry was going to shake it.

But Landry played the gentleman. "I know the name. You were once in business with Miss Bosarge." Landry withdrew his hand. "Until you were sent to prison," he added.

Perry's smile flattened. "How nice of you to bring that up."

"I believe in laying out all the facts."

"Spoken like a typical accountant," Perry observed. "Bet you're a blast at parties."

Landry crossed his arms. "Yep, we nerdy types also believe in having plans. What's your game plan? Must be hard finding employment with a felony record."

Perry shrugged. "Something will come up. It always does. Besides, I'm doing my best to talk my girl into going back into business with me."

His girl? Jet stepped away from Perry's overly tight hold.

Landry swept his hand over the room. "Looks to me like she's got other ideas for earning an income. Guess

Miss Bosarge could always hire you temporarily to help with shipments and inventory as her supplies arrive."

Jet almost snorted. Perry work as a lowly stock boy? Not happening.

"I have a higher standard than that," Perry scoffed.

The air between the two men crackled with animosity, all pretense of politeness worn thin. Time to break it up. Jet headed to the door, motioning to Landry. "I'll have that paperwork for you no later than tomorrow," she promised. Of course, she had access to the papers. The problem was that most of them were bogus.

Landry followed her while Perry leaned an elbow on the front counter and watched them.

At the door, he handed her a card with his phone number. "My teenage brother is staying with me a few days. A temp job would give him something to do while I'm at work. Think about it and give me a call later if you'd like to meet him."

Suddenly, Landry bent down and whispered in her ear, "Don't do it. Don't go back into business with that guy. You're better than that."

Jet gasped at the feel of his hot breath at her ear, the touch of his cheek as he temporarily pressed against her neck. Even with the protective scarf to hide the gill markings, the silky material only served to make the contact more provocative.

Landry pulled away, his blue eyes inches from her own, intense and full of warning. Without waiting for an answer, he abruptly exited.

"Looks to me like that IRS dude is interested in more than your tax returns," Perry drawled after Landry shut the door. "What gives?"

"None of your business," she snapped. "Why did you

come by?" She sat on a bar stool next to Perry and rubbed her temples.

Perry smoothed back her hair behind one ear and ran a finger along the marking. "Let him get too close and he'll wonder about this."

Jet slapped his hand away, hard enough that Perry winced slightly. "That your way of saying I should stick with you since you know my deep, dark secret?"

"It should weigh in my favor that I know all about you and it doesn't bother me."

"Of course it doesn't. If I weren't a mermaid, you'd still be collecting penny-ante treasure crumbs all by your lonesome."

"That's not true. I want us back together," he said huskily. "The way it used to be in the beginning. Remember?" He leaned in and softly kissed her lips. "I remember. And while I was in that stinking prison I thought about you every single night."

It wasn't true. He'd never written or called. And when he got out, he took plenty of time getting back to the bayou. He nuzzled the tender flesh of her neck and rubbed her shoulders. "I missed you. C'mon, baby. Give me another chance."

Don't do it. You're better than that. Landry's whisper drowned out Perry's coaxing. Jet sighed. "We can never be business partners—or anything else—ever again."

His eyes narrowed. "Is it because of that accountant nerd? I saw the way he looked at you."

Jet's heart gave an odd tug at the idea. "Don't be stupid. We just met."

"Doesn't matter. I heard him ask you to hire his brother. That's his way of keeping an eye on you."

"We were talking about us." She took a deep breath. "It's over." There, she'd said it.

A deep red flush lit his pale face and his jaw clenched. "You don't mean it."

Jet stood. "Yes, I do." She held out her hand. "Good luck with whatever you decide to do in the future."

Perry grasped her hand. "Do this one last job with me. Help me get back on my feet."

"No, but I'll help you out." Jet shrugged out of his grasp and lifted her backpack from a shelf. "I'll write you a check. Enough for you to move and set up in some new business."

Perry's mouth dropped open and Jet smiled inwardly. He'd obviously expected her to fall into her lap. She found a pen and opened her checkbook.

Perry grabbed her writing hand. "I don't want your money. I want you to go with me to Tybee Island."

Jet jerked her hand away and gazed at him in surprise. "Since when do you not want my money?"

His flush deepened. "I like to earn my money and this is a big deal at Tybee."

"I don't have time for this. I'm opening the shop back up and moving on with my life."

He rolled his eyes. "Bor-*ing*. You'll be stir-crazy in two weeks."

"Shows how little you know me." She signed the check with a flourish and handed it over.

"I told you I don't want your—" Perry read the dollar amount and paused. "On second thought, I'll take it. Thanks." He grabbed the check and stuffed it into his white jeans. "But I still need you for this job."

Jet snorted. What had she *ever* seen in this man? "I gave you enough money to start over doing something else."

Perry stood. "This is your last chance. Say no, and I'm never coming back."

"Have a good life."

Perry's lips clamped together so tightly a thin white line edged the rims. "You'll be sorry," he warned.

"Get out," she said flatly.

He stared at her with an unfathomable expression. At least he didn't stoop so low as—

"I love you, Jet." His eyes softened. "And I'm begging you. Let's go now, right this minute. Forget your shop."

Don't do it. Landry's whisper echoed in her brain. *You're better than that.*

Yes, she was.

"No," she said firmly.

He stiffened. "If that's the way you want to play it." Perry slapped the countertop. "But you'll regret that decision before the week is out. Consider yourself warned."

Chills skittered down her spine at his set face. There was something there behind the words, something twisted. Something more than Perry believing she would miss him.

She picked up the invoice stack Landry had looked through, determined to get right to work and set her mind on business instead of worrying. A strong scent of baby powder tickled her nose and she lifted the papers to her face. Hmm, why would paper smell like powder?

The shop door slammed shut as Perry left, chimes exploding in a riot of discordant clangs.

Jet no longer cared. Landry's expressed faith in her character harmonized in her heart, outweighing Perry's threat and pique.

Chapter 4

A long rock guitar riff assaulted Landry's ears as he entered the house.

"Hey," he shouted. "Turn it down."

Seth sprawled on the sofa, lost in the music, a crumpled bag of chips and half a sandwich by his side. Landry winced at the thought of meat grease staining the expensive leather.

He unplugged the cord and Seth jumped at the resulting quiet. "Wha—"

"Little loud for me. Is this what you've been doing all day?"

Seth sat up straight and stretched. "I got up about two o'clock, fixed a sandwich and listened to my iPod. Jeez, it's so boring out here."

"What do you usually do all day now you're out of school?"

"Hang out with friends. You know."

No, he didn't know. He'd worked nights and summers since he was sixteen and put himself through college. And after college he'd been busy with his career. "What's your game plan until summer school starts?"

Seth gave an elaborate shrug. "More of the same, I guess."

The kid would drive him nuts. "We need to establish a few house rules." Landry pointed to the food refuse. "Pick up after yourself and get in bed by midnight. Or at least turn the TV on low or read a book."

"Read a book?" Seth snorted. "Yeah, this week is going to be a blast."

Oh, hell, he could make more of an effort to be hospitable. A few days wasn't forever. Landry regarded Seth's bored, impassive features and sighed, trying to remember what he liked at that same age, besides the all-consuming testosterone-raging obsession with girls. He'd been a serious kid, always retreating from his noisy family and working jobs for some cash.

"How about a temporary job? I know a lady who might be interested in hiring you."

Seth grimaced, as if tasting sour lemon. "Why would I want to do *that?*"

Right, whatever you want you can shoplift. "It's not so bad. Be nice to have your own spending money."

"Nothing I really need."

"What about a car or money to take out a girl?"

"Don't have a girlfriend and I could never save up enough for a car. Guess I'll try to join my dad on the oil rigs in a couple of years. Might as well be a bum while I can."

Landry thought quickly. "You could save up enough for a used car. Tell you what, whatever you save in the next six months, I'll match it."

It was easy to read the mistrust in Seth's eyes. "Why would you do that?"

"You're my brother."

"Half brother," Seth corrected. "And I haven't seen much of you in the last few years."

Landry fought down the guilt that flared in his gut. "You should take the job. She needs a temp to stock. There's a shipment of goods coming in tomorrow, so she'd need you right away."

"Oh, all right," he said with a complete lack of enthusiasm. "I don't see why she can't do it herself, though. Is she old or something?"

Landry snorted. Jet Bosarge was the complete opposite of old and frail. "She's younger than me by at least five or six years."

"She your girlfriend?"

The question took him aback. Jet's sharp features sprang to mind. She was way too...*intense* for his taste. There was a storm in her eyes, a tightness and electricity in her every move that was disturbing. Everything in her manner suggested a hard, unbending nature. Despite it, there was no denying most men probably found her type alluring. He wasn't one of them. He liked women that were more nurturing with soft, curvy bodies that promised a hot night in bed. And out of bed, he wanted the kind of woman with whom he could relax at home on quiet evenings. God, he sounded like a chauvinist. No wonder he was single.

"Well?" Seth asked. "Is she your girlfriend or not?"

"Not. Definitely not. I only met her yesterday," he said way too loudly, pushing aside the memory of how they had almost kissed in the shop. "And I need a favor. Don't tell her I'm with the FBI. She thinks I'm an IRS auditor."

Seth scowled. "Why'd you lie?"

"It's not a lie—it's an undercover job."

"Uh-huh. So you want me to spy on her."

Landry's jaw tightened. "Of course not." Did the kid think the worst of everybody? He hadn't considered it but... "If you do see anything weird, you could let me know."

Seth snatched up the chips bag and stalked toward the kitchen.

Landry followed him, picking up a used drinking glass and an empty box of crackers. "And speaking of weird—have you noticed anything unusual going on around the house?"

"No. What do you mean?"

Landry felt the back of his neck heat. "Like things not being where they're supposed to be and strange noises. Stuff like that." Seth's blank face reminded Landry why it was always better to just keep his mouth shut. "Never mind. How about we go out? We could swing by Miss Bosarge's house so she can meet you, and then go to Mobile for pizza and a movie."

"I guess."

His brother's lack of enthusiasm was irritating, but at least he hadn't refused. During the fifteen-minute ride to Jet's, Landry looked at Bayou La Siryna with new eyes. Much as he appreciated the lonely, mysterious swampland, which suited his own loner nature, it didn't offer much for a teenager. If Seth stayed the whole summer, he might lose his mind from boredom. Landry pulled into the Bosarge driveway, glad Perry's Mustang was nowhere in sight.

"Cool house," Seth commented, sliding out of the BMW. "She rich?"

"Yep. Her family has a whole lot more money than we'll ever earn in our lifetime." The thought rankled. Jet's wealth was one of a dozen reasons why he shouldn't get involved with her. They were from different planets. Everything he had, he'd earned through hard work and disciplined savings, while she'd been raised in a life of ease.

They walked up the steps onto the wraparound porch of the large Victorian home. Wicker rockers graced the open space and large ferns hung from wooden rafters. The place didn't reflect Jet at all, much too girlie. He rapped on the pale blue door and waited.

Loveliness, incarnated in human form, opened the door. She had long blond hair, green eyes, perfect skin and full, lush lips. Seth sucked in his breath beside him and Landry smiled. This must be Jet's cousin Shelly, because Jet's sister, Lily, had been gone for months. Whereabouts unknown. "I'm here to see Jet," he said.

Those ocean-green eyes widened a bit. She opened the door and waved them inside. Some *thing*—some mixture of rat, possum and hellhound—scrabbled his way over, barking and snarling.

"What is that?" he asked.

"Our dog, Rebel." Shelly commanded him to sit and the thing complied.

Landry looked at him closer. "What's wrong with him—besides the mange? He's covered in cuts and scars."

Shelly scratched his hairless ears. "He doesn't have the mange. He's a Chinese Crested Hairless. Jet and I rescued him. We found him tied to a tree where a group of kids were stoning him to death."

"Glad you found him in time." No creature, no matter how hideous, deserved that fate. He followed her into the den. "Nice place," he commented. Now, this was more like Jet, especially the collection of swords over the fireplace. "I hope we haven't come at a bad time."

"Not at all. I'll get Jet." She smiled warmly at Seth,

who still looked a bit dazed. "Have a seat. Can I get you a Coke or something?"

"No, ma'am." His voice squeaked and he sat down quickly.

Landry shook his head and sat, as well. What had he been thinking yesterday about wanting to be younger? Seth made him remember that adolescence sucked sometimes.

"This place is cool," Seth said, eyeing the swords.

"Then you ought to like working for Jet." Landry ran a finger over a brass antique compass lying on a coffee table. The magnetic needle jerked and spun frenetically in circles and he hastily stuffed his hands into his pockets.

Seth's gaze turned from the Confederate sword he'd been studying. "This is the kinda stuff she sells? I thought it would be clothing or makeup crap."

"I promise no makeup crap," Jet's voice rang out.

The air in the room crackled as if a high voltage of positive ions had been released, like a smell after a heavy rain at the beach, bracing and refreshing. She wore a pair of cutoff denim shorts and a gray T-shirt with Alabama Crimson Tide stamped across the front.

Landry stood and pulled Seth to his feet. "Hello again, Jet. This is my brother Seth."

"Half brother," he mumbled.

Jet shrugged. "Whatever. I could use some help tomorrow with a big shipment of furniture from Mobile. I'd only need you a day or two. You up for it?"

"Guess so," he muttered.

"Tell me what time you need him at your shop," Landry said.

"About ten o'clock."

Seth's mouth dropped open slightly. "That early?"

Landry elbowed him. "He'll be there."

Shelly walked up beside Jet. "What about school, Seth?"

Seth straightened and a dull red flush crept up his neck. "I'm done for the year."

Shelly absently swirled a lock of honeyed curls. "I see. Since you're at loose ends for a bit, I've got someone I want you to meet. Do you swim?"

Landry shifted uncomfortably, hoping Shelly wouldn't ask him the same question because he hated lying. What thirty-five-year-old man couldn't swim? It was ridiculous. Yet he sank like a stone every time he tried to learn.

"Of course I can swim," Seth answered.

"Then I want you to meet Jimmy Elmore at the YMCA pool. His grandmother Lurlene is one of my senior clients."

Shelly turned questioning eyes to Landry. "Mind if I introduce them? Jimmy's a good kid. You'll see."

"Sure. Seth could use some company his own age."

"I'll set it up now while you two talk business." Shelly steered Seth out of the room. "Let's call Jimmy now and work out a time." Her voice became fainter, from the kitchen. "Then I want to show you our knife collection. Some of them are over one hundred years old—"

"My cousin loves kids," Jet said. "Looks like she's taking Seth under her wing."

Landry couldn't tear his eyes from Jet. For the first time, he noticed her dark eyes were rimmed with flecks of gold and green, like chips of orange citrine and emeralds. He stepped closer, watched them widen with a sudden wariness.

Jet fingered a red scarf draped on the sides of her slender throat as she inched backward. "Why are you staring at me?"

Good question. What the hell was he doing? Jet was

a possible felon and might be involved in some big-time scam if she and Perry Hammonds were working with Sylvester Vargas. He had never—ever—looked twice at a woman with a shady background. They were persona non grata in his rule book.

"I'm not," Landry lied, running a hand over the back of his neck. This was inexplicable and frustrating. Everything about this woman was a mystery. And he hated mysteries.

Or so he'd once believed.

"I have those documents you wanted." Jet walked away and he watched her long, slender legs cross the room. She leaned over slightly to yank open a drawer in an old rolltop desk. He stared at the slight curve of her hip framing a heart-shaped ass. The rest of her tall body might be thin and muscled, but her bottom was lush. He imagined gripping a handful of cheek and—

She spun around, an armload of paper cradled at her side, and frowned. "You're staring at me again."

Caught red-handed.

Landry pointed at the papers. "Those for me?" Nothing like a little deflection when denial was pointless. What was the matter with him? He didn't go around gawking at every pretty girl that crossed his path. Yet around her, all he could think about was drawing her body to his.

"Every freaking year accounted for." She marched to him and held out the stack. "All yours."

"How did you get them so quick?" Damn. Hounding her about the paperwork was merely a ploy to test the waters about her relationship with Hammonds. Good thing she'd hired Seth, so he'd have an excuse to hang around her shop. He riffled through the stack—each item had a provenance form with date of origin, location found, date sold and more. On the surface all appeared normal, but how could one woman be so lucky finding sea treasure? He discounted Hammonds as a factor in their success. Perry the Prick was nothing but a useless hanger-on. Anyone with half a brain could see that within minutes of meeting him.

Except Jet.

She folded her arms and matched his stare. Only now, the veiled hostility of yesterday was missing. Her expression was hard to fathom, a mixture of curiosity, sensuality and challenge. Maybe she, too, remembered that moment in the shop when their mouths had been inches from kissing.

He tried to remember all the reasons why this woman was off-limits, but he couldn't name a single one. Everything about Jet fascinated him and stirred his sensual appetite like it hadn't been in years. The pale glittering skin, full lips and unusually dark eyes framed by black hair were so different from any other woman, especially his blonde, blue-eyed ex-fiancée.

No, screw that memory. The past would not haunt him anymore.

Jet crackled with energy and a directness that cut through his usual barriers and demanded sole focus on her own unique qualities.

She leaned closer, a glint of desire sparkled like pixie dust in her enlarged pupils, and Landry's jaw clinched at his body's immediate tug to draw closer. "What did you tell Perry today?" he ground out in a voice harsh from the tightness in his lungs and chest.

Jet blinked. "I told him we were done."

"You really mean that?" If she was truly finished with Hammonds, maybe they could be together. He hadn't found anything—yet—that proved Jet was involved with

Sylvester Vargas or had plans to illegally salvage something on a large scale.

She gave a lopsided grin. "Cost me a few thousand, but he finally accepted I won't do any more treasure hunts with him."

Landry frowned, fingers curling into his palm. "Don't tell me you had to pay Hammonds to get rid of him." What a low-life scum bucket. Someone that mercenary and manipulative had no ethics or morals. Someone like that was dangerous. He hoped Hammonds would take the check and leave town, but instinct and experience warned there was little possibility of that scenario playing out.

"Forget I said it, then." Jet shrugged and her eyes again shone with heat. "The important thing is that it's over between us." She touched his chest with one hand, and even through his thick cotton shirt, the heat of her skin traveled downward, and his stomach clenched.

All reason fled. He had to feel her, taste her, claim her—

Landry lowered his face and kissed the top of Jet's scalp, inhaling her warm, earthy scent. If he'd read the signals wrong, she could back away now. But she didn't rebuff him. Instead, Jet wrapped her arms around his waist and pulled him closer, setting his groin on fire.

His body hummed with need. Landry tightened his hold on her before at last claiming her lips. They were as soft and yielding as he'd imagined. Their mouths parted and he tasted liquid warmth as their tongues danced, tentative at first, then with increasing urgency. He ran his hands down her lean, tight back before palming that cute ass he'd been eyeing moments earlier. The contrast of the lushness there, compared to the muscled tightness on the rest of her body, made the soft flesh even more enticing.

Jet let out a noise somewhere between a moan and a

sigh and the sound inflamed Landry's senses. He had to explore another area of soft flesh. His hands reached under the flimsy T-shirt until he palmed both breasts, which—thank goodness—were harnessed only by an athletic bra that he easily pushed upward and out of the way.

Although many men might prefer bigger breasts, Landry found Jet's perfect, exactly suited for her tall, athletic frame. He trailed kisses down her throat, reckless with need.

A door slammed shut and the sound of voices entered the hall. *Shit.* Abruptly, Landry pulled Jet's bra down over her breasts and stepped back. He inhaled deeply, trying to control his heavy breathing. Jet appeared stunned by his sudden withdrawal and wrapped her arms across her chest.

"So bring your swim trunks and a few towels—" Shelly entered first, glanced at them both sharply and resumed talking "—because Jimmy will meet you at the Y as soon as you get off work tomorrow."

Landry slowed his heavy breathing with an effort, incredulous at his lack of composure. This woman's effect on him was downright uncanny.

Seth came in directly behind her, running a hand through his wind-tossed hair. "Cool." He grinned at Shelly, looking happier than Landry had seen him since he arrived at the bayou. "It'll be awesome to have someone to hang out with."

Huh? Little brother could actually be agreeable and talkative. It hadn't even occurred to Landry to try to introduce Seth to guys his own age; he'd only been concerned about getting through the visit without the two of them wanting to kill each other. Landry shifted uncomfortably at a little pang of guilt. He didn't know anyone around Seth's age, and besides, Seth would go along with anything Shelly suggested. The kid was obviously spell-bound by her looks.

"You can leave work whatever time you want," Jet said to Seth, settling down on the sofa and crossing her long legs. "The schedule's flexible."

Landry stole a glance at her from the corner of his eyes. Jet appeared cool and composed, like she had when they first met. Only the faint darkening of her lips indicated she'd been thoroughly kissed.

To hell with always following procedure and all his rigid rules and preconceived ideas about his perfect type of woman. He'd thought his ex was perfect for him. All those quiet evenings spent at one another's place watching television or reading books. There'd been no drama, no fights. So what if it had been a bit dull? They had settled into a comfortable companionship he imagined would last forever until the day she texted and told him she'd found someone more exciting.

Landry took a deep breath. Nothing about Jet would ever be boring or fade to a companionable kind of relationship. He dropped his gaze to those shapely, smooth legs and wanted to lick his lips. He could almost feel them wrapped around his back as they made love. Maybe once that happened he could regain control over his traitorous body and stop mooning over Jet.

Soon, very soon, he promised himself.

Chapter 5

Seth's thin forearms and biceps knotted into muscled cords as he and the deliveryman carried a Duncan Phyfe sofa into Jet's shop, The Pirate's Chest. Despite his slightly sullen attitude around Landry, Seth had proved to be a hard worker. The teenager's chin-length hair was washed and shining and he'd shaved the face stubble. No doubt the sudden interest in grooming was to impress Shelly, whom he seemed quite taken with last night.

Last night. Little sparkles of happiness tap-danced along Jet's spine whenever she thought of Landry's kiss. Amazing that chemistry ignited when they were together, considering how and why they met. He'd been so antagonistic at first. Yet, even then, she'd been drawn to the crisp blueness of his eyes and the solid strength he emanated. Biology was a very weird thing.

"Set it over here in this corner," Jet directed Seth. The floor space was filling up quickly, yet several large pieces remained on the delivery truck. Funny, her stockpile of nautical salvage hadn't looked so gargantuan in the huge industrial warehouse.

Shelly, perched on a bar stool reclaimed from an old ship, shook her head as she surveyed the ever-increasing piles of stuff. Ripples, like sun bouncing off water, shimmered through her golden curls. "You should have measured everything first, like I suggested."

"Nobody likes people who say 'I told you so.'" Jet lifted a handful of her sweaty black hair to cool her neck and then remembered the nearby strangers. Drat. She let go and arranged some chunks around her neck to cover the faint outline of gills. Too bad all humans weren't like Eddie, Shelly's soon-to-be brother-in-law. Around Eddie, she didn't have to worry about any oddity. "I'm not worried about the space," she added. "Once I hang up some of the merchandise, there will be plenty of room in the aisles for customers to browse."

Eddie stood as unmoving as an ice sculpture in the middle of the chaos. His head was thrown so far back, only his long neck and the tip of his chin were visible. Jet followed his gaze up to where a four-hundred-pound chandelier glimmered with thousands of prisms, each casting variegated dots of pastel hues on the coppered ceiling.

"Rainbow," Eddie pronounced.

Jet nodded. Eddie was wrapped up in his own autistic world, but when he spoke, he often had a unique perspective.

"So, are you expecting Landry to stop by today?" Shelly asked with a knowing smile. "Maybe y'all can finish what you started yesterday."

Her cousin was far too perceptive. After Landry had left last night, Shelly had gone on and on about what a nice guy he was, such an improvement over Perry, he had such a safe, secure job, etc. The biggest positive, in Shelly's eyes, was that Landry demonstrated a caring nature, since he took his little brother under his wing— much like Tillman watched over his kid brother, Eddie.

Jet sighed; she'd been hoping for Landry to contact her all morning but hadn't heard a word. "No, I haven't seen him, but Perry's called a few times. I didn't answer the phone."

Shelly's green eyes darkened. "That bastard," she hissed.

"That bastard," Eddie mimicked, eyes still glued upward.

Jet laughed. For Shelly to use that language was unusual, especially around Eddie.

"Very funny." Shelly rolled her eyes. "Hope he doesn't repeat it around Tillman later."

"Even if he did, Tillman wouldn't care. He thinks you are Miss Perfect." Jet bit her lip, hoping Shelly didn't catch the whiff of bitterness. Her cousin was one lucky woman and deserved every bit of happiness. She had been through hell last year after witnessing a serial killer dumping a body at sea. The killer had hunted her down, but Shelly and Tillman defeated the man and fell in love in the process. By the time Tillman had discovered Shelly was part mermaid, it didn't stop him from loving her and proposing a lifetime together.

Shelly snapped her fingers as inspiration struck. "Hey, want me to have Tillman run Perry out of town? As sheriff, he could find a way to do it."

"I can handle an ex-boyfriend," Jet said with a sniff. She didn't mention the desperate measure of paying Perry off to get rid of him. Humiliating enough that she'd slipped and admitted it to Landry last night.

As the movers loaded a ten-foot-high mahogany armoire onto a dolly, Jet glanced around, assessing where to best make room. The only hope for it was to take the sofa and move it into a middle aisle so the armoire could be placed against the far wall. She hoisted the sofa, raising it a good two feet off the ground. As she walked forward, she spotted Seth and the deliveryman, who had both stopped rolling the furniture and stared at her, mouths agape. Behind them, Shelly grimaced at the careless, giveaway slip.

Uh, oh. After spending weeks doing nothing but training undersea and attending the Poseidon Games, she was forgetting all the little subterfuges necessary to not draw attention from landlubbers. Good thing Landry hadn't witnessed her strength. The man was way too observant for her comfort.

"How did you lift that all by yourself?" Seth's voice squeaked a bit at the end. He cleared his throat. "It took both of us to drag it in."

Jet dropped it immediately. "I wasn't thinking." She placed a hand on the small of her back and sank down onto the sofa's scratchy wool upholstery. "Oh, my back," she moaned, hoping it sounded convincing.

"You're always trying to lift things that are too heavy." Shelly rushed over with a distracting display of concern and bent over Jet. "Your back will hurt for weeks because of this. When will you ever learn?"

"Good job," Jet mumbled in her ear.

"Play along," Shelly whispered back as she put an arm around Jet's shoulder and pretended to support her. "Come sit up front with me. I've got some Tylenol in my purse."

Jet hobbled around the men and waved her hand

vaguely in the air. "Fit everything in here as best you can."

Seth and the mover looked slightly appeased, though their male pride had undoubtedly taken a hit.

Once they were both seated, Shelly pointed to a cardboard box on the long, scarred oak counter. "I'm about halfway through cataloging the contents." She patted a stack of papers. "I've already printed out the inventory for all this." She swept her hand over dozens of old coins, cuff links, and other odds and ends. "You can finish going through this box while you are…um…convalescing that injured back."

"Where are you going?"

"Back to the YMCA." Shelly glanced at her watch. "Next class starts in fifteen minutes. My senior swimmers already have a low opinion of the younger generation. Don't want them to lump me in with the slackers."

Jet snickered. "Those old folks adore you. All your clients do, especially Eddie." Her cousin was a popular woman in the bayou. As an aquatic therapist, Shelly helped the elderly and special-needs persons with their challenges. And by the end of summer, she would be married to Tillman. The merfolk might look down on Shelly because she was half mermaid, half human, but she'd come to terms with her shape-shifting heritage, found a man who loved her and established her place in the community.

Too bad Jet couldn't say the same for herself.

She might be all mermaid by birth, but Jet, like Shelly, had never felt comfortable around other mermaids, either. Jet sensed a distance between them, knew that behind her back they exchanged raised eyebrows or knowing looks of disdain. Growing up, she'd attributed it to her mother insisting she and Lily spend so much time with humans in the bayou. But Jet suspected more was afoot and this year she would demand the truth. She fingered the golden trident nestled against her chest on a chain. As soon as her mother came home for their annual family reunion, she'd use her one wish to find out why the merfolk shunned her.

As far as her love life… Jet bit the inside of her lip. *Don't get too excited over Landry. He'll only disappoint you like Perry.* She let out a deep sigh, stifling the depressing thought. It might be foolish, but she couldn't help hoping this time might be different. Landry was the complete opposite of Perry. You couldn't get any more safe or predicable or stable than an accountant. And she was so tired of being alone. Surely there was no harm in yielding to her carnal desires. Landry's pull was magnetic and she didn't want to fight it.

Only two obstacles stood in the way of them exploring a relationship. One, Perry needed to go away and, two, Landry needed to close his audit file. That high-priced attorney assured her everything was in order with her taxes and she had nothing to fear. Landry might be a bit suspicious but he could prove nothing illegal. This whole matter of an irregularity in the tax records should be dropped as soon as Landry reviewed the paperwork.

Seth gazed after Shelly as she left with Eddie. If he was this entranced by Shelly, the kid would be totally lost if he ever met Lily.

Finally, the delivery was complete and they both sank onto chairs by the window.

"I don't know what I would have done without you today," Jet began.

Seth gave a half smile and pulled one leg on top of the opposite knee. "You probably would have lifted everything by yourself and been finished—" he yawned broadly "—by lunchtime."

Jet let the remark pass without comment. Seth might be a teenager, but he was pretty sharp. "Good thing I met your brother."

Seth shrugged. "You done with me? I can help you move shit—" he stopped and reddened slightly "—I mean move *stuff* around."

"I could use some more help. I'll treat you to lunch first. Let me freshen up and I'll be right back."

Seth ambled out of the chair and went to the counter where she'd laid out dozens of knives that had yet to be cataloged. "These are way cool."

Jet smiled faintly. *Cool* and *awesome* seemed to comprise a large part of his vocabulary.

"Yeah, they're cool," Jet said, sweeping by the display. Once ensconced in the tiny employee bathroom, she retrieved a comb and ran it through her tangled bob. Not her best look, but it would have to do. She'd secretly hoped Landry would show up and go to lunch with them, but he must be busy.

As Jet reentered the store, she halted in surprise at Seth's furtive glance behind him as he held up the dagger he'd admired earlier. Jet noiselessly stepped behind a bookshelf and watched as he hesitated and then quickly stuffed the weapon into an inside pocket of his baggy camouflage jacket. Her heart plummeted. She'd planned on letting Seth pick out one from the collection as a gift before he left town.

Takes a thief to catch a thief. Jet shifted in the shadows, annoyed the thought popped into her mind. She didn't steal anything, only told half-truths in reporting where and how she found sea treasure. *A half-truth is the same as a lie. Don't kid yourself.* How disappointed would Landry be if he knew all her secrets? Of all the people to fall for, it had to be an IRS auditor. He was sure to view the world like he did financial ledgers, with everything either black or white. And she was definitely a shade of gray. Jet remembered his urgent whisper, *You're better than that,* when Perry tried to persuade her to take one last "sure thing" salvage venture.

She shrugged off the battle with her conscience and stepped out from behind the bookcase, prepared to confront Seth. But before she said anything, he took the dagger out of his jacket pocket and laid it back down on the counter.

"Good choice," Jet said crisply. The words seemed overly loud in the cramped space.

Seth jumped and faced her with wide, stricken eyes. "I...I..." He gulped and couldn't say any more, his entire body rigid and unmoving.

She couldn't help but feel sorry for him. "It's okay. I won't tell your brother."

He relaxed only slightly. "I'm...uh...sorry." Seth's face turned red and he stared at the floor. "Guess I'm fired, huh? I'll call Landry to come get me." Still unable to look her in the eyes, Seth walked to the door with his head down.

Damn, she probably felt as bad as he did. "Wait," Jet called out.

Seth stopped, but kept his back to her.

She walked over and motioned for Seth to sit down in a chair by the door. Pulling up another chair and sitting across from him, Jet leaned close. "Look at me."

He crossed his arms, scooted backward and leaned so far over that he balanced precariously on the two back legs of the chair. His brown eyes might be different from Landry's, but he had the same remote expression down pat. The defensive stance screamed you-can't-hurt-me and Jet would recognize it an ocean away, considering this was how she reacted when cornered.

"You didn't take the dagger and that's what matters. We're—what's your word?—cool."

"You're saying that 'cause you have a thing for my half brother."

Observant guy. "Everyone's redeemable," she mumbled.

Seth regarded her blankly. "Huh?"

"What I mean is…what matters in the end are the actions we take." Holy Poseidon, she was talking about her own situation. No wonder Seth wasn't following her train of thought.

She ran a hand through her hair. "Never mind. Let's forget this whole thing happened. You're not fired and I want you to keep working. Now, how about lunch?"

"No need." Seth craned his neck to look past her out the front window. She'd taken down the paper covering on all the doors and windows to let in the sunlight. "My half brother's here."

Jet turned and watched an expensive BMW being expertly maneuvered between two other vehicles as the driver executed a perfect parallel-parking feat.

"Did you two have plans to meet for lunch?"

"Nope."

Landry entered, polished and neat in a navy suit, eggplant-colored tie and crisp white shirt. The atmosphere shimmered with the heat between them. Jet suddenly became aware of how grubby her jeans and T-shirt were. She sneaked a glance in the mirror at the far end of the front counter. Her black hair had sticky spikes shooting out at odd angles and her face had a sheen of sweat that culminated in a drop of perspiration above her lips.

She lifted an arm to swipe at her face, but checked the motion. Landry found her attractive as she was; he'd shown that last night. And the sweat was from trying to make an honest living.

Well, starting *today* she was trying to make an honest living. If you didn't count the few odds and ends for sale that were collected from the bottom of the sea.

Landry gave a low whistle. "And to think yesterday this place was nearly barren. You both must be beat." His eyes went immediately to the six-foot-high mermaid masthead hanging on the opposite wall. "Wow. That wasn't here yesterday. It's incredible. Where did you get this?"

The elaborately carved ship masthead was one of her favorite pieces and definitely not for sale. Instead of the dreamy perfection of most artists' mermaid renditions, this mermaid's features were fierce. In her right hand she held a raised sword, as if defying Poseidon himself as the lone protector of the ship she guarded. The bold cut of her features, as well as the detailed carving of her tail-fin scales, were so precise that Jet often wondered if the artist might have once had a close encounter with one of her kind.

She couldn't keep a bit of pride out of her voice. "I have my sources. That masthead is dated from the late 1700s and is carved from suar wood."

He drifted down an aisle toward the masthead, fingering a few select pieces of brass hull plates from salvaged ships, antique dive helmets and rare, colored-glass floats. He swiveled abruptly to Jet. "I'm surprised Bayou La Siryna has enough high-end clientele to support a store with such expensive items."

"We have a few wealthy families. Last time I had the shop open, we drew a significant customer base from

Mobile and Pensacola. Nautical-salvage stores are a novelty. Besides, I sell lots of merchandise over the internet too." Jet rose slowly and remembered to put a hand at the small of her back.

Landry immediately strode toward her, frowning. "What's wrong?"

"You should have seen her," Seth broke in. "Miss Bosarge lifted a big ole sofa all by herself. Thing must have weighed two hundred pounds."

Landry arched an eyebrow. "Did she, now?"

Jet went to the front counter, away from those piercing eyes. She pulled out a bag of old coins from the cardboard box and fired up the laptop to enter it into the store invoice. "Seth has been great. In fact, I'd like him to return after lunch and we can discuss the possibility of him working the whole time he's visiting you.

Seth scrunched his face. "I'm not going to be here long."

"What's this?" The low rumble of Landry's voice beside her caught Jet by surprise. A prickle of sexual awareness tingled down her spine. His large hand closed over one of the artifacts scattered on the counter, an old, sheathed dagger.

Jet's gaze traveled up his arm and into his eyes. Damn, it had been much too long since she'd made love to a man—or a merman, either. Her pheromones were in overdrive and the memory of his touch fueled the fire.

She wasn't alone in feeling a sexual tingle. The pupils in Landry's eyes were so enlarged that the irises had shrunk to a razor-thin rim of blue. Her own dilated eyes were reflected in his like a black mirror image of lust.

Her heart flip-flopped in her chest like a tiny minnow caught in the jaws of a shark. She drank in every detail of his face...the squared jaw, the light brown hair that waved ever so slightly at his earlobes. Jet curled her fingers into her palm to keep from reaching up and again exploring the curve of his jaw, the golden tips of his light brown hair, those firm lips. The stinging imprint of her nails inside her palm reminded Jet that right this moment was not the time to indulge her curiosity.

Landry lowered his face a fraction. The same electricity that sparked every time they were together returned stronger than before. She'd put it off as nerves at that first meeting, but after last night she'd been forced to acknowledge that it wasn't a mere case of apprehension. It was him. Something about Landry drew her, excited her, as primitive as the need to immerse her body undersea during a full moon.

"Check this one out." Seth stepped between them and pointed to the dagger he was so taken with.

Landry straightened abruptly and withdrew his hand.

Jet picked up the dagger and handed it to Seth. The slight tremble in his fingers made her inwardly wince. He was trying hard to act as if nothing was wrong.

The rusty squeal of steel brushing against steel rang out as Seth removed the dagger from its scabbard. He reverently ran a finger down the worn, pitted twelve-inch blade. He pointed at the scrolled engraving on the handle. "Is this gold?"

Jet smiled. Every man who entered her store would walk right past the furniture and accessories and head straight to the knives and swords in the display case up front.

"Sorry, it's just brass."

Seth's face lit up for the first time that morning. "Then maybe I can afford to buy it."

Landry frowned. "Might still be too expensive." He turned to Jet. "Is this another one of your antiques?"

She nodded. "It's early twentieth century but I haven't been able to trace the exact origin."

"How much?" Seth asked, eyes wide with interest.

Poor guy. Jet doubted this trinket would be in his price range. "About eight hundred dollars," she admitted reluctantly. "But I could discount it to four hundred if you really want it."

"Nah, that's okay." Seth's thin shoulders drooped as he replaced the dagger in the scabbard.

Landry slapped him on the shoulder. "You're saving your money for a car. Remember?"

"Yeah." The light died in his dark eyes and his lips turned down at the corners, the same mulish expression he wore when Landry had dropped him off in the morning.

"That's great," Jet said, trying to lift the kid's mood. "All the more reason to work for me while you're in the bayou."

Seth shrugged. "It doesn't matter. I'll never be able to save enough money for a car." He faced his brother. "Even if you really did pay half."

Landry's jaw tightened. "I said I would."

"Whatever."

As Seth went to the door, Landry rolled his eyes and Jet shared a secret smile with him. There was no doubt in her mind, if Landry said he would do something, you could consider it a done deal.

"I came to invite both of you to lunch," Landry said. "Where would you like to go?"

"McDonald's," Seth cut in before she could reply.

Landry gave Jet a wry smile. "I was thinking of something a little more upscale."

This new, easy manner of Landry's, outside the confines of the IRS office, warmed her heart far more than it should. Besides the physical pull, she actually *liked* this man, enjoyed his company. Too bad she hadn't met him before Perry. Bad boys were way overrated.

"I'm not crazy about fast food," Jet admitted. Actually, she couldn't metabolize red meat, and the fries and other stuff on the menu had the texture of sawdust on her mermaid tongue. "There's a restaurant one block away that serves great fried shrimp."

Seth jerked his arms into his coat pocket. "I hate seafood. It stinks."

Landry frowned. "You can't live off of hamburgers and strawberry milk shakes."

Jet tried to ease the tension. "You two go ahead. I'll order something and keep working. Seth, let me know after lunch if you want to work more while you're in town. I've got a ton of stuff that needs to be either shelved or hung on the walls."

Landry reached into his suit pocket and pulled out a set of keys. "You go ahead, Seth. I want to treat Jet to lunch."

Seth grabbed them quickly, a huge grin transforming his bony face. "Thanks, see ya," he said, practically running out of the store.

"Wait." Jet hurried behind the counter and grabbed a key ring. "Take this spare store key in case you finish lunch before we do." She tossed it to him and he deftly caught it one-handed by the entryway.

The stunned look on Seth's face was priceless. "You really giving me a key?"

"I trust you." If he had no conscience, he wouldn't have returned the beloved dagger.

Seth blinked and the usual aloofness in his eyes softened, making him appear like the young teenager he was. "Hey, thanks, dude," he mumbled.

Landry raised a brow. "Jet's a *dude?*"

Seth didn't bother answering and they watched as he eased the BMW onto Main Street.

"How does he stay so skinny the way he eats?" she asked.

"Metabolism," he said decisively. "What I wouldn't give to have a teenager's ability to burn fat."

His body looked pretty smoking hot as far as she was concerned. And it felt pretty damned hot, too. But then she'd suspected all along that beneath his tailored suits and veneer of reserve, Landry was a passionate man.

Jet hoped to find out just how passionate he was.

The sooner the better.

"How did you and Perry meet?"

Jet almost choked midswallow. She set down the water glass. They'd been having a fun conversation about Alabama football and their mutual fascination with horror movies and Southern Gothic tales until Landry slipped that question in.

"He'd been sailing around the bayou in his Catalina. I'd pulled my motorboat into the harbor at the same time he was securing his boat," she said reluctantly. She flushed remembering how she'd been so taken, so besotted, with Perry that within a week of meeting him she'd rashly confided her mermaid secret, something she'd never done before or since.

"Did you go into business soon after you met him?"

Jet shifted in her seat. "Pretty quick," she admitted, pushing aside her plate. Why couldn't he just finish his audit and let all that go? He kept chipping away at that stone barrier she'd put in place about her past. "What about you?" she asked, deflecting more questions. "How long has it been since you were in a serious relationship?"

"Not very subtle," he said with a one-sided smile. "But I'll play. It's been a while."

"Divorced?"

"Never married, just engaged once."

"What happened?" Jet's hand flew to her mouth, as if to stuff the words back inside. She was as bad as he. "Forget it. You don't—"

"She found somebody else." Landry's features hardened like chiseled stone.

That must have hurt like hell. She lowered her voice. "How long ago did this happen?"

"Five years."

About the same time she met Perry. She wasn't the only person who'd suffered a betrayal of sorts. Jet lightly touched his arm. "I'm sorry."

He shrugged as if it were no big deal. "I can see now that we weren't meant to be together. What we had was more along the lines of a friendship and we tried to make it something it wasn't. Besides, nothing ever lasts. You can only depend on yourself."

"Right." Jet straightened her silverware. How often she'd made the same remark. But to hear it from someone else's lips…well, it sounded so desolate. And unbelievable. "At least we have our families," she said with a small laugh. "They're stuck with us no matter what."

His eyes shifted to the window. "I wouldn't say that. Don't count on anyone. Not friends, not girlfriends, not family."

"Really?" Jet chewed her lip. What the hell was wrong with Landry? "You can't mean that. Surely there's someone in your life that you love and trust."

Landry shrugged. "The only one to ever fit that bill was my grandmother. And then she died."

The bleakness in his eyes made her want to do something foolish. Like throw her arms around him and tell him she understood.

He'd hate that. Landry probably thought his aloofness hid the loneliness inside. Or, even worse, he didn't realize he carried the hurt like a shield every day to ward off anyone else getting too close.

Just like me. Jet's fingers curled tightly around the water glass. "What about your parents and brothers and sisters?"

"Dad split when I was five and I haven't seen much of him since. Mom is…" He hesitated. "She's hard to explain. I've got six half siblings and about as many ex-stepdads. Easy to get lost in the chaos."

He looked out the window and continued, his voice wooden and hollow. "We were always broke and scraped by day to day with food stamps, child support and the occasional odd jobs."

"That's awful." Made sense he chose a solid, respectable, steady profession like accounting.

She'd taken her own family's wealth for granted, couldn't imagine worrying about basics like food, rent and utilities. Money never had been, or would be, an issue in the Bosarge household. Although they didn't live ostentatiously and often worked stints in landlubber jobs to fit into society and not raise eyebrows, sometimes the immense wealth made her feel guilty. Like when she witnessed the struggles of the bayou shrimping families, eking out an existence that never lifted them above poverty level. The lucky residents worked for minimum wage in the stinking seafood processing plants, gutting fish and shucking oysters all day, every day.

"It must have been hard to live that way," she said at last.

He shrugged again. "I survived."

"After everything you went through growing up, seems like you would be extra close to your brothers and sisters."

"You'd be surprised."

"What about Seth? The two of you must get along pretty good if he comes down here to spend time with you."

"I barely know him. He's staying as a favor to our mother, who's under the delusion he needs a little male guidance to straighten out his attitude. Frankly, I think she's just tired of dealing with him. He's the last kid at home and she's ready for the empty-nest gig."

"A bit harsh, don't you think?" she asked lightly.

"I know her pretty well." His dry tone suggested she back off with that line of questioning. "I try not to judge my mother too much. She's been through stuff no mother should have to suffer." Landry leaned back in his chair and folded his arms. "But enough about my family. What's yours like? I'm guessing it was a whole lot different than mine."

"As far as money, yes. And there was stability at our house. Maybe too much—living in the bayou is pretty isolating."

"Why's that? I spent summers here and loved it. I got to fish and putter around the backwaters all day in my grandmother's old boat."

She could hardly tell him the truth. They lived between two worlds. Humans weren't allowed to get too close for fear they would learn their secret. Her mother preferred they lived on land, so Jet didn't get to spend much time with the merfolk. Although she suspected there was some other reason the merfolk didn't offer her their friendship, even before Orpheous's poison words during the Games.

Her kind shunned Shelly as a TRAB—a traitor baby born of a mixed couple—and Jet found the exclusion infuriating. But at least she understood that the merfolk viewed all TRABs in the same biased light. Yet they adored Lily and wanted nothing to do with Jet. Was it because Lily was gifted with a siren's voice? Or was there more to it than that? Orpheous's blue face flashed again in her mind. *Ever suspect you are one of us?* Jet fingered the golden trident, her key to the answers.

"Jet? You okay?" Landry's voice cut through her errant thoughts.

"Oh, sorry. I was thinking how best to explain my family. Like you, my dad never played a big role in my life." *Ha.* Mermen were notoriously promiscuous and free-spirited. Most never acknowledged or knew their offspring. "My mom traveled a lot." She didn't mention her mother often took Lily along, but seldom herself. Her excuse was that as a siren, Lily attracted too much attention with landlubbers and needed periodic escapes at sea. "When she was gone, different aunts and older cousins took turns watching us."

"So you didn't have the idyllic family, either."

"But I have a sister, Lily, that I'm close to. My cousin Shelly came to live with us in our late teens when her parents died, so I'm pretty close to her also. Maybe you and Seth will grow closer during his visit."

"Doubt it. There's a huge age difference between us and I've never been around him much. Tell me more about your mother."

"Of course, I love her," Jet answered much too quickly. *Even if I'm not the fair-headed golden girl she loves best.* Being known as the older, ugly sister of Lily Bosarge— both on land and at sea—wasn't easy. "She's an amazing woman—smart, beautiful, confident. The kind of person who walks into a room and takes charge." She couldn't believe how easy it was to open up to Landry; it was something that did not come naturally to her.

"Lucky you." Landry pasted on a grim smile. "No point rehashing childhood memories." He leaned across the table and whispered, "Who's that old lady behind you that keeps staring at us?"

Jet deliberately dropped her napkin. Bending down to pick it up, she casually straightened, eyes traveling slowly upward until they slammed into a pair of brown eyes nearly as dark as her own. Wearing her signature purple turban, the woman was as exotic as snow in the bayou. She gave an almost imperceptible nod to Jet with a mysterious half smile twitching the corners of her round face.

Jet nodded back in acknowledgment and faced Landry. "That's the one and only Tia Henrietta, the bayou's own voodoo queen."

Chapter 6

"Ah," Landry said with a grin, "a voodoo priestess. I should have guessed. The resident psychic I've heard about over the years."

"Or local crackpot, as most people call her."

Landry tapped a finger against his lips. "What do you make of her? Do you believe in the supernatural?"

Jet almost choked on a bite of shrimp. "Me?" she gasped out. She swiftly reached for her glass and gulped down water to clear her throat. "I have an open mind," she managed. "Things might not always be as they appear on the surface." *Ha.* "I don't suppose you would agree. You seem to view everything in terms of black-and-white—which I guess is a useful trait for an accountant."

A shuttered expression settled on his face. "My profession doesn't define me."

Just when she thought she had him pegged, wham, Landry threw a curveball. Jet gave a one-sided smile.

"So you do believe in the possibility of magic? Maybe I should have guessed it when you mentioned Edgar Allen Poe and Stephen King are your favorite authors."

"Magic? No." Landry's face tightened. "I wouldn't go that far. Most times, if something is out of the ordinary, there's a perfectly logical explanation."

"Most times? But you aren't saying there's *always* a natural explanation."

"Not always," he agreed softly. "Have you ever encountered something that defied all logic?"

Her heart thudded painfully against her rib cage. *You have no idea.* "Yes. And you?"

He rubbed his jaw and gave her a considering look, as if debating whether to tell her.

"Go on," she encouraged. "I promise not to laugh or call you nuts."

"Okay." Landry folded his hands on the table. "But remember you promised not to laugh."

At her nod, he continued.

"When I was about twelve, I fished almost every day at an inlet three miles from Murrell's Point. As much as I enjoyed the freedom and quiet, I mostly fished because each afternoon when I went to the small island, I'd find presents left for me on the sandbank, sometimes old coins or bits of sea coral. The best gift was an antique spyglass from the early 1800s. I'd like to imagine it was used by a pirate."

All gifts from the sea, she noted uneasily. "Why do you think they were presents meant for you? They could have been things that just washed ashore."

He shook his head. "No. Every day they were placed in the same spot where I tied up my boat. And each gift was left in a carefully crafted circle of seashells."

"Maybe your grandmother put them there as a treat."
She didn't believe it, though.

Landry snorted. "She never set foot in that old boat.
Said with her luck, the motor would die and she'd get
stranded at sea."

"Oh." Jet licked her dry lips. "Then yes, I'd say you
had unexplained weirdness in your childhood."

"I haven't got to the really weird part yet."

"You haven't?" Her mind spun in dizzying swirls.
Had he actually seen a mermaid? What would she say
if he did? Should she deny the existence of her race and
scoff at his story?

"One day I went out on the boat when I shouldn't have.
The wind had kicked up and a storm was predicted. But
I told myself I had time for a quick ride to the sandbank
to check and see if there was a gift waiting for me.

"Big mistake. That trinket, can't even remember now
what it was, damn near cost me my life. Instead of riding out the storm on the sandbank, I got back in the boat
and headed home. My grandmother had forbidden me
to go out that day but I'd snuck out anyway when she
took her nap."

Holy mackerel. I see where this is heading—

"Anyway, I never would have made it home except…"
He hesitated a moment before plunging on. "Except I
wasn't alone. Someone or something below the boat
guided it to shore."

"Divine providence?' she whispered.

"Maybe," he acceded. "That's what I've tried to tell
myself over the years anyway. I was young, I was scared
and too imaginative for my own good."

"Imaginative?" That didn't fit him.

"What kid dreams of being an accountant when he
grows up?" Landry's smile was wry. "I was quite the

fanciful kid who retreated into daydreams to deal with… things."

"Makes sense. But you've done a hundred-and-eighty-degree turnaround since then."

"By high school, I knew that if I ever wanted to rise above a hand-to-mouth existence, the key was to make good grades and get a college scholarship."

"Admirable." She meant it. Without a clear motivation to do well in school, she'd merely drifted. Outside of school Jet pursued subjects she was interested in, like marine biology, maritime history and cartography.

She leaned forward in her chair. "Sorry, I can't stop thinking about your story. What do you think guided your boat that time—do you have any theories?"

"I know it sounds preposterous but I thought I saw—just for a couple of seconds—a sea creature that was half-human." He shook his head. "I can't believe I'm telling you this. I've never told anyone before."

The air pressed in on her and her lungs felt as porous as a sea sponge. *Deep breaths. He doesn't know my secret.*

His brows drew together. "You okay?" Landry's hand ran up and down her chilled forearms, his touch thawing some of the frozen slush in her veins.

"You sure it wasn't some kind of illusion?"

"Must have been. Crazy, huh? Goes to show what a wild imagination can dream up when your body is flooded with adrenaline."

Jet clenched her jaw to stop her teeth chattering and managed a tight smile. "Right, crazy," she agreed, ready to change the subject. "Well, aren't you full of surprises?"

"Honey child, we are *all* full of surprises."

They both looked up, startled, at the deep, gravelly voice by their table where Tia Henrietta stood in all her eccentric glory. Jet had forgotten all about the old woman. Jet inwardly winced, hoping Tia hadn't heard the crackpot reference.

The old woman clutched at the gold shawl draping her olive-colored skin and smiled with an amused glint in her black, faintly almond-shaped eyes.

Jet regarded her curiously. She'd seen Tia around town, but the old woman had never struck up a conversation, and Jet had never driven down the bayou back roads to Tia's cottage, where she reportedly eked out a meager living reading palms and tarot cards.

Tia was an enigma, although she'd lived in Bayou La Siryna since anyone else could remember. No one knew where she came from or if she ever had family. Indeed, no one could even determine Tia's ethnic heritage; with her deep olive skin and almond eyes, it was possible Tia was distantly related to the many Vietnamese who worked in the fishing industry. Or she might even be Creole or African-American, or some mixture of several races.

"Yes, ma'am," Landry said, rising from his chair. He motioned to the empty chair at their table. "You're welcome to join us."

Jet approved the respectful gesture. Landry was a true Southern gentleman, a quality sorely lacking in Perry.

"Thank you kindly, but I must be moseying on."

Jet tried to pinpoint the accent, which itself was a regional hodgepodge. Southern, Gullah, Cajun… None of it quite fit Tia's arresting, unique voice.

"Besides," Tia added, "y'all need lots of alone time together if you're ever gonna figure out each other's secrets."

Jet's jaw tightened. No matter how much time she and Landry spent together, it would be a dry day under the sea before she would again tell another human her biggest secret. Honesty was not always the best policy, even if the man already believed in mermaids. "A woman's got to have a little mystery," Jet said, raising her water glass in mock salute to the elderly woman.

"No one would ever say Miss Jet Bosarge is lacking in mystery." Tia Henrietta made an odd clucking sound with her tongue. "And as for *you,* Mr. Landry Fields, things aren't always what they seem on the surface."

Landry's eyes narrowed a fraction before he offered a glib smile. "And how many secrets do you have, ma'am?"

She laughed a deep, throaty clucking noise that made Jet picture a demented chicken. "I'm right nigh filled to the brim with my secrets and the secrets of all the bayou people who visit me with their problems and questions."

Landry signaled the waitress. "Everybody wears a public mask," he said lightly. "Hardly any earth-shattering supernatural observation."

Jet studied him closely and noted an edge of white around his compressed lips. The genial, Southern manners were being used to suppress a show of annoyance. What could Landry possibly have to hide? He was probably right; Tia merely spouted basic truths of human nature under the guise of psychic revelation. If it kept the old woman entertained and provided a means of supplementing her Social Security check, let Tia have some fun. If she really knew what she was about, Tia would have singled her out, not Landry. After all, she was the one who led a secret life.

Tia Henrietta waggled a long, bony finger at them. "Day of reckoning coming soon. Mark my words." She grinned broadly, exposing a gold crown on one front tooth. She patted Landry's shoulder. "By the way, she's trying to communicate with you, you know. But you refuse to listen."

Landry froze and Jet leaped to his defense. "He does listen to me when I talk."

"Not talking about you, child," Tia said, her eyes glued on Landry. "I'm talking about the spirit of a little girl long dead."

Jet expected Landry to laugh off the preposterous claim but the grim set to his jaw and the wintry gleam in his eyes were more pronounced than when he'd first questioned her business records.

Tia faced her. "And I am no crackpot." With that parting sally, she exited the diner, her bold, Egyptian-printed sarong swishing mightily over her considerable girth and chunky bracelets rattling.

Crazy witch, Jet thought ruefully as Landry paid for their meal. But even crazier, Tia had zapped the fun out of their lunch as much as Landry's mermaid story. His playful attentiveness was again shuttered behind icy-blue eyes. "Let's go," he said in a clipped voice.

Jet raced to keep up with his long stride as they walked the downtown streets. Their return to The Pirate's Chest was somber, despite her attempts to lighten Landry's mood. They had actually been having *fun* until Tia Henrietta squashed it with her cryptic remarks. He'd let her glimpse his feelings behind the steel shell he presented to the world. She'd recognized the lonely child whose grandmother's love had provided a haven, because she had experienced the same sense of separation with her own mother. And even though his mermaid story made Jet uncomfortable, it demonstrated Landry could be open to that which was hidden.

A little girl long dead. It couldn't be. He didn't believe in spirits and ghosts and wanted nothing to do with hocus-pocus nonsense. He'd buried that side of him as a child, choosing instead to focus on the real world, on what could be seen with the eye and touched and heard. As an FBI agent, Landry relied on facts. Concrete, observable data that lead to logical answers and correct decisions. It had served him well over the years and he'd trained his mind to strictly focus on only the present reality, smothering any reminders of the past.

Those painful memories needed to stay buried deep in his psyche, as deep in the dirt as his sister's grave.

But…what about the porcelain cat in the fridge, books falling off shelves, weird electrical malfunctions…?

Coincidence, he insisted to the inner whispers. *Coincidence, coincidence, coincidence,* he repeated grimly, until the whispers evaporated under the blistering assault of his will. "Coming back to the bayou this time was a mistake," he muttered.

"Why do you say that?"

Landry started at Jet's question, hadn't realized he'd spoken aloud. That old lady had really gotten to him. Somehow, she had made the connection of his grandmother's name and the crime from long ago. Fakes like Tia found information and used it to convince the gullible to fork over money for messages from The Other Side.

"Never mind," he said nonchalantly. "Carnival acts like the one we just witnessed from that old woman are a pet peeve of mine."

Jet gave him a sharp glance. "Hit a nerve, did she? Must be a reason her comments got under your skin so bad."

"Nonsense."

"Keep an open mind. After all, you did have a supernatural experience once. Who's to say there aren't more unexplainable phenomena in the—"

"Like I told you, the whole thing was some stress-induced illusion."

He shouldn't have told her. What the hell had gotten into him lately? He'd never even told Mimi what he'd seen that afternoon. Jet must think he was loony tunes. He even questioned his own sanity when he recalled that childhood experience and tried his best to suppress the memory.

And since when did Jet's opinion of him start to matter? He was in Bayou La Siryna to catch a criminal, not find a lover. Worse, Jet was still technically a person of interest.

But he didn't believe that anymore. The woman had gone so far as to pay Perry Hammonds off in a desperate attempt to get him out of her life. Jet Bosarge was a decent, caring person who loved her family, donated a small fortune to charities protecting animals and the environment, and was starting a legitimate business when she had no need for gainful employment. During lunch, she'd opened up and admitted to some painful childhood memories of her own.

Landry walked briskly, brewing over his newfound loquacious streak. Matters had gone from tricky grounds to eerie nether regions when old Tia what's-her-name told Jet he had a secret. How was Jet going to take it when she found out he wasn't the IRS auditor she thought he was? She'd think he was a liar, that was what. A crazy one to boot.

"Slow down. I can't keep up with you." Her voice was breathless from trying to match his pace.

"Sorry." He stopped momentarily as she slipped her hand into his. Her touch felt good, right. As natural as if they belonged to one another.

"Don't let Tia Henrietta ruin your day." Her deep

brown eyes were bright with worry. "And don't deny that she did. You were in an awful hurry to pay the bill and leave."

They were a mere block from her shop. Landry was filled with a sudden urge to tell her everything. All about the weird incidents that plagued him and that had reached an alarming pitch since his return to the bayou this year. The fact that he wasn't who she thought. Landry opened his mouth and then snapped it shut. Just a few more days. Time to concentrate his efforts on finding the Vargas/Hammonds connection. Time to confront Perry head-on. Time he sent her idiot ex packing—and cancel payment on that check she wrote him if it wasn't too late.

"It's okay," Jet said at his hesitation. Her eyes slid downward a microsecond. "Like you said, we all have our secrets."

Landry ran a finger across her full red lips. He'd love to pry Jet's every little secret from those tempting lips, wanted everything bare and open between them. "Tell me yours and maybe I'll tell you mine," he said lightly.

She gave a shaky smile. "You go first."

"I'm not so easily fooled."

"Me, either."

The longer he put this off, the harder it would be when she discovered the truth. This was a small town; word always managed to get out.

He would do it.

"Okay, me first. The thing is, Jet…" He took a deep breath and looked past her right shoulder, avoiding eye contact. Didn't want to see the kindness in her eyes return to the antagonistic contempt of when they first met. "I need to clear up—" His mind registered the fact there was a county sheriff's car parked in front of Jet's store. "What the hell?"

Jet followed his gaze. "I wonder what Tillman's doing here?"

Out on the sidewalk, the sheriff talked to Seth, a stern expression on his face.

What had the kid done now? He never should have let his mother talk him into letting Seth stay. He sent her a hefty sum of money every month, had done more than any other of his siblings. Wasn't that enough?

Of course it wasn't; it was never enough. Landry raced down the street, past gawking store owners and people milling on the sidewalks. Even through his anger, he worried Seth would say or do something stupid that would aggravate the situation. If Seth just kept his mouth shut, he might be able to help him, ease things over with the local law enforcement and get him an attorney. Whatever was needed.

His brother was in trouble.

Chapter 7

"What did you do?" Landry asked as soon as they got within fifteen feet of The Pirate's Chest. His voice was loud enough that several people passing by shot them curious glances and slowed down to check out the commotion.

Seth didn't respond, his face stoic with what Jet imagined to be false bravado.

Tillman nodded at her in an all-business manner. "Let's go inside and talk this over."

She quickly unlocked the door and pushed it open, the three men following her inside.

"Tell me what happened," Landry demanded as soon as the door closed, pinning Seth with a withering gaze.

Jet wanted to shiver and back away from the frost in his eyes and couldn't fathom what Seth must be feeling under the stern condemnation.

"Nothin'," Seth mumbled. He didn't go so far as to roll

his eyes, but his stiff posture and unrepentant expression screamed "stoic teenage boredom" in the face of whatever disaster brewed.

"Why don't we all have a seat at the front counter?" Jet suggested, trying to ease the tension.

Everyone ignored her.

Tillman's hands went to his hips. "It might be nothing at all." He got straight to the point. "I got an anonymous phone call this morning from a man who would only identify himself as a curious citizen. He claimed that a new employee here, named Seth, had stolen valuable knives and coins and hid them inside his jacket."

"That's a lie!" Seth said, bursting out of the indifference act. "Who said that? No one even knows me around here."

"Officer, I'll reimburse Miss Bosarge for the costs of any stolen items," Landry volunteered in a tight voice.

Tillman held up a hand. "I don't know if it's true or not. I came down to talk to Jet and found this young man attempting to enter with a key. I asked if he would mind a few questions."

Seth's face flushed in anger. "And I said *no way.*"

"Be quiet and let me handle this," Landry warned.

"But I didn't—"

"He's a minor," Landry said to Tillman, dismissing Seth. "Surely you can—"

"I'll prove I didn't steal nothin'." Seth took off his jacket and threw it to Landry before turning the pockets of his jeans inside out. "C'mon, you can search me."

Jet pursed her lips as she studied Seth, noting that he cared more about proving his innocence to his brother than the sheriff.

"Damn it, kid. We'll talk about this later," Landry muttered.

"I didn't do anything." Seth turned beseeching eyes to Jet. "I swear it."

She wanted to believe him, had imagined they'd established an understanding before lunch when she'd caught him with the dagger. But why would someone call the sheriff's office and report a false crime? It didn't make sense. Who would do such a thing if it wasn't... A flash of red whizzed by in her peripheral vision. Jet narrowed her eyes and looked out the front window, catching sight of a red Mustang whipping around the corner, a block from the siren statue.

Perry.

Perry had found out Seth worked here and he didn't like it.

And in that moment, Jet knew Perry would never give her up. She was too valuable to him. He viewed her as a lifelong meal ticket. She took a deep breath, feeling claustrophobic, as if she were lying on a bed of sand and the weight of the ocean pressed on her lungs.

"Well, look what we have here," Tillman said, pointing to a glint of brass poking through the torn lining of Seth's camo jacket. He reached over and pulled out an eight-inch knife, sheathed in brass, which gleamed golden under the store's chandelier. Several gold and silver coins spilled onto the floor from the ripped lining, the metallic sound clanging loud as cannon fire in the sudden silence.

Jet eyed the knife, relieved it was *not* the dagger Seth loved. If Seth was going to steal something, it wouldn't be this item.

"I'm getting you an attorney," Landry said, breaking the appalled quiet.

"There's no need for a lawyer," Jet spoke up. "I'm not pressing charges."

Tillman narrowed his eyes. "Sure that's what you want to do?"

Seth took a step back. "You can't arrest me! My half brother's with the FBI."

What brother? Jet looked at Landry for clarification. He'd told her over lunch that he had half a dozen siblings, so it must be one of them.

Landry ran a hand over his face before facing her inquisitive gaze. He didn't say a word, his face composed, impassive.

Oh, hell. Landry was the FBI agent. Bits and pieces from their first meeting flashed through her mind: her initial impression that he didn't fit with the shabby surroundings, his questions about Perry and Gulf Coast Salvage, and his insistence on a personal follow-up meeting.

Jet felt as if she'd been rammed in the solar plexus by a giant swordfish. She'd been falling for the guy, especially after their talk at lunch when she'd glimpsed the loneliness beneath his tough exterior—so like her own. And there was his belief that she was above the low-life Perry, his sharp intelligence and, until this moment, what she thought to be his honesty.

Not to mention those hot kisses that flamed her insides. Would she ever learn not to trust humans?

She pulled herself together and turned to Tillman. "Of course I'm not pressing charges. I gave the dagger and coins to Seth as a gift."

He lowered the brim of his sheriff's cap and frowned at the obvious lie. "Why are you protecting—"

Jet started forward, swiftly passing Seth's incredulous face and Landry's inscrutable blue eyes.

"Where are you going?" Tillman asked, but Jet never turned as she headed out.

"Jet, wait," Landry called.

She ignored him, too. As she exited, she overheard Tillman berate Landry for not having the professional courtesy of letting him know a fellow law-enforcement agent was in town.

Outside, she sucked in the windy, briny air and kept walking, hoping to burn off steam. Tia had tried to warn her at lunch. *You don't know each other's secrets yet... Day of reckoning coming soon.*

She wondered if Landry had any more secrets. At least her own secret was still safe, her mermaid nature hidden as always. She smiled with no mirth. Landry might be the only person in the world she could tell about her shape-shifting, since he'd seen a mermaid before, as much as he tried to deny it to himself. Jet halted at the base of the siren statue and looked up at the mysterious face that was no doubt modeled after an early ancestor seen by a human and now immortalized. Had this ancestor ever been in love with a human? Ever been disappointed by falsely placed trust?

Jet reached through the spraying water at the statue's base and touched the cold, wet edifice, closing her eyes. The forewarned day of reckoning had come early. She tried to convince herself it was better this way, better to know the truth early before her heart invested too heavily.

Landry Fields was a rebound thing, she tried to convince herself. She'd been in emotional turmoil over Perry's return, and for a brief moment, Landry had felt like a safe harbor, like someone strong, steady and good in the midst of corruption, chaos and callous betrayal.

Had he been playing her all along? Pretending an attraction to unearth more about her less-than-stellar past with Perry? Sure, she'd played fast and loose with the humans' maritime and reporting laws, but what she'd done was small-time compared to larger salvage companies and huge corporations with their overseas tax shelters. And why now, years after any wrongdoing, was the FBI digging into all this?

The fountain's mist sprayed cool drops of water on her arms, neck and face, providing a touch of liquid comfort. What she desperately needed at the moment was a good swim at sea, to immerse her body in Earth's amniotic fluid and swim with the fish. Or she could pay Dolly another visit. Scratch that. Dolly's predicament was too sad to deal with at the moment. The dolphin would pick up on her churning emotions, not good for Dolly or her unborn calf.

A good, long swim might be in order. She hadn't swum much since returning from the Poseidon Games. It would be good to have an activity in which she had the utmost confidence in her abilities. Swimming was something she excelled at, something at which she depended only on her own strength to succeed in.

Forget fitting in with humans. She should turn her attention back to her own kind again. Now that she'd won the golden trident, she'd finally have an answer about her heritage. Her mother couldn't refuse her request for information if she gave up the trident's one-wish magic to know *why*. Why she never fit in anywhere, not at sea nor on land. Why other mermaids pulled away from her, why Lily was the favored one with the gift of the siren's song and why Jet looked nothing like her family or other mermaids. If she knew why, perhaps she could fix whatever was wrong and spend more time at sea—away from lying human men.

If she had those answers, Jet believed she might discover a way to fit in better with her own kind and find some peace. Shelly and Lily maneuvered happily between land and sea, but maybe that wasn't her path.

So why wait? She could swim southward tonight and perhaps meet Mom and Lily returning home from the Games. The store opening could be delayed. It would give her a break from her problems and during the long swim she could devise a plan for getting Perry permanently out of her life. If she was lucky, maybe Landry Fields would lose interest in her and go away. For an FBI agent, there had to be bigger fish to fry. She groaned inwardly at the unintentional pun.

As if her thoughts had summoned Landry, Jet sensed him approach. Landry had an aura of power and stability that was unmistakable. She kept her eyes closed, not sure she could keep the hurt from shining through. The clean scent of water, soap and male pheromones enveloped her like a refreshing wave. Emanations of solid strength drew closer until at last a tentative hand touched her shoulder blades.

She wanted to lean back, sink into the warmth of human skin, feel his hands running through her scalp and caressing the sweet, vulnerable spot at her nape. Jet tilted her head back, enjoying the cool spray of water on the front of her neck and the heat of Landry's hand on the sharp plane of her right shoulder blade.

If she left tonight, this might be the last time she saw Landry. Anything could happen while she was away. The possibility this might be their final meeting made her chest tighten painfully.

"Look at me."

Jet felt the rumble of his voice vibrate down her spine. Two hands were on her bare arms, gently guiding her toward him. She kept her eyes closed, chin tilted upward. He laid a finger over her lips and then his own brushed against hers. "Jet," he whispered, part question, part regret.

She opened her eyes and stared into the burning blue of his, frozen-hot like the sting of ice on bare flesh.

"What do you want from me?" She'd intended for the question to be confrontational, but instead it escaped from her mouth like a sigh of defeat. Everybody wanted something, some little piece of her soul.

Landry hesitated.

"The truth," Jet insisted, calm yet firm.

He removed his hands from her arms and indicated a nearby park bench. After they sat down, each stared ahead at the statue.

"I didn't mean for you to find out this way. I apologize."

"Then what Seth said is true? You're an FBI agent?"

He reached into his back pocket, pulled out a billfold and flashed a shiny badge. It glinted like a silver talisman of doom in the midday sun.

"Why are you after me?"

Landry ran a hand through his wavy hair with the light brown curls at the edge of his collar. "It's not so much you," he admitted grudgingly. "It's Perry Hammonds."

Jet swallowed hard, a knot of fear in her stomach. Had Perry managed to do something spectacularly stupid only a few weeks out of prison? Was he trying to draw her into danger? "Because of our past business venture?" she asked, hoping Perry wasn't presently involved in anything sinister. But she'd heard prisons were training grounds for criminals to learn and graduate to ever more serious felonies. Perry didn't deserve her sympathy, but she only wished him gone—not in serious trouble.

He waved a hand dismissively. "That's not so important." His brows drew together in disapproval. "It's true there's something strange about your past treasure findings and sales." He paused, as if waiting for her to deny it.

When Jet kept silent, he resumed talking. "Look, I don't believe you've knowingly committed a major crime or have ever been involved in a crime ring. So I'll tell you what I'm really investigating. Three weeks ago we received a report that a known international gangster had arranged to spring an American citizen out of a Chilean prison. Ever hear of Sylvester Vargas?"

She shook her head.

"Vargas owns Gulf Coast Salvage, the company you did business with and own substantial stock in."

Jet's fingers curled into her palms. Perry had picked the company and handled the administrative end of their ventures. It felt as if she would never be free from her past. "I don't know anything about this. Have you questioned Perry about it?"

Landry regarded Jet through hooded eyes. "Not yet," he conceded. "I've been observing him, gathering additional information from known associates and waiting for him to make a move. What has he told you about his future plans?"

"He wants us to work a site near Tybee Island, Georgia. I told him no. Even though I gave him enough money to start his own business, he still might not give up trying to make me change my mind."

Landry's eyes chilled. "Time I confronted him."

The continuous spray of the water fountain gurgled and stopped momentarily before suddenly shooting up a stream twice as tall as the mermaid statue, as if an underwater geyser had exploded. She'd never seen that happen before.

They both watched until the stream became a normal-size spray once again.

Jet shrugged at Landry's threat to confront Perry. It

sounded as if they didn't have much to go on yet. But maybe the questioning would scare Perry off for a while.

So Landry was an FBI agent. Had he lied about anything else? She'd been so worried about protecting her own secrets that she didn't suspect he might harbor a few of his own.

Jet was hard to decipher. When he'd found her by the statue and she opened her eyes and looked at him, the vulnerability and sadness he glimpsed lashed him like a whip. He'd fully expected her to be furious and scald him with righteous indignation at his misrepresentation as an IRS auditor.

Misrepresentation? It was a downright lie. Jet had every right to be angry. He'd never apologize for the undercover work; that was his job. But he shouldn't have let it get personal between them until the case was resolved. Yet instead of anger, she looked defeated. His guts churned at the sadness in her eyes. At their first meeting, he'd thought of her as invulnerable and much too cocky and prickly. And yet he was drawn to her despite it. When she let down her guard, Jet was irresistible. She brought color and vitality into his black-and-white, rigid world.

Jet's spine suddenly stiffened, as if a new idea had struck her. "Now I see."

"See what?"

"You planned on using me to find out what Perry is up to." She folded her arms across her chest. "Why expose who you really are when I can do the dirty work?" Her full lips twisted in a scowl.

This was more like Jet. He'd much rather deal with her anger than hurt. "Something like that. At first anyway."

Her dark eyes flashed in challenge. "What's changed?"

Indeed. What had Jet done to him? Everything was

changing. She'd gone from being a suspect of possible criminal mischief to a woman he cared for and wanted to protect from danger. Damn, the admission made him squirm. "What's changed is that I got to know you," he admitted. "I don't believe you have any idea what your ex-lover is up to."

Jet's shoulders slumped and she let out a deep sigh. "Thank God for that at least."

What kind of a jerk did she think he was? "If I thought you were a criminal, I wouldn't have—" His voice drifted off and he gazed down at her lips, dropping his eyes to her chest, where her shirt was slightly damp from the fountain. He remembered the evening before, the feel of her breasts and her hard body pressed tight against him. "Well, I wouldn't have kissed you, touched you." He swallowed hard, fighting the impulse to draw her to him immediately, in broad daylight in a public place. But if he did, he was afraid he couldn't stop at a quick hug or peck on the cheek.

Her eyes widened and her pale face flushed, either remembering the shared passion or guessing his thoughts. Landry wasn't sure which.

Jet abruptly pursed her lips and asked, "So now what? If you planned to have me trick Perry in some way and lure him to a convenient confession, then you're on the wrong track. Perry and I are done."

He felt a lightness in his body at the words.

Jet held up a hand with crossed fingers. "On my end anyhow."

"What's that's supposed to mean?"

"It means I want Perry out of my life but I don't think he'll ever cut me loose."

"Why not?"

She hesitated only the briefest of moments, but Landry

had interviewed enough people over the years to recognize that pause as someone carefully crafting their words. "Because Perry needs a job, an income."

"He can find another treasure-salvage company," he said harshly. "The man at least has an uncanny knack for locating sites."

Jet stared at the mermaid fountain, seemingly transfixed by her fractured reflection in the rippling water.

"Unless," he added slowly, "*you're* the one who found the best sites."

She didn't face him. "At lunch, you mentioned a supernatural encounter, something unexplainable by human logic."

Landry stilled, almost not daring to breathe. "Go on," he urged.

She turned to him. "I'm the one who finds the shipwreck sites. Not Perry. He's nothing without me."

"Figures Perry didn't contribute much to the partnership, besides his connections and shady sales." He leaned closer. "Tell me how you find treasure."

"Let's just say I have a sixth sense."

"Let's not."

Her brows rose.

"Sounds a bit far-fetched. You trying to say you take out the boat, wait for some mysterious vibe and then dive to explore?"

Jet jumped to her feet. "Of course it's not that simple. I study history, oceanic maps, old ship cargo manifests—all the things others in the business do."

Landry rose off the park bench. "Go on. What's your special edge? I admit I've been curious."

"Forget I said anything. You'd never understand."

"Try me."

Jet didn't move and he stood stock-still, afraid of scaring her off. The fountain splashed and gurgled in front of them, children shrieked at play and cars drove by, usual sounds at the park, but they seemed far away, as if he and Jet were at a precipice. An island of two where no one and nothing else mattered.

A strong breeze blew back a chunk of her shiny black hair and lifted her loosely tied scarf. Jet adjusted it quickly, but not before he noticed a few distinctive white scars on both sides of her neck. How odd. If he didn't know better, he'd say they resembled fish gills. A chill settled deep in his bones.

She wet her lips and a ghost of a smile danced across the sharp planes of her face. "Why should I explain? You've given me no reason to trust you." With that parting volley, she spun and strode quickly back toward the downtown shops.

"Wait a minute." Landry caught up to Jet and held her arm. "How did you get those scars on your neck?"

She flinched and jerked her arm from his grasp. "Childhood accident," she mumbled.

"Don't go back to work. Let's talk this thing through."

"I'm done talking and I'm not going back to work. I'm going home."

"But what about the shop?"

"Seth has the keys. Let him close up." Jet opened the door of her rusted truck. "And give the kid a freaking break. Families should stick together. You were awful rough on him. He didn't steal anything."

"How can you be so sure?" Of course, Jet didn't know Seth had stolen before. He should never have suggested Seth working for her. This was his fault.

"Don't be so quick to judge, Landry. We all screw up. Just because someone makes a mistake in their past doesn't mean they'll make bad choices the rest of their lives."

"Are we talking about you or Seth?"

She regarded him with pursed lips. "Haven't you ever messed up big-time?" she asked.

"Of course, but I've never stolen from anybody."

"For Seth's sake, try not to come across as such a self-righteous prig when you apologize."

Heat flushed his face. Prig? That was harsh. "Why should I apologize? You don't know all the facts. This isn't the first time—"

Jet cut him off. "If Seth had stolen anything, it would have been the dagger he admired earlier. Your brother was framed."

That didn't make sense. No one even knew his brother was here. "By whom?"

"Perry, of course. He was parked across the street the whole time watching Tillman bring Seth into the store. He's desperate to drive a wedge between us. Some FBI agent you are." Jet slammed her door shut and drove off in a cloud of noxious fumes.

Landry coughed and rubbed the back of his sweaty neck. Maybe he *had* been too hard on his brother, too quick to jump to conclusions. Had he really turned into a prig? The label stung. He returned to The Pirate's Chest, the door chimes jingling behind him.

Seth was unpacking boxes behind the counter and continued working without glancing up. The sheriff was already gone, irate that Landry hadn't shared information on why a federal agent was in Bayou La Siryna. This was the sheriff's jurisdiction. But Landry knew Tillman was engaged to Jet's cousin and wouldn't risk the FBI investigation by testing the man's loyalty to family.

Landry cleared his throat. "Seems I owe you an apology." Seth still didn't look up. This wasn't going to be easy. Landry tried again. "I know you didn't steal anything."

"Great. *Now* you believe me? After the cop leaves? Thanks a lot."

"Sorry. But you can hardly blame me, since Mom said you've stolen before."

"So I'm automatically guilty the rest of my life?"

Almost the same words Jet had used. "No. It's just that in my job I see the worse in people. I'm paid to be suspicious and prove a case against them."

Seth paused unloading the box. "What made you change your mind?" He shook his head and went back to work. "Jet must have stuck up for me."

"She did. Said Perry Hammonds, her ex-boyfriend, set you up."

"Why? He doesn't even know me."

"It's not about you. He's doing what he can to keep Jet and me apart."

"Glad to see you finally admit she's your girlfriend," Seth said sarcastically.

"She's not my girl," he automatically denied. "Okay, recent development."

Recent history, more likely, now Jet knew he'd lied about his job. It was way past time he interviewed Hammonds.

"She's too good for you," Seth mumbled.

"I didn't know you were such a fan."

"She isn't as hot as her cousin but she's nice."

Landry leaped to Jet's defense. "She's just as hot as Shelly. Hotter, actually." What a stupid conversation. Seth was dragging him down to teenager level.

"Mom says you'll be a bitter, single man the rest of

your life 'cause of some girl that dumped you for another guy."

The hits just kept on coming today. "Ouch."

Seth regarded him from the corner of his eye as he continued pulling out merchandise from boxes and unwrapping newspaper casings. "Sorry I spilled your secret. Is Jet mad at you?"

"Furious." Landry sighed and pulled up a chair. He grabbed a pair of box cutters and sat beside Seth. "I'll give her a little time to cool off and then go see her tonight."

They worked together silently while Landry brooded on Jet's markings. Those scars were too symmetrical for an accident. Not only that, there were identical scars on both sides of her neck.

The memory from age twelve arose for the second time today—the one he'd never forget, had dreamed about a million times.

He hadn't told Jet every detail. For a few seconds he'd seen the invisible force that had guided his boat to shore in the storm. Seconds burned into his brain forever when a sea creature had slipped out from under the boat and he saw it…her. A pale face gazing at him through a foot of salt water, blue eyes unblinking. Long, white hair had fanned upward and a torso had morphed into a glittering tail fin where legs should have been. Tiny flaps on the sides of her neck opened and closed, while her lips stayed clamped together and curved upward in a secretive smile.

Those neck markings were the same size and location as Jet's.

Landry put down the box cutters and rubbed his jaw. Was Jet like that long-ago creature who'd saved his life? If so, was it possible for someone to live both on land

and at sea? Sure would explain her uncanny ability to find sea treasure.

He arose and paced the shop, examining antique coins, daggers and an eclectic mixture of maritime-themed knickknacks. A familiar flash of red sparkled on a low shelf and he came to an abrupt halt. What the hell? It wasn't hers; she hadn't owned the only red se-quined coin purse ever made. But as Landry picked it up and opened the tiny clasp, he knew damned well what he'd find inside.

Sure enough, the letter *A* was etched in black marker on the purse's white lining. A child's large and wobbly penmanship to mark the purse as unmistakably hers. It held one corroded copper penny, dated 1979.

The year of her death.

Landry rounded on Seth, holding up the child's purse, which was nearly engulfed in his fisted hand. "What's this doing here?" he bellowed. "Did you bring it from my house?"

Seth came over and took a look. "Noooooo—" he said, drawing out the word, as if talking to a deranged asylum escapee. "I've never seen it before." He frowned. "Are you accusing me of stealing or something?"

"No." Landry slowly lowered his arm and stuffed it into his pants pocket. "But it doesn't belong here."

"Okaaaay," Seth drawled, evidently back to thinking his older brother was an idiot. "Whatever."

Landry turned away from him and rested his elbows on the front counter, his breath shallow and rapid. A few moments to collect his composure and then he would get on with his federal case and make a little side trip to try to get to the bottom of this weirdness.

Why was all this happening again? He'd packed away the past and stuffed the memories into a trunk, like an old woolen sweater. Now someone or something had unpacked that trunk. The smell of mothballs was in the air and the threads were unraveling.

His fingers brushed against a stack of business cards by the register with the store's name printed in large blue letters. The Pirate's Chest, indeed. The words conjured images of a seventeenth-century Blackbeard kind of rogue. He tilted his head up and observed the mermaid masthead mounted on the wall above him. The determined, passionate set of the carved face favored Jet.

Could Jet be a mermaid?

Preposterous. Besides, *everything* reminded him of Jet these days. Couldn't possibly be true. He was losing it to even consider the possibility that Jet could jump into the ocean and transform into a mermaid.

But in some dark area of his mind, questions whispered like tiny yet pesky ghosts.

Chapter 8

By the time Landry arrived at the rental cottage, his anger hadn't cooled. If anything it had escalated as he replayed two images frozen in his brain: Seth's crumpled posture of defeat at his false stealing accusation, and Jet's scathing indictment of his deceit that shone in her dark abyss eyes.

All Perry Hammonds's fault. And right now, Landry couldn't control his need to confront the bastard. It overrode years of law-enforcement training and his own sacred creed of following the rules—work hard, obey protocol, keep it impersonal… FBI regulations he'd slowly allowed to become law in all areas of his life.

Until now. Until Jet.

He bounded toward the front door, catching sight of Hammonds peeking through a set of blinds. Before Landry could knock, Hammonds unlatched the door a crack and stared out with bleary eyes, as if he'd just been awakened from a nap.

Landry pushed on the door and Hammonds's wobbly legs careened backward. He entered the den and glared at the man who'd dare threaten Jet and Seth. "Don't you ever come near or say a word against Seth again," Landry said with a growl.

Hammonds managed a smile of bravado. "Who's Seth?"

"Don't play games with me." He grasped and twisted the collar of Hammonds's stylish dress shirt.

Hammonds threw up his hands and gave an unsteady laugh. "Whatever. We're cool, dude," he said, trying to placate him.

Landry let go and stepped back, breathing hard. "By the way, it didn't work."

"What didn't work?" Hammonds sank onto the couch and rubbed his temples.

The guy looked as if he could use a beer and some BC Powder.

"Cut the innocent act. Jet saw you taking off when Tillman and Seth were inside the shop. That red Mustang stands out like a scream in the night."

Hammonds switched tactics, brows drawing together as if in anger. "Why are you after Jet? I was with her first. She's mine."

"She doesn't *belong* to anyone. Jet's her own person."

He pasted on a grin that held no mirth. "Jet loves me. Always has, always will."

Disgust gurgled like burning tar in the cauldron of his gut. "Bullshit. She paid you to leave town. Why haven't you?"

A flush of color tainted Hammonds's pretty-boy face

and Landry was unsure if he was furious, embarrassed or perhaps a mixture of both.

"That check she gave me was for new equipment and setup costs for the new site we're going to work together soon."

"Is that so?" Landry drawled, instantly on the alert. Maybe he could draw him out; Hammonds mistakenly viewed him as nothing more than a meek bean counter, a mild nuisance. "What kind of work did you have in mind? Jet's busy opening up her shop at the moment."

"None of your business. Go back to your books."

He regarded Hammonds thoughtfully. "Jet's through with the marine-salvage business. Just as she's through with you."

"You poor, deluded sap." Hammonds rose, putting his hands on his hips. "Jet could never be content with someone like you. She craves adventure, passion—things you can't provide."

Landry wanted to knock the sneer off the guy's face. Wanted to shake, shake, *shake* him until he took back those words and spilled his guts about what he and Vargas were plotting. Some last-recalled shred of FBI protocol stayed his hands, which he fisted at his sides. He hadn't blown his cover yet, but if he stayed much longer, Landry wasn't sure he could keep his temper in check. Some glimmer of uncertainty on his part must have slipped out because Hammonds advanced toward him.

"I know things about Jet that no one else does. We understand one another."

Landry kept his features guarded, refused to give credence to Perry's words of poison. "Stay away from her and my family."

Hammonds snickered. "Or else what?"

Landry leaned in, his face inches from Hammonds's.

"Or else I'll have my revenge," he whispered in a voice as frigid as a glacier. To his surprise, Hammonds didn't say another word as Landry turned and exited the cottage, slamming the door behind him for emphasis.

Landry got in his BMW and turned on the engine of the sleek machine, a few degrees less angry than before he'd confronted the jerk. To be fair, and Landry was excruciatingly honest with himself, all of today's recriminations weren't entirely the fault of one Perry Hammonds. Some of the fault was his own. He'd failed to be a stand-up kind of brother for Seth and he'd failed to level with Jet once he believed she was no party to whatever Vargas had planned.

He vowed to do better in the future.

Jet sat at the kitchen table and scribbled a terse note for Shelly, explaining she was going out for a long swim and might be gone a day or two. No sense upsetting her cousin by an unexplained absence, although Shelly was so caught up in planning the upcoming family reunion that she might not notice Jet was gone.

No, that wasn't fair. Shelly was kindness itself. It was Jet's own damned fault that being around the happy couple Shelly and Tillman presented only emphasized her own loneliness. Jet took another bite of a protein bar. She needed the high-calorie sustenance for the prolonged swim.

The crunch of ground shell in the driveway made her jump. Had Landry followed her home? She squashed the involuntary tingle of anticipation running up her spine. More than likely it was Perry. She stole a cautious glance out the window. If it was Perry, she wouldn't answer the door. He couldn't get in with all the new dead bolts and other security precautions they'd taken after last summer's break-in by the killer.

Shelly's golden curls sparkled in the midday sun as she ran up the porch steps. Jet groaned. She'd been only five minutes from a clean getaway. What she needed was physical exertion to burn off the hurt and anger churning in her gut. Talking it out, sharing her emotions, was Shelly's thing, not hers. What good did talking do? She'd kept the pain of Perry's betrayal to herself and she would do so with this latest. She had her pride to protect.

Her cousin burst through the door and hurried over. "I came as soon as I heard the news. Are you okay?"

Jet folded her arms across the front of her body. "Let me guess, Tillman told you all about the little scene in my store."

"Tillman's furious that an FBI agent came to work in Bayou La Siryna and didn't have the professional courtesy to check in with him."

"Yeah, well, he's not the only one who's angry."

"I know it looks bad that Landry lied about being an accountant." Her green eyes widened with earnest concern. "But I'm sure he had a really great reason."

"Sure he did," Jet spat out. "He was investigating my old treasure-salvage company. Evidently, Perry's into some scheme with scary, big-time criminals."

"And his return to the bayou made it look like you might be a part of it." Shelly shook her head in disgust. "That jerk's been nothing but bad news from the start."

"Took a while, but I finally figured that out for myself. Look, there was no need for you to rush home." Jet nodded at the note on the table. "I'm taking off for a day or two."

Shelly bit her lip. "Don't go. Remember you have a mighty big secret yourself that Landry doesn't know about. Talk to him instead of running off. He—"

"You mean well but I don't want to talk with anyone. Even you."

"It's not good to keep your feelings bottled up like you do, Jet. Don't rush off without giving Landry a chance to explain."

"None of that matters," Jet cut in. "He lied to me and led me on, just when I was starting to fall for the nice-guy act."

Shelly put her hands on her hips. "How do you know it's an act? You wouldn't know a nice guy if he bit you on the ass—" Her face reddened. "Um, you know what I'm trying to say."

"You're defending him because you're desperate to steer me away from Perry. Don't worry—I wouldn't go back to that slimeball for anything." Jet started for the back door.

"That's not the only reason." Shelly followed, undeterred. "Think of his positive qualities. First, he's in law enforcement, so we know he's moral and—"

"Like our fine deputy sheriff, the corrupt Carl Dismukes?" Jet snorted.

"And *second,* we know he cares about family or he wouldn't have taken on Seth."

Jet stopped at the door and faced Shelly. "Don't you see what you're doing? The outer circumstances are so much like Tillman's that you mistakenly believe Landry has all the qualities you love and admire about your fiancé."

Shelly's jaw slackened. "Guess you might have a point," she admitted grudgingly.

"Bye, Shell. I won't be gone long." Jet hurried to the shed before her cousin thought of more reasons to delay her. Jet *needed* the swim, needed the water's caress to soothe the hurt.

"Hey," Shelly called out as she neared the shed. "What about your store?"

Jet cupped her hands over her mouth. "Seth can do more of the setup work if he wants."

She unlocked the shed and quickly slipped inside, kicking off her sandals. Leaning her back against the door, Jet sighed as her toes curled in the sandy floor. *Alone at last.* The sound of lapping water called to her from the secret portal where, for centuries, Bosarge women shape-shifted between land and sea. What appeared from the outside to be an ordinary shed actually housed the portal and served as a changing room.

Quickly, Jet stripped naked and approached the small opening, about the size of a manhole on a city street. She inched in her legs and they instantly morphed into a glittering tail fin. Jet admired the mixture of pastel and bold teal sparkles before plunging into the narrow tunnel, part of an undersea cavern, which led to the sea.

Down she went for several feet until the tunnel emerged into open waters. She pushed onward past their vegetable garden of sea cucumber, kelp and water chestnuts and the deep, winding roots of turtle and wigeon grasses lining the bayou banks. Sea turtles feasted on a colony of sea grapes. Jet plucked the green fruit and popped it into her mouth, savoring its peppery flavor. She grabbed a handful and stored them in the sporran she always wore belted at her waist. In it, she kept a knife in case of sudden predators who might view her as a tasty meal.

Jet swam south, fighting against the gulf current pulling her eastward. She might spot Mom and Lily returning from the Games for the family reunion. She kept up the rhythmic pattern of swimming, crunching her abs and thrusting out her tail fin. She knew the action reflected an effect like undulating ripples of sea grass. Fish brushed against her, attracted by her large, sparkling tail fin.

At last, her tattered emotions were lulled by the physicality of movement, the beauty of swarming fish and the antics of dolphins. Poor Dolly. What fun it would be to have her swimming alongside her. Jet lost sense of time, not sure if she'd been swimming an hour or ten hours. Without the protection of other mermaids, she'd had to pay careful attention to the thrum vibration of boats. But all she heard was the constant cacophony of marine life: the high-pitched clicking of dolphins, sand crabs scurrying along the ocean floor and schools of fish cutting through the sea in constant search for either mates or a meal.

Moonlight danced shadows on the waves above and a huge colony of lantern fish glowed like fallen stars. Jet relaxed and drifted in the current, peaceful for the first time in days. The salty sea enveloped and cradled her weary body, the eternal thrum of the ocean undertow a lullaby to her low spirits. She was used to being alone and lonely. No big deal.

But the lie chaffed. Until she met Landry, she didn't realize how hollow and superficial her life had become. She'd existed as a shell of her former vibrant self, betrayed and cast aside by someone she thought she'd loved. But she hadn't known the meaning of love until she'd seen the genuine love Shelly and Tillman shared. Until Landry came along and the hope of new love erased some of the past pain and gave her the strength to resist Perry.

What was Landry doing right now? Was he thinking of her as she was of him? The earlier anger was spent, burned somewhere in the gulf waters.

Yes, he had lied to her, same as Perry. But his reasons weren't for selfish monetary gains. Checking her out and scrutinizing her business had been a necessary part of his job. Landry was on the right side of the law. Shelly had a point there.

The sight of lobsters jolted her out of her musings. Hundreds of them marched single file along the ocean floor—like ants on land—which might mean a storm was brewing. They formed a long line, positioned head to tail, stirring up tiny sediment particles. She dived closer and observed a few stragglers. Those would most likely be the next meal for parrot or triggerfish. Jet eyed a lone, stray lobster, its antennae swaying in the current. She was *really* hungry. She reached out a hand, hovered it over the unfortunate creature.

No, she couldn't do it. Most mermaids ate raw fish and other seafood, but she stuck to kelp and other sea vegetables while undersea. On land, she had no compunction about cooked seafood. Mostly raised as a dirt dweller, Jet blamed her mom for her weak mermaid stomach.

"Guess you're safe," Jet said, sending bubbles gurgling from her mouth. She pivoted and swam to an area abundant with kelp. Not delicious, but it would have to do. She picked a handful and ate, regretfully watching the lobsters march away.

An eight-foot octopus oozed close and she scowled. A few more feet and the thing would be able to reach her with one of its long tentacles. She studied it closely for any sign of agitation but it didn't change color or exhibit papillae over its dark, horizontal pupils. When erect, the papillae resembled horns, giving it the appearance of a gelatinous devil.

But this one seemed merely curious. Jet relaxed and slowly extended her hand, knowing it wanted to taste her with its suckers and detect what manner of creature she was. "Don't you dare give me a case of giant hickeys all over my arm," she warned. Whatever would Landry think if he saw this? She laughed. He was so full of surprises and so open to the supernatural, he'd probably think it was cool.

Its right eye swiveled in its socket, as if weighing potential danger. Jet didn't doubt its huge brain contained a highly intelligent being. All those millions of neurons must serve some kind of intelligent purpose. If an octopus's life span were as long as a dolphin's—twenty, instead of only three years—it might have evolved into the ocean's smartest life-form.

The octopus reached out one of its eight tentacles and wrapped it around her arm. It probed, caressed, tasted, trying to figure her out.

A sudden sizzle in the water set Jet's sonar sense ablaze. The giant octopus released its hold, turned red and shot away. From the west came a conglomeration of light and sound unlike anything she'd encountered in all her travels. She'd heard tales of what disturbed jellyfish were like, but doubted she'd ever witness such a scene.

Bolts of electrical flashes lit the indigo water like a lightning show on a Kansas prairie in the dead of night. A colony of angry jellyfish lashed at one another with thousands of poisonous tentacles, producing a bioluminescent display worthy of the grandest Fourth of July fireworks exhibition on land.

"Holy Triton," Jet muttered. She was more used to moon jellyfish colonies floating like white, placid bubbles in oceans of blue, or like clouds in the summer sky. But true of most things undersea, the more beautiful something was, the deadlier it was. Best to keep her distance from the warring turmoil.

Jet veered northward toward home, disappointed to have heard nothing from Mom or Lily. If they'd been anywhere near one another, Jet would have heard Lily's magical voice singing, its crystal purity riding the currents for miles. Same old story. So many times she had swum out as a child, hoping to hear her family returning—only to go home alone.

That old sharp pang from the memories didn't pierce as deeply. Landry had faced far worse. Opening up and swapping stories with him had helped. Perhaps Shelly was right. It was good for her to talk about what lay buried in her heart.

And maybe—just maybe—she'd been unfair to lash out at Landry. Time and expended energy had gained her perspective and she viewed the revelations in a newer, calmer light.

Besides, it wasn't as if she'd been entirely truthful with him. She had her own secrets.

Chapter 9

Landry shook his head in bewilderment at the plethora of sea-treasure sites. He was accustomed to using the computer for criminal or missing-person searches, not for shipwrecks. Astonishing the number of wrecks caused by war, error or weather over the centuries.

He kept looking, determined to discover what Perry was so intent on finding with Jet. He didn't believe the con man for a minute when he claimed Jet wanted to keep working with him and that the check she gave him was for purchasing supplies. But it felt like a gut punch when Perry confidently claimed that Jet still loved him and always would.

Maybe Jet couldn't help herself; maybe she was one of those women drawn to the bad-boy type. He'd met many over the course of his career. Landry shook off the disturbing thought. He was giving Jet a chance to cool off a bit while he continued his investigation. She didn't have any more information on the Sylvester Vargas/Perry Hammonds connection. He'd call her again later today. He'd tried to reach her last night but she wasn't returning his calls. Her anger and shock should have melted considerably by now. He'd go to her house tonight.

He concentrated on the search. Tybee Island had a rich history, as the French and Spanish had fought to obtain the barrier island. Pirates, including Blackbeard and Captain Kidd, were also frequent visitors to the Georgia and South Carolina coastlines. Despite being a well-known treasure-hunting site for avid amateurs who searched for Spanish galleon, none of the known wrecks around Tybee indicated a huge, unclaimed treasure awaiting discovery.

Landry rubbed his jaw. How did Jet find so much treasure? She'd been close to revealing her secret method. If only Seth hadn't spilled his own secret about being an FBI agent. Landry glanced over at the sofa and frowned at the pristine cleanliness. No potato chips lay scattered across its black leather, no cans of soda littered the coffee table and no sandwich crumbs marred the gleaming, waxed floors. In fact, there were no signs anyone lived here but himself.

In the past, this would have pleased him. Now the place seemed hollow and empty. Seth was spending most of his time with Jimmy Elmore, the kid Shelly had introduced him to. This should have thrilled him, yet he missed Seth's companionship, strained as it had become after the false shoplifting accusation. They'd struck a truce, but Landry still felt guilty for not believing Seth at first. Their mother had made him out to be a lying, no-good nuisance who couldn't be trusted. Jet had shown him that wasn't true.

It was way too quiet. He pushed back his chair and

went for the TV remote, turning the volume high to soak up the silence.

Much better. Landry returned to the Tybee Island search and almost scrolled past a web link until the word *bomb* caught his eye. Quickly, he pulled up an old newspaper article from 2011 about residents at a special town meeting airing concerns of an old hydrogen bomb jettisoned near the island in the 1950s and never recovered.

His pulse raced. The makings for a dirty bomb would interest Vargas. If he found it, no doubt some foreign country would pay hundreds of millions to get their hands on such a weapon. But was there really a bomb nestled in the ocean floor? And if so, was it even feasible to find and recover it? The whole thing reeked of intriguing conspiracy theory, wrapped smartly in military history and glittering with the shiny gold bow of a treasure hunt.

He scanned everything he could for quick answers. Yes, it had really happened. On February 5, 1958, a B-47 bomber collided midair with an F-86 fighter jet during a simulated combat mission. The pilot jettisoned the H-bomb so he could land the plane without crashing with the bomb on board. His action prevented a nuclear explosion on the barrier island, which was less than twenty miles from Savannah.

Navy vessels and divers searched the ocean for ten weeks before the military declared the bomb irretrievably lost. It was now one of the dozen or so nuclear bombs commonly known as Broken Arrows.

As recently as 2001, the United States Air Force reported the bomb was probably buried anywhere from five to fifteen feet in silt and posed no hazard if left undisturbed. The area where the bomb was believed to have dropped was extremely murky and no radiation readings were ever obtained by navy divers in the initial search.

If left undisturbed. A mighty big *if,* in Landry's mind. There was so much new technology developed since the '50s, he was surprised the government didn't search again. Maybe recovering the 7,600 pound bomb, labeled Number 47782, would be prohibitively expensive even for Uncle Sam's deep pockets.

But researching further, he read that the estimated recovery costs, if the bomb was found, would be roughly five million dollars. Not cheap, but certainly doable, if nothing more than to reassure Savannah citizens that possible uranium leakage wasn't contaminating their public water system. If he lived there, he'd be worried about heavy-metal poisoning.

And what about the environmental danger for marine life? He remembered Jet's frequent visits to the dolphin at the water park and her substantial donations to Save the Oceans and other such charities. She would be appalled to know that a potential menace to the entire gulf was buried in less than twenty feet of silt.

Suddenly restless, Landry got up, poured a fresh cup of coffee and grabbed his binoculars before walking out onto the cottage's second-story deck. As he did at least twice a day, he aimed it at the cage across the bay where he put out fresh fish daily, in hopes of luring the pregnant feral tabby. Yet again, the cage door was open and the fish gone. He shook his head and grinned. Damned smart cat. Even if he couldn't tame and spay her, at least she was getting food for herself and the unborn kitties.

The sea surface gleamed with millions of rainbow prism droplets swaying from underwater currents. Number 47782 was one of the earliest thermonuclear devices, designed to be a hundred times more powerful than the Hiroshima bomb. What kind of devastation would erupt from an underwater mushroom cloud? How many species of aquatic plants, mammals, fish and other creatures would be boiled alive—wiped out forever?

He wasn't a scientist, couldn't begin to guess how all that would affect human lives as well as... The creature of his youth came to mind. For the first time in ages, Landry stopped trying to fight remembering. Too much had happened in the past couple weeks to keep discounting the possibility that something lay beyond the ordinary. Whatever the creature had been, it had seemed human, a sentient, sympathetic being. Who knew what lurked far into the ocean's uncharted depths? It was as mysterious as any galaxy light-years away.

Countless times he'd stood on this deck, staring at miles of watery realms. The sea had depths no human had ever entered, its deepest ocean floors more mysterious than the moon. It held power and mystery, could be savage or serene; each wave held an enormous store of energy as it crested. There might be any number of sentient beings that existed undersea.

It stretched farther than his eyes could encompass, yet Landry strained to search beyond the point where ocean met sky in a flat line of mixed blues and grays. A pang of loneliness squeezed his chest.

Where was Jet?

He needed to hear her voice. At once.

He tried calling again, but got no answer. It had been nearly two days now since she'd discovered his lie. Plenty of time for her to recoup from the surprise and hurt. He hated the way she'd found out, but he'd been doing his job the best way he knew how and he'd make Jet understand that. Filled with resolve, he grabbed his car keys and headed to the Bosarge home.

During the short drive, Landry worked himself into a state of agitation. Jet claimed she had a sixth sense for finding sites. What if Hammonds and Vargas wanted to exploit her talent to find the missing hydrogen bomb? He pulled into their driveway and quickly skidded to a stop, overcome with urgency. Her red truck was there, a good sign. He rapped at the door sharply, but was disappointed when Shelly appeared.

"Where's Jet?" he demanded.

"She's not here."

Dread prickled the back of his neck. "Where is she?"

"Jet's gone," Shelly answered evasively, moving to shut the door.

He grabbed the handle. "Hold on a minute. What do you mean, she's gone? Do you know where she went?"

It was the kidnapping nightmare all over again—the defining incident of his childhood. That damned red sequined purse was the last physical link, an albatross from the past that warned life could be snatched away in an instant. One unguarded moment and all was lost forever.

Panic and despair from years ago washed through him. What if he never saw Jet again? He'd have to live the rest of his life with the memory of the hurt in her eyes when she'd found out he was an FBI agent. Wasn't it bad enough he'd lived through this same kind of hell once before? The gods were surely punishing him for some unfathomable reason.

Shelly frowned. "Why? You come to arrest her? Jet's done nothing wrong."

"No. Of course not. I'm worried about Jet. When is the last time you saw her?"

She stiffened. "Are you questioning me in an official capacity? 'Cause if you are, I'm calling Tillman to—"

"No," he interrupted hastily. "I just want to make sure she's okay." Landry swallowed hard. "Please."

Shelly's face softened. "She's okay. You really care for her, don't you?"

He started to deny it. But the idea of Jet going missing had frightened him to his very core. The memory of The Incident from his childhood washed over him. "You're sure she's okay and not in any danger?"

"Positive." Shelly's eyes narrowed. "Now answer my question. Do you honestly care about Jet? If you're using her to get at Perry, I promise Tillman and I will make you regret it."

"I care." The admission made him uncomfortable. He'd have to deal with those emotions later. What was important was making sure Jet was safe. "Tell me where she went."

"She's on an out-of-town trip."

"When will she come back?"

"I'm not sure. Anytime now."

Shelly was insufferably evasive. Never mind, he'd dig up the facts. Landry nodded at the red truck. "She didn't take her vehicle."

Shelly blinked those wide green eyes and said nothing.

He'd check the Mobile flight lists when he got back home. He'd also need to notify his supervisor about the Tybee Island bomb possibility. The bayou would probably soon be swarming with officers from both agencies. It wouldn't look good if Jet was MIA in the midst of it all.

Landry's frustration built. His duty was clear—notify his boss about his suspicions. But how could he do that if it meant Jet would be treated as a suspect when he knew she was innocent? She'd never forgive him for an ordeal with the federal government.

A more sickening thought assailed Landry. If Perry couldn't sweet-talk Jet into the Tybee Island excursion, he might force her to cooperate. A deep fury pounded through his veins at the very idea. Low-life scum like Perry were capable of anything, especially when desperate for money. "Look, Shelly," he said urgently, "Jet could be in deep trouble."

Her eyes widened farther. "What kind of trouble?"

He pulled his very best officer intonation. "I am not at liberty to say."

"It's Perry, isn't it?" She put her hands on her hips and sighed. "We always knew he'd be back one day, causing more problems."

"Then help me help Jet."

Shelly bit her lip. "I'm really not sure when she'll come home. Like I said, it could be anytime."

"I need to find her immediately and warn her of a possible danger."

The sound of a door slamming shut drew his attention to a shed located about thirty feet from the side of their house. As if he'd conjured her from his own desperation, he saw Jet had returned. She was dressed in a white terry-cloth robe; her black hair clung to her neck as if she'd just emerged from water. She adjusted a lock on the shed door and then turned toward the house, walking slowly, shoulders slumped, as if she'd finished a million-mile marathon.

How odd. Landry looked around the yard, puzzled. What had she been doing in a shed? There was nothing in her hands to suggest she'd gone out for a tool or some other necessity. Instead, it appeared she'd had a shower and was exhausted. At least he knew she was okay. The relief nearly made him weak in the knees. He knew Perry was in town, but one of Vargas's men could have easily slipped her away. Landry silently vowed to keep an eye on her until all this was resolved.

Shelly quietly closed the front door, but he stood

rooted on the porch, eyes on Jet. Her pale, wet skin shimmered under the Alabama sun.

He'd never seen a more beautiful sight.

Through an exhausted haze, Jet's skin prickled with awareness. She was being watched. She raised weary eyes and found Landry's frosty eyes pinned on her. Had he seen her come out of the shed? Of course he had, she admonished herself.

The long swim had drained all her mental and physical energy. All she needed now was sleep and lots of it.

Landry hurried toward her, face grim and harsh. "Where the hell have you been?" he demanded as he bore down on her.

She shrugged. "What does it matter? I'm back."

He grabbed her shoulders and hesitated, as if debating whether to shake her or hug her. Concern etched worry lines in his brows and the corners of his eyes. "Don't ever do that again," he said gruffly.

"Do what?"

"Don't leave me."

He pulled her to him and pressed her tightly against him. She rested her head on his shoulder and let him support her weight. It was the first time in days Jet had felt such calm comfort. It struck her again that Landry's touch was like finding an oasis in the desert. She hoped it wasn't all a mirage.

It sure felt real.

She listened to the steady thump of his heartbeat and felt her own heart hammer like a resounding metronome in perfect time with his. If she could, she'd curl into a little ball and slip into the crook of his arms, her face resting against his chest. The sound of his heart and the echo of waves in the background felt like a perfect union of land and sea—like a home she'd always wanted and never had.

"Okay," she mumbled into his chest. "I won't leave again."

He held her out at arm's length. "Promise?"

She was bereft without his hold, chilled in the middle of a hot, humid Southern sky. "Promise," she agreed quickly, needing his arms around her again.

He complied with urgency, a quickness that was stunning. What had gotten into him? Jet inhaled the soapy, male scent that she loved. The why didn't matter; she needed him now and was too drained to ask questions. *Later,* she promised the last questioning voice in her brain that didn't want to be quieted, until at last it shut up and left her in peace.

The sun's warmth, coupled with Landry's body heat, made her groggy. She was safe at last.

"I'm sorry I had to lie to you about my job," he whispered into the top of her scalp.

"It's okay. I don't like it, but I understand."

Landry gave her a quick squeeze. "Thank you," he said simply.

"Uh, um, Jet." Shelly's voice broke through her reverie. Jet reluctantly raised her face away from the haven of Landry's chest to find Shelly holding out an overnight bag.

"I think you're going to need this," she said.

"What do you mean?"

Landry took the bag and nodded at Shelly. "She'll be safe with me."

"What the hell are you two talking about?"

Shelly gave her a quick hug. "I packed several days' worth of clothes, your charged cell phone and all the essentials."

"I'm not going anywhere except to bed." At Landry's raised eyebrow, she flushed. "To *sleep*," she elaborated. "I'm dead on my feet, in case you all haven't noticed."

"And starving, too, no doubt," Shelly said. "Call me later," she added, before walking away.

Landry guided Jet toward his BMW, but she dragged her feet.

"Where do you think you're taking me?"

"I know you love shrimp. What would you say to a shrimp-and-lobster smorgasbord?"

Her mouth watered and her stomach grumbled. "But I'm not up to going out," she said regretfully.

"Who said anything about going out?"

She gave up and followed him, taking the path of least resistance. At the car, he opened the passenger door and tucked her in as if she was precious cargo. She sank into the soft leather.

He came around the other side and started the car. "I'll grill the seafood and boil some corn on the cob. I think I have the makings of a salad, too."

"No need for all that. All I want is shrimp and lobster."

"You got it."

Jet laid her head back on the headrest and soon the steady drone of the car tires was like a lullaby. She sighed, slipped out of her sandals and placed a hand on Landry's right thigh. Beneath her fingers, his muscles felt strong and tight. A small smile escaped. And to think that when she first met him she'd imagined his body would be soft and flaccid like a geek's. Landry was full of surprises.

She rather liked that.

Chapter 10

Jet awoke and blinked in unfamiliar darkness. Through deep shadows she looked around the small, pristinely neat room. She would have called the style minimalistic except for a collection of neatly piled quilts at the foot of the bed. On the nightstand a lamp sat atop an old-fashioned doily that was slightly yellowed with age.

Under the nightstand she at last saw a familiar item, her blue overnight bag. Memories besieged her brain like pieces of a quilt—returning from that long swim, Landry overtaking her on the lawn, Shelly handing her the bag.

She stretched, grateful for the peaceful sleep on a mattress instead of some sandy shore. Jet swung her long legs over the side of the bed.

Her long, naked legs.

Jet's hands flew to her chest. Gone was her old terry-cloth robe; she was completely naked. She groaned, searching in the shadows for her robe. She spotted it folded neatly in a chair on the opposite wall.

Had Landry seen her naked? Her skin heated and flushed until an even worse realization hit. He might have seen her exposed gill scars. She tried to quell a surge of fear. Surely most men would be much more interested in other parts of a woman's body than their *neck,* for heaven's sake. No, he wouldn't have undressed her. She must have taken off the robe herself but was just too tired to remember.

Quickly, she donned the robe, turning up the collar as best she could. Her nose led her from the hallway to the kitchen, where Landry stood at the stove, his back to her. The light illuminated streaks of gold in his hair. He seemed competent in the kitchen, as he did in every situation.

Jet inhaled deeply as she entered the room. "I hope it's time to eat. I'm starving."

He didn't even turn around, as if he was able to merely sense her presence. "Have a seat. Everything's almost ready."

She sat at the kitchen table, already laid out with plates and condiments, then poured a glass of water from the pitcher and drank. She tried to quell the nervous fluttering in her stomach. The man was probably going to grill her with questions. Maybe even want to know what was wrong with her neck. She considered going back to the bedroom and sinking into oblivious sleep.

"Where's Seth?" she asked.

"Staying with Jimmy Elmore, the guy Shelly introduced him to. They really hit it off."

"Is that his room I slept in?"

Landry snorted. "No way. His room is disgusting. Bed

unmade, dirty clothes on the floor." He shook his head. "Hard to believe we're brothers."

Landry set a platter of shrimp and lobster on the table.

"I don't know what you like to eat with them, so there's a little bit of everything here." His hand swept the table. "Melted butter, cocktail sauce, ketchup—"

Jet eagerly filled her plate and began eating, trying not to make a fool of herself and gobble it up too quickly. But all too soon, the plate was empty. She reached for more and caught Landry's bemused eyes upon her.

"How did you work up such an appetite?"

The questioning had begun. Jet shrugged and carefully dunked a shrimp in butter, eating slower. "Swimming."

He nodded. "Where at?"

She waved a hand. "Oh, a good ways south of Bayou La Siryna."

Landry nodded again and proceeded to ignore her as he ate.

The silence began to unnerve Jet until at last she had to know. She pushed away the plate. "You said I was in danger. What's happening?"

He rose. "Let's sit out on the deck and talk."

She picked up her plate and headed for the kitchen sink to wash it, but he stopped her.

"I'll get those later."

She gave him a half smile. "Must be serious if you don't want to do dishes first. Your house is immaculate."

"I do like to keep things in a certain order."

"Then let's clean up. It won't take long with both of us working together."

Working together. Had a nice ring to it, Jet mused. She took in details of the kitchen and den as she rinsed and loaded the dishwasher. In spite of the overall modern ambience, there were whimsical touches that seemed out of place: old canning jars lined against the backsplash, cat figurines in a curio cabinet and kitchen towels trimmed with crocheted embellishments.

She picked up one of the mason jars and read the label aloud. "Ginger-peach jam. Who canned these for you?"

"Mimi, my grandmother. She left this cottage for me when she died."

Ah, that explained the homey touches. "How long ago did she die?"

"About seven years ago."

Landry possessed a sentimental streak to hold on to her things for so long. She liked that about him. At least he'd loved one person in his life. She secretly watched him as he efficiently put condiments back in the refrigerator and wiped the table. "Did you enjoy every summer you spent with her?"

"Every single one. I used to count down the days during the school year. Mom's house was always full of too much drama."

No wonder the guy loved order and solitude.

He reached under her and took out some dishwasher detergent from the lower cabinet. "Go on outside while I start the dishwasher. Want some wine or beer?"

"What kind of wine do you have?"

"Merlot okay?"

She nodded. "I'll get it. Tell me where everything is." Jet poured a glass and briefly returned to the bedroom to change into shorts and a T-shirt Shelly had packed in the overnight bag. She retrieved her wineglass before stepping into the warm night air swirling on the balcony. Nice view where the salty gulf waters edged the property. She sat in a rocker and the nerves from dinner dissipated. The warmth, the full stomach and the gentle rocking soon had her yawning. It would take a couple more days of deep sleep to recoup. She set the merlot on a coffee table and closed her eyes.

A scrape from the sliding glass door had her bolting upright. Landry's tall figure emerged from the shadows and he eased into a chair across from her.

"Did a little research today on what kind of shipwreck might be off the coast of Tybee Island," he began, direct as always.

Jet sipped the merlot, curious as to what he'd discovered. She'd never bothered to read that library book or search the internet. Opening the shop and manufacturing the manifests Landry had requested had taken all her free time. Besides, she'd had no intention of going anywhere with Perry again. "What did you find?"

"Something highly unusual." The glacier chips of his eyes glowed in the darkness. "Nearly eight thousand pounds worth of unusual."

Jet snickered. "You think Perry wants to excavate the remains of an entire ship? We—that is, *I*—don't have the right equipment to excavate something as large as a ship's hull."

"Exactly. I don't think he intended for the two of you to work alone."

She tilted her head to the side, recalling Perry's words. "I don't remember him saying we'd work with a crew. We never have before."

"You really don't know what lies buried out there, do you?" He paused, gazing at her thoughtfully. "What about your, um, special abilities?"

Jet stiffened, not sure if he was mocking her. "That's only good once I'm in the water. Not before."

"How good are you at finding something buried several feet in sediment?"

"It would be harder, but I could probably do it." Her

mermaid sense of smell was even stronger than her excellent night vision. Highly developed sight and smell were necessary for navigating murky or deep waters. You had to know what danger might lurk.

He whistled. "Impressive."

She took a long, fortifying swallow of the rich wine, savoring its tang. "Now tell me what's going on. You said I'm in danger."

"I can't prove anything yet. But after a little digging I discovered there's a missing hydrogen bomb believed to be buried offshore."

"Bomb?" She gave a disbelieving laugh. "How the hell could that happen?"

"A military mishap from the '50s. Navy divers tried to find it, but had no luck."

She shook her head, setting down the drink. "And you think Perry wants us to find this? What the hell would we do with a bomb?" The notion was ludicrous.

"It's worth millions to the right buyer."

"Maybe. But neither of us has international connections. Everything we did was fairly small-scale."

"Until now," Landry insisted stubbornly.

"Coincidence." Jet stood and walked to the edge of the deck railing. The news of a bomb rattled her inside. "Do you think so little of me that you believe I'd sell a bomb to the highest bidder?" she asked, her back to him. Her hands gripped the railing as she fought waves of disappointment.

The scrape of wood on wood was loud as he rose from his chair. "Not you. I can believe anything of Perry Hammonds. But not you."

The pressure of his hands suddenly rested on her shoulders, searing her with heat.

"I told you before," he began, hands lowering to her

hips as his mouth found her neck. "You're better than that," he whispered. His breath sent tingles of desire exploding through her body.

Jet leaned back, sinking into Landry's steel chest. She closed her eyes, inhaling his clean scent while she listened to their heartbeats and the ocean waves pound in an inevitable union. She started to turn in his embrace but as she did so, a flash of orange across the lagoon drew her attention. Jet narrowed her eyes, adjusting to the darkness, until she made out details.

An orange-striped tabby—extremely fat—stared back, eyes aglow. Even at this distance, the cat had zoomed in on her with its acute, predatory olfactory sense. Damned stray cats followed her everywhere she went in town. How long had it been watching her? She allowed her nictitating membrane to lower a fraction for better vision. The extra eyelid was useful undersea as well as on land at night. She spotted the outline of a gray cage.

Outrage pushed aside passion. "There's a caged cat out there." She pointed at it.

Landry squinted in the direction she pointed. "How can you tell in this darkness? I can't see it."

"I have perfect vision." *To put it mildly.* "Why would anyone trap a cat? We've got to help it."

Landry ran a hand through his hair, as if composing himself. "Guess I better go get it, considering I'm the one who set the trap."

"Why would you do such a thing? I hate seeing animals in cages!" Her nightmare pricked in the back of her mind.

"I'm trying to help it. She's a pregnant feral cat. I'd like to see the kittens be adopted at the shelter."

"Oh, I see." If only it were this easy to help Dolly and her calf.

Landry started toward the door. "Let's go get her. It won't take long."

Jet hurried after him as he sped downstairs for the carport. She heard him mumble something about *damn cat* and *why now of all times.* "I'll wait for you here," she called out.

He was walking across the lawn to a small fishing dock with an old johnboat attached to it. "Come with me," he said, waving an arm toward the boat. "Won't take long."

"But I'll get wet."

He turned at that. "The first day we met it was pouring rain and you lingered outside with no umbrella. Now you're worried about getting wet?"

Jet struggled for an excuse. If so much as a drop of salt water landed on her legs, the gig was up and the freak show would begin. "I feel like I'm coming down with a cold," she offered lamely. Desperately, she scanned underneath the carport, at last spotting a pair of knee-high wading boots. That should do the trick. "I'll borrow your boots." She hurriedly put them on. Landry started the boat motor as she clumsily made her way to shore.

He raised a brow at the boots but didn't comment. He threw her an orange vest and grabbed another for himself. "Put this on."

As if. "Don't need it."

He frowned. "It's the law."

"Seriously? It's just you and me in the middle of nowhere. Besides, I have an *in* with the local sheriff." She gave him a wink. "We're good."

His fingers stilled on the jacket straps. "What if the boat tips over?"

All hell breaks loose, that's what. She wanted to go

back inside but didn't want to draw questions about her motives.

"If it tips, we swim," she answered grimly. What a relationship killer that would be.

"The thing is…" Landry spoke hesitantly, his voice trailing off.

Jet glanced at him sharply, surprised to see a flush of red in his cheeks. "What?"

He slowly snapped closed the jacket fasteners. "I don't swim."

She gaped at him, astonished. "Why not?"

He expertly guided the boat out toward the cat. "I can't, okay?" he answered testily.

She couldn't imagine not knowing how to swim; it would be like a human saying they never learned to walk. Of course, she'd heard some people couldn't. Shelly even taught a few adults at the YMCA who'd never learned how.

They continued in silence until they reached the bank on the opposite shore. Jet carefully maneuvered out of the boat, avoiding water as best she could, even with boot protection. Landry squatted down in front of the large, wire cage. "We meet at last, little mama," he said in a soft voice. "You put up a good, long fight, I'll give you that."

Jet bent over, eyeing the tabby, which instantly hissed and began growling.

"She was fine a moment ago," Landry said, brows knitting.

"I have this weird effect on cats. Sort of a mutual non-admiration society."

"I thought you loved animals. Anyone that could love that ugly mutt of yours—"

"Leave Rebel out of it," she warned in mock sternness. Reb couldn't help the cruel joke nature had played on his appearance.

Landry picked up the cage, the tabby crying and spitting its disapproval. "Sorry, girl. The ride over won't be fun, but we've got some leftover shrimp you're going to love."

Although Jet did her best to not even look at the cat on the boat ride home, the thing mewled like a banshee from hell. At the dock, Landry donned a thick pair of rubber fisherman's gloves before picking up the cage and hauling it to the cottage.

"Smart thinking," Jet said, watching the cat flay its claws out the cage slits, ready to do damage.

"It's not the first time I've done this. I'm fighting a one-man battle to end the bayou's feral cat population."

"Why?" she asked in surprise.

"Because most end up living short lives filled with both disease and serious fight wounds, or else they starve."

She followed him upstairs. "Where you taking her?"

He set the cage down in a small utility room. "I'll take her to the shelter when I get a chance. They can take care of her until she has the kittens." He left the room. "Be right back. I promised her shrimp."

Jet dropped to her knees and eyed the tabby, which glared and hissed in response. "You better start acting lovable," she warned. "Nobody wants a wild hellion."

The tabby growled louder and spit.

"I see no progress has been made," Landry observed, carrying in a plate of shrimp and a bowl of water.

"How do you plan on getting that in the cage without being clawed?"

He shrugged. "I don't. I'm letting the cat out." He got down on a knee beside Jet and set down the food and water. "Maybe you should back away. You seem to make her more agitated."

"Fine." She rose and watched as Landry opened the cage latch. She expected the cat to dig in on the peeled shrimp, but the tabby backed into a far corner, eyeing them with suspicion.

"Thought you said wild cats were usually starving. She's not acting hungry at all."

Landry rose, grabbed a large plastic container and filled it with kitty litter. "Be patient. It takes time. When I check on her in the morning, the plate will be empty." He turned to the door. "Let's leave her in peace to get used to her new surroundings."

Jet's mouth dropped open. "But you can't leave her locked in here!"

His mouth twisted in a wry smile. "Better here than in a cage at the shelter anyway."

"Then maybe she's better off in the wild." She folded her arms across her chest. "Let's release it."

He leaned against the doorjamb, eyeing her with curiosity. "What is it with you and caged animals?"

"It's just…" Her mouth went dry and she swallowed hard. "It's just like this dolphin at the local water park. She's with calf and instead of being with her pod, she's trapped and alone."

"You mean Dolly?"

She gave him a sharp glance. "You know her?"

"*Know* her? That's an odd way to put it. I visited the water park once. You go there a lot so I wanted to see the main attraction. I still don't see your objection."

"Never mind, you wouldn't understand." She went to the door, but Landry blocked the exit.

"Try me," he said.

She lifted her shoulders casually. "I have a recurring dream where I'm stuck in a tank, er, I mean a cage."

He nodded wisely. "Probably a guilty conscience symbolically urging you to break all ties with Hammonds before you end up in prison."

"Don't analyze me with that FBI profiling crap," she snapped. But then she caught the stirrings of a smile playing at the corners of his mouth. She ran a finger along the edge of his strong jawline. "Whoever would have thought the uptight FBI man had a sense of humor behind that stiff exterior?"

The amusement faded. "Is that how I come off?"

"Most definitely," she assured him. "Serious, hardworking and uptight."

"I'll show you uptight." He pulled her against him and kissed her long and hard, until Jet was breathless with need.

"I retract my statement," she whispered in a shaky laugh.

His hands lifted her T-shirt and caressed her breasts. He cupped them, thumbs brushing her nipples. Sexual need hot as lava erupted in her core. But in spite of the erupting desire, Jet was conscious of the gill markings.

"Let's go to your bedroom," she gasped.

He drew back, incredulous. "That's so predictable," he said. "Now who's the uptight one?"

But he picked her up in one efficient, effortless move and carried her to the last bedroom down the narrow hallway. Once inside, he flipped on the lights but at Jet's protest turned them back off.

"Never figured you as the shy type," he said huskily. "I wanted to see you. All of you."

"Later," she promised. She wanted to see his naked body, too, but didn't want their first time marred by probing questions. All she needed tonight, truly needed, was to merge her body with his. From the first time they met, Landry had stirred her passion. Something about the penetrating chill of his blue eyes made her want to fuse it with her own heat.

He laid her gently on the bed. Jet flung off her shorts and T-shirt in the darkness, heard the sound of metal scraping metal as Landry unzipped his pants and the whooshing of fabric against skin as he ripped off his shirt. She scooted over and he eased down alongside her, stroking her breasts and then the plane of her abdomen. She'd never considered her stomach an erogenous zone, but Landry's hands on her flat abs inflamed her body's internal temperature even more.

Jet placed one leg over his, running the tender flesh of her instep along his sleek, muscular thighs. Beneath his conservative attire, Landry hid a body as hard and muscular as a professional athlete. The man was full of surprises. She snuggled closer, the small mounds of her breasts pressing against his broad chest. Curly hairs tickled her nose as she inhaled the fresh scent of soap and clean skin.

His hands moved upward and her scalp prickled as Landry ran his fingers through her short hair. In the darkness she couldn't tell where he would touch her next and that added to the excitement. Everywhere he touched sent her nerve endings tingling with fever. Each moan and ragged breath Landry released was amplified and echoed, as if they were alone in some deep, black cave.

But what amazed Jet most of all was the tender eroticism of his caresses. All her senses surrendered to his touch. His hands moved from her scalp and traveled down her spine until he located the curve of her hip and gently pushed her back against the mattress. Landry kissed the hollow at the base of her throat, his tongue lapping the indentation before trailing his mouth over her breasts, kissing and licking. When Jet thought she couldn't wait another second, he pursed his lips over the soft bud of one nipple while he gently squeezed the other between his thumb and forefinger. Her fears and insecurities gave way to raw desire.

Burning spasms of need flared between her legs, as if a hidden toggle switch existed between her nipples and core. Jet moved her hands to his erection, wanting him to be as desperate as she for release. His manhood was hard, ready. Landry groaned and pressed into her exploring palms.

"Let's do it," Jet whispered in a ragged whisper. "Now!"

"So soon?"

"There's always next time for more foreplay," she promised.

He made a noise that was half moan, half chuckle. "You bet."

Landry parted the folds of her core and entered slowly.

He was driving her crazy. She needed him now, would shatter into a million pieces if he took his time. She bucked her hips underneath him and he increased his pace. Tension coiled in her stomach, an unbearable need.

Jet flipped Landry so that he was on his back, she astride him. She cringed at his quick inhale. Damn, she'd shown too much of her inhuman strength. She hardly dared move, waiting for Landry to demand an explanation.

"Don't stop," he groaned. He placed his hands on either side of her hips, urging her to continue.

He was as desperate as she for release. Jet momentarily reveled in the knowledge before rocking her core and taking in his manhood, until all thought abandoned her mind once again. The only thing that mattered was the gathering storm at the apex of her thighs. "Landry," she cried out, needing the sound of his voice, her orgasm crashing like tidal waves against a granite cliff.

"I'm with you, baby," he assured her, body taut and straining as he matched her quickened pace.

Jet knew the instant he found his own release as he moaned and shuddered before lying completely still, breathing hard and fast. She laid her head against his chest, listened to his deep breathing as he stroked her hair.

"That was incredible," he murmured against her ear.

"Mmm," she agreed, suddenly too tired for conversation. Landry rolled her over and rubbed her legs in relaxing massage strokes. Exactly what she needed. Every muscle ached from her swimming binge. "Oh, that feels so good."

"Relax and take a little nap," Landry encouraged. He chuckled. "I want you well rested for next time."

"Whatever," she said, concentrating on the muscle relief. She'd probably agree to almost anything right now.

"And next time—" he lightly patted her ass "—it will be with the lights on."

Momentary alarm flared at his words, but Jet decided to deal with that problem later. Right now was pure bliss, the aftermath almost as incredible as the sex—something she'd never before experienced.

His hands continued their magic, comforting and healing Jet. She snuggled against the pillow, breathing in Landry's scent as he massaged her body, all the way down to her toes. Who knew toes needed love and attention, too? Landry, that was who. She nestled her face into the pillow. Her breathing slowed and grew deeper under Landry's expert touch. Jet experienced the same sensation as when she swam under a full moon—her body was fluid, responsive, in the flow of being exactly where it needed to be.

Sweet Triton, she never wanted to leave Landry's bed.

Chapter 11

Landry eased out of bed, careful not to awaken Jet. He pushed open the bedroom door and light from the hallway spilled into the room. Her pale skin seemed to shimmer in the semidarkness. He leaned over to smooth a lock of hair from her face and again noticed the faint etchings of some past trauma that had left small white scars on the sides of her neck, so eerily like the mermaid of his past that it disturbed him. Jet's ebony hair framed the patrician features of her face. Full red lips were curved as if she were having sweet dreams. She looked like a dark angel, he decided. A very *sexy* dark angel.

He frowned at the direction of his thoughts. Jet Bosarge was getting to him. Getting to him *bad*. First, he went into overprotective mode to keep her from Hammonds. Second, the news she was missing had scared him shitless. And then tonight when they'd landed in his bed, he'd been flooded with mixed feelings of tenderness and passion. It was so much more than mere physical need. Frankly, it made him nervous as hell.

He grabbed his discarded clothes from the floor and left the room, shutting the door quietly behind him. Jet appeared to be exhausted from wherever the hell she'd been. Time enough to question her later. He still needed more concrete information before he went to his supervisors.

Something had been tickling the back of his brain. Something he couldn't quite catch, like trying to remember a dream fading away as soon as you awakened.

Landry quickly dressed, booted up the computer and read more on the hydrogen bomb. After nearly half an hour of reviewing the material, a name jumped out at him—Brian Tindol, copilot of the plane that scuttled the H-bomb to land.

He'd heard that name before today, Landry was positive. It was unusual enough to catch his eye. But where? He pulled out the files on Vargas and Hammonds, searching for a connection. He would try Hammonds's phone list first, since there were fewer names and numbers to scan. Twenty minutes later, Landry neatly tucked the phone records back in the Hammonds file and determinedly started on Vargas's records.

Bingo! Vargas had been in extensive communication with one Jim Tindol. He'd bet his house that Jim was related to Brian. Satisfaction settled deep in his bones now that he had a connection between the H-bomb and Perry Hammonds. He'd call his supervisors in Mobile in the morning and let them run a background check to confirm the Tindols were related. The sooner he laid this case to rest, the sooner he and Jet could put Hammonds behind them.

* * *

Perry smirked, his brown eyes taking on the sly look of a fox that had cleverly sneaked into a chicken coop to survey the easy prey. "You're mine. All mine," he said in a singsong chant. "Forever and ever."

Bubbles of frustration spewed in Jet's gut, before rising and clogging her throat in a stifled scream. Not again! She couldn't, wouldn't be tricked by Perry and turn into his treasure-hunting slave.

"There's no escape. Mine, mine, mine."

Jet jumped off their boat and swam from his voice as fast as she could, but had only gone a few yards underwater when something sharp grabbed her ankle. She kicked, but even her strength was no match against that steel grip. She turned, staring into Orpheous's blue-green face with its smile exposing sharply pointed teeth. "Told you I'd find you one day and make you mine," he said with a leer. "You belong with me and the Blue Clan. Together, we will mate and produce fine specimens. Our sons will become elite warriors and our daughters fitting mates for Blue Mermen. Our family will be pivotal in forcing other merfolk to serve our cause—domination of the seven seas."

Jet's limbs were useless appendages, as paralyzed as her vocal cords. *No, you deluded maniac,* she tried to protest, but no sound emerged. Orpheous shook her like he would shake seaweed off a dead fish before biting into its flesh with his jagged teeth. But instead of biting her, Orpheous flung her deeper undersea. Jet found herself in some kind of pit where electric eels encircled an invisible border she could not cross without being stung.

Beautiful mermaids passed, pointing and laughing. Even their cruel laughter held a beauty, an allure that she could never attain. Jet glanced down. Her beautiful mermaid's tail had transformed into pale human legs. It was all wrong; she shouldn't be human down under the sea. She was more of an outcast than ever.

"You don't belong," one voluptuous mermaid sang out, and the others immediately joined in a chorus. *Don't belong, don't belong, don't belong.*

Again she struggled to move, and this time she was rewarded with a reconnection to her limbs.

Soft sheets rubbed against her naked flesh and she opened her eyes, staring into a strange room. Confusion gave way seconds later to recognition. This was Landry's bedroom. She stretched out an arm and found the space beside her empty. Quickly, she found her cast-off clothes on the floor and dressed before she entered the living room. Landry sat in front of the computer, but his hands gripped a framed photo. The profile of his tight jaw and the white knuckles drew her curiosity. He didn't move as she walked barefoot and stood behind his back.

A small girl grinned from a tire swing mounted to a tree. The picture was slightly blurry, as if she'd been in motion when the camera snapped. Something about the blond curls and the shape of her nose and mouth suggested a strong family connection. A daughter perhaps?

"Who is she?" Jet asked, laying a hand on his shoulder. His muscles tensed beneath her palm.

"My sister. Her name was April."

"I caught the resemblance—" Jet paused as the word *was* sank in. "Was?"

Landry carefully set the frame down beside the computer. "She died less than a month after that picture was taken."

"That's…that's awful. What happened? She doesn't look sick in that photo."

"April was kidnapped. Went missing one summer afternoon from our own front yard. Mom had gone into the house for something and when she came back out a minute later, April was gone." He pointed to the photo. "That tire swing was still in motion."

Jet's throat closed up and she couldn't speak. Words were so inadequate anyway. She rested her chin on the top of Landry's scalp and wrapped her arms around his chest.

"April's body was found a month later by a fisherman, under a clump of pines along the Mobile River."

In the silent stillness, she heard the eternal motion of waves lapping against shore. Lace curtains billowed from the open window like pale ghosts. "I'm so sorry," she whispered.

"My first vivid memory, at age five, is of Mom screaming."

The bleak, deep timber vibrations of his voice traveled from his chest to her fingertips and on up through her arms, past her rib cage and into her heart, where it pinched like a monster sea crab. His sorrow was her sorrow.

"I'll hear it forever," he continued. "Those screams echo in my brain every damn day, with every new case."

"It's why you became an FBI agent," she answered past the ache in her throat. "To stop crimes from happening to anyone else."

"Exactly. When I see this photo, see that happy grin on April's face, it's a reminder that in a minute—a mere sixty seconds—one evil person can snatch a loved one and destroy their life and their family's lives."

Jet moved around Landry's side and sat in his lap, stroking the nape of his neck and the small wisps of light brown curls he always tried to keep combed down.

"It broke up our family," he continued. "Dad moved

out three months later, away from the scene of the trauma, the looks of pity on everyone's face. Away from April's dark, closed-off bedroom, her empty chair at the kitchen table. Away from the shadow person Mom became."

"And from you." Jet simultaneously hated and pitied Landry's father. "He deserted you, too." No wonder Landry loved coming to visit his grandmother every summer. It must have felt like a prison furlough from the house of misery, a respite from haunting memories.

He shrugged as if his father's absence were no big deal. "I learned to live with it. Mom's method of coping was keeping a steady stream of new boyfriends and more children." He shook his head with a rueful smile. "Lots of children."

"Keeping busy." She gave a small smile of understanding. "Kids will ensure your mind stays occupied all day."

Landry nodded. "My mother never stopped *doing*. We never sat down in the evening to watch TV or movies like other families. She was always busy—going out, cooking, cleaning, whatever." He fell silent a minute before giving a weary sigh. "But at least she didn't run away, not physically anyway. I try to be patient and remember what she went through, but it hasn't been easy."

How difficult it must have been growing up as the eldest with a slew of half siblings while he was the one that favored April in appearance. Every time his mother looked at him, she must have remembered her dead sister.

"Enough about me," he said resolutely. "I don't know why, but I end up telling you things from my past that I don't speak about with others, and stuff I try not to dwell on even privately. Besides, we need to talk."

Jet groaned and stood up. "Sounds ominous."

"It's serious, not ominous. Go ahead and sit. Want something to drink first? Coffee?"

"It's too late for coffee. Just some water for me."

"Coming right up."

Jet tried not to stare at April's photo as Landry went to the fridge. She was still rattled about the news and her own intense response to his pain. His sister's tragic murder explained so much about Landry—his strong sense of justice, his need for order and his self-contained reserve that she at first mistook for aloofness. Everyone in his past had deserted him in one way or another, so he learned to rely on no one but himself.

Would he ever fully open up his heart again and risk being hurt?

Could she do the same? Fear lanced through her brain as she again recalled Perry's betrayal when the Chilean marine police had sneaked in through the fog and caught them.

The blasting marine foghorn had jolted them awake from a nap. Naked, they had leaped to their feet and tried to cover their loot with an old tarp, frantically kicking the rest of it under the seats. But it was too late. Three skinny officers dressed in navy uniforms boarded their boat, shouting a high-pitched volley of foreign words.

"Americano?" one of them had asked, leering at her breasts. "You speak English?" he'd added in a thick accent. An officer spotted antique jewelry scattered on the deck and pointed. After a moment of incredulous silence, their voices rose in a chorus of excitement. The shortest policeman, who sported a long, twirling mustache, flung the tarp aside. All three dropped to their knees, picking up handfuls of expensive artifacts. She hoped they would take the loot for themselves and leave. But one of the officers returned to the patrol vessel to radio in the find.

Perry pointed a finger at Jet. "It's her!" he'd screamed,

eyes wild with fear. "This is *her* boat and *her* stuff. The woman's a freaking mermaid."

Jet had stared at that pointing finger, transfixed at the betrayal.

"Mermaid?" The shortest officer asked, mustache twitching in confusion.

The three spoke rapidly to one another until Shorty beat a hand on his chest and said, *"Sí. Soy el Capitán Hook."*

Jet stood transfixed as they laughed. This was so not a Disney moment for her.

"Captain Hook, *comprendes?*"

"It's true," Perry insisted. "She really is a mermaid, and I can prove it. Capture her and you'll be rich!"

The officer beside Shorty, the one who had been leering at her breasts minutes earlier, pulled out a set of handcuffs.

No way in hell.

If Perry was bailing on her, exposing her secret, she had no choice. Jet had dived off the side of the boat. That long, long journey home had been more physically demanding than ten Poseidon Games races put together. She'd returned to Bayou La Siryna skinny and frail and exhausted and emotionally shattered.

"Here's your water."

Jet jumped at the sound of Landry's voice.

"What's wrong?" he asked, placing a warm hand at the back of her neck.

"Nothing. Just thinking," she said hastily as she sat, gesturing for Landry to join her. No need to dwell on Perry's miserable betrayal. What Landry had been through was so much worse. She opened the water bottle and started to take a sip when she recalled Tia's words.

"The little girl who's trying to talk to you!" She grabbed his arm. "It's your sister, April. Right?"

"Maybe," he said with a frown. "I wanted to dismiss the old woman as a charlatan. Wanted to believe that she remembered the old news of my sister's death and used it to pretend she had secret knowledge."

"Why would she do that?"

"I've seen it several times in my career. Fake mediums who—for a price—will help families locate missing children or communicate with a dead loved one for clues on where to find their body or who murdered them."

"You said you *wanted* to think that," Jet noted. "Has something happened to make you believe Tia's telling the truth?"

Landry gave a rueful, one-sided smile. "More crazy stories. You up for it?"

She shook her head at the irony. If he knew he was sitting across from a shape-shifting mermaid… "Nothing would be too left-field for me," she said drily. "Trust me."

Landry stood and picked up something from the sideboard. "Ever seen this before?" he asked.

She squinted at the old red coin purse before also rising and taking it from him. "No," she said. "No offense. But it's nothing valuable." She ran a finger over patches of missing sequins and its scarred clasp. "Oh, did it belong to your sister?"

He took it from her hands and laid it gently back on the sideboard. "It was found on the grass by the tire swing. April carried it everywhere. She drew her initial on the inside and carried a lucky penny in it."

Some luck, poor kid. "Damn," she muttered. "I don't know why you think I've seen it before, though."

"Because it was in your shop a few days ago."

"Impossible."

Landry raised an eyebrow. "Exactly. For the past couple of weeks weird crap has escalated—broken clocks, electrical malfunctions, moved objects, even the scent of baby powder when there shouldn't be any."

"Those papers you touched," Jet said in wonder. "You went through some paperwork in the shop and after you left I smelled baby powder, too."

"April always smelled like talc. Mom put some in an old saltshaker and called it pixie dust. April hoped she'd attract fairies if she sprinkled it everywhere." A ghost of a smile crossed his face.

"You said everything's escalated since you came to Bayou La Siryna. Why now?" Jet asked softly.

"No clue. Creepy stuff happened before, but not as often or as strange."

"You can't dismiss it anymore. Let's find out what April wants."

The twisty back road grew narrower and Landry inwardly cursed. Even driving Jet's truck, the tires whirred ominously in the looser, less-compacted sand. Early-morning sunlight slipped through oak-tree limbs and Spanish moss that smacked and scraped against the truck. "Between the sand and the potholes, we're likely to get stranded out here in the boondocks," he said.

"Better hope not." Jet gave a casual shrug of her shoulders. "There's no cell-phone signal to get towed if we do."

"Terrific. You sure this is the right way? 'Cause I keep expecting to drive into a swamp at every bend in the road."

"I promise we won't end up as gator food. Shelly gave me exact directions."

This was a bad idea. Landry couldn't believe he'd let Jet convince him otherwise. For once, he'd been caught up in the moment and pushed his job aside. Jet's enthusiasm and his own curiosity had temporarily got the best of him. "I'm wasting time chasing ghosts when I should be working. I didn't tell you what I discovered earlier about Hammonds. He and—"

"There's the house," Jet interrupted.

Some house. The clapboard structure more resembled a shack with its tattered roof and dangling shutters. The headlights exposed a maze of potted plants and other assorted junk spread out front. Oh, well. He'd see what Tia had to say and then he and Jet would decide on a strategy before he called his supervisor today. Landry wanted to leave Jet out of everything as much as possible.

He pulled up close and hurried to open Jet's door. "Hold on to my arm so you don't trip. It's tricky with all this crap lying around."

"I can see fine. You don't need to…" She hesitated. "Okay, great."

He guided her through the maze of junk and up dilapidated porch steps. The door swung open with a screech of rusty hinges before he knocked.

Tia beamed at them. "I knew you two were a-coming this evening. Welcome."

Landry's eyes watered from a hit of burning incense as they entered the cramped, yet clean, den. Tia pointed to an old, battered sofa, where a cat napped on a lime-green afghan. "Have a seat."

The cat rose up, arched its back and glared at them resentfully, hissing at Jet before racing out of the room.

"Bad kitty," Tia said, clicking her tongue. "But he powerful good company on a lonely night."

A card table was set up by the sofa. Candles burned at all four corners and a strange game board with symbols and letters lay open.

"What's all this stuff?" he asked as they sat down, Tia across from them.

"The Ouija board. Spirits tells me most of what I need to know through it."

By the looks of her shabby abode, Tia should be asking the spirits for winning lottery numbers.

Jet squeezed his hand. *Open mind,* she mouthed at him while Tia Henrietta shuffled a deck of cards.

"The tarot cards fill in details the spritis may not have or don't want to tell." Tia held out a wrinkled hand, palm up. "Give me April's purse."

Landry's breath caught and the room went fuzzy. He turned to Jet and his vision righted as he watched her pull it from her backpack. She'd been right in thinking to bring it; Tia wanted to touch an object that had belonged to April.

Tia laid the purse on the table. "I just needs to get me a few more details," she said, spreading out a row of colorful cards with pictures of dragons and angels and other fantasy images. "Mmm-hmm, that's what I thought," she mumbled. Tia closed her eyes and hummed, a deep, guttural sound that vibrated the flimsy table.

Landry clenched his jaw to hold back a snicker. The medium act was as hokey as he feared. This woman knew nothing of April other than what she'd heard of the murder years ago. Another minute and he was walking out. This was ludicrous, a travesty, a—

Tia opened her rheumy eyes, the grayish film a shroud over the too-perceptive stare. "I have a message from your sister," she announced in a deep, dark voice that was surprisingly vibrant for a woman of her advanced years. "But first—" Tia fixed her gaze on Jet "—you must leave."

Jet pasted on a smile and stood. "I can take a hint. I'll go sit on the porch."

"Sorry, this won't take long," he promised.

Tia said nothing more until the front door closed behind Jet. "April's skipping for joy she finally got yer attention."

He threw up his hands. "I have no choice but to concede that she's nearby. Too much has happened."

Tia tilted her head to the side as if hearing a voice. "She says you weren't this way when you were both young'uns. Says you both used to try and sneak up on fairies in the garden."

A faraway memory tickled his consciousness. The two of them playing outside, the sun shining on her golden hair, the same shade as his own. Carefree, happy days before everything changed. "Is she—okay?" he asked. Stupid question. April was dead.

"Oh, she's just fine. Don't you worry about her," Tia said. "Your little sister be prancin' about with the angels. Mimi watches over her, as well."

He'd never given much thought to his sister's afterlife. Could only imagine April's last minutes on earth ending in terror and pain. Preventing the same crime from victimizing others was the sole reason he'd become an FBI agent and worked crazy hours every week.

"Forget that last day," Tia said sharply, either reading his thoughts or guessing them. "'Twas a long time ago. That's why she's here. To tell you to move on. She sees the bitter, rigid man whose heart and mind are closed to love and magic."

"I'm not—" He wanted to deny it, but couldn't. Landry cleared the lump in his throat. "Why now? Why after all these years is she communicating with me?"

"Because, way April sees it, you got a mighty big test

comin' up. You either pass it or you're doomed to go through life lonely and empty-feelin'."

He tried to lighten the spooky miasma. "Doomed?" he asked, grinning.

Tia's face grew sterner. "Doomed," she repeated.

"I want more details. What test? When will it occur?"

"April says that's just like you to starting cutting straight for the facts." Tia gave a throaty chuckle and handed him the coin purse. "Magic don't work like that." She blew out the candles and rose.

Landry stood also. "That's it? Will April still hang around?"

"She's always around her big brother." Tia moved toward the door, dismissing him.

"I've been an agent for years. Can't expect me to just change," he muttered, digging out his wallet.

"There's plenty things to investigate besides violent crimes round this bayou. Weirdness you ain't never dreamt of," Tia said with a mysterious smile.

Landry slapped a handful of twenty-dollar bills on the table. From the looks of things, Tia Henrietta could use the money. Outside on the porch, Jet stood and gave him a questioning glance. He gulped in the fresh, briny air, his lungs grateful at the change from the smoky interior.

"Everything okay?" Jet asked.

"Fine." In his haste to get away, he forgot to dodge the junk in the yard and stumbled over a collection of conch shells. Damn, no, he wasn't okay. He wasn't sure how he felt about this visit—confused, relieved, intrigued, curious, uncomfortable, but no longer a skeptic. He started the truck and they began the tortuous path out. Driving, even in these conditions, was a familiar, safe distraction.

"Tell me what happened," Jet said. "Did she know why April's trying to get your attention?"

Landry shot her a sideways glance, took in her bright eyes and pale, gleaming skin. Love and magic? He needed time to mull over the evening and process the information. It was too new, too strange. Jet had shaken up his world, made him question his beliefs, forced him to remember the past and the young child who'd been gifted sea treasure and had been saved in a storm by an unknown *something*.

He shrugged, reluctant to share all that Tia Henrietta had mentioned. "Tia said the usual occult things. April is on The Other Side and doing fine. And there's some kind of test or trial coming up soon."

"That's it? No startling world-shaking information?"

He grinned at Jet's disappointment. "I wasn't expecting any. This isn't my first go-round with a medium. We get them all the time at the agency, volunteering their services when news of an unsolved crime gets lots of media attention."

"Don't you believe April's spirit is here with you?"

"I do," he said promptly.

"That's a start," she muttered.

"Start of what?"

"Oh, nothing." Jet looked out the window, avoiding his eyes.

They rode on in silence. A few miles from his cottage, Jet spoke again. "Before we left for Tia's, you said we needed to talk. What gives?"

He frowned, berating himself for losing focus on his job, even if it was for a short length of time. The most important thing for now was to solve this case and keep Jet from danger. Afterward, he could consider April's message.

She raised an eyebrow. "You look as serious as you did when you interrogated me about my tax records." Jet gave a teasing smile. "Should I call my attorney? Am I in trouble?"

He didn't crack a smile. "If you're talking about a few petty, past legal violations in the salvage business, the answer is no. None of that matters. But you are in danger. I've found a connection that directly ties Hammonds with Vargas and the missing hydrogen bomb at Tybee Island. I need your help to stop them."

Chapter 12

It had been hard convincing Landry to let her leave yesterday. What with the annual family reunion and setting up the new business, Jet had no time to be sequestered away from home. Landry worried Perry would whisk her away before he had a chance to prove his case and arrest Hammonds. In the end, she'd persuaded Landry that carrying on as usual would keep anyone from suspecting they were onto their possible plan to retrieve the missing bomb.

Today her place was overrun with Bosarge women. Everyone had returned from the Games for their family reunion, always held after the Poseidon Games to celebrate their victories and spend time together. Mom, Shelly, Lily and a couple of the older cousins lounged in the den while the younger cousins roamed the house, exploring treasure crammed in every bureau drawer from generations of Bosarge hoarders.

Jet took a swig from her water bottle, surveying the den awash with golden hair and luminous, pearlescent skin. All the women wore pastel sundresses with long strands of pearls and abalone-shell earrings. Mother-of-pearl bracelets jingled as each sipped water from delicate antique teacups. Each had model-lovely hands, gracefully holding their cups, opal rings glittering to advantage.

It was like being dropped into a living advertisement for *Town & Country*. Jet stretched out her bare, unpedicured feet and inwardly sighed. She wore cutoff jeans and a crimson-colored University of Alabama T-shirt. Her only jewelry was a pair of stud ruby earrings and the golden trident necklace.

"You should have heard Lily sing. I declare, she's more mesmerizing every year." Adriana Bosarge beamed at her youngest daughter. "The other mermaids didn't stand a chance." Her cobalt eyes settled on Jet. "Darling, couldn't you have stayed another couple of hours at the Games to watch your sister? You're always in such a rush."

"I had Orpheous on my tail. Literally."

Mom raised her chin and waved a hand dismissively. "As long as you were with us, in the crowd, no harm would have come to you."

Lily laughed, trilling delicate whimsical notes that made everyone around her involuntarily smile. Except Jet.

"Yes, you should have stayed," Lily said, suppressing a giggle. "The Blue Merman was besotted with you."

Jet shrugged. "Not after he heard you sing."

"That's true." Lily patted the lavender folds of her dress. "I don't think you need worry about him chasing after you for a long time. When we left, he was muttering something about taking you down next year."

Shelly caught Jet's eye and gave her a knowing nod

of sympathy. She pointed to Jet's pendant. "Isn't it awesome that Jet won the Undines' Challenge?"

Lula Belle, a great-aunt, set down her teacup, pulled an old-fashioned opera glass up to her faded blue eyes and squinted at the necklace. "I see you haven't used your wish yet."

Jet stared at her mother across the room. "No. But I know exactly what I want to use it for."

Lily hopped up and spun in the center of the room. "Look what I got for winning the Siren's Song again." She held out a conch shell made of solid eighteen-karat gold with diamond dust glittering in its folds.

As everyone oohed and aahed, Jet crossed her arms and watched them cluster around Lily. She had never felt so distant, so left out from her family. No matter what she accomplished, it was never as good as what came naturally to Lily. She didn't fit in. Why, why, *why?*

Jet's cell phone pinged and she checked her messages. Landry had called three times already today, as had Perry. She skimmed Perry's messages, each increasingly desperate for her to meet him, but focused on the last one from Landry.

Did you read my earlier texts? I was called in to the Mobile office today and will return this evening. Respond so I know you're okay.

Jet quickly scanned Landry's previous texts, filled with warnings to stay hidden from Perry while he made the entrapment arrangements they had agreed upon yesterday. Worrywart. If Perry caused her any trouble, she could flip him and throw him to the ground in a second, and well Perry knew it.

A whiff of amber mixed with coriander tickled her

nose. Adriana settled into the chair beside her. "What's got you scowling? Trouble already with your new boyfriend?"

"I see you've been talking with Shelly. I wouldn't call Landry my boyfriend yet." Jet turned off her phone.

Worry clouded her mom's face. "Shelly also told me that worthless Perry Hammonds is in the bayou again. Please tell me you aren't entertaining going back into business with the jerk."

"Of course I won't."

Adriana patted her arm, as if Jet was still a five-year-old. "Good girl."

"Mom, we need to talk."

A slight veil shuttered the brightness of her irises. "Maybe later. We're all exhausted from our trip right now." She arose and yawned delicately. "I'm going to take a little nap."

Typical evasive move, but this time Jet wasn't giving up. She waited a good five minutes after Adriana left and then headed upstairs.

Portraits hung on the landing, depicting generations of Bosarge women. Their eyes seemed to follow her movements, like a galley of creepy *Mona Lisa*s. They might as well have been painted with an index finger pressed against their full, luscious lips, a warning to all mermaids to guard their secrets.

Jet studied them in a new light. Interspersed among the blue-eyed blondes were a couple of redheads and a chestnut-haired beauty with kiwi-green eyes. Not a black-haired, brown-eyed one in the bunch.

She rapped softly on the guest-room door before sticking her head in. "Mom?"

Adriana sat up in bed and sighed. "I can tell by the

determined gleam in your eye you want to have *that* conversation again."

"Da—" Jet clamped her mouth shut. No need for vulgarity and a lecture from Mom. "Right." She sat next to Adriana. "I can't help feeling there's something you're not telling me. I'm so different from Lily and every other blue-eyed blonde in our family." Jet paused. "Why is that?"

Mom wouldn't quite meet her eyes. "We don't all have the same eyes and hair color," she argued. "Some have green eyes like Shelly, and I have a great-niece with hair the color of red algae. And remember your aunt Melusina? Her hair was a lovely shade of turquoise."

"I'm not just talking physical appearance. I'm not like any of you. I have no siren skills and I'm freakishly stronger than any other mermaid I've ever met." Jet got up and paced. "Besides, whenever I'm at the Games or around other merfolk, something about the way they look at me and whisper behind their hands, it makes me think something must be terribly wrong with me."

Adriana stoically crossed her arms. "Nonsense."

You are one of us. Orpheous's words ran in her brain like an endlessly looping tape cassette.

Jet tried again. "I've told you before. If I have a different father than Lily, I'm cool with it. I've only seen Dad a few times in my life. He takes no notice of me. I won't be upset if someone else is my father."

Mermen were notoriously neglectful fathers. Mermaids outnumbered the male species of their race almost five to one. As a consequence, mermen recklessly impregnated mermaids and swam on their merry way to the next conquest.

Her mother frowned. "We've been over this a hundred

times. If anyone is judgmental toward you, it's because of all the treasure you've taken."

She didn't expect that. Merfolk were taught as children that what fell to the sea belonged to its own. "What do you mean? Everybody does it."

"Not to the extent you have. Not only did you take huge quantities of valuable artifacts, but you did it for Perry's profit. It's not like you needed the money. And if we all did that, there would be nothing left before long. Even worse, it was obvious you'd told him our mermaid secret."

The heavy censure in her voice made Jet inwardly wince, but she wouldn't back down. There had to be more to it. "I'm out of that business now, have been for years."

"Merfolk have long memories," Mom insisted.

"You leave me no choice." Jet unclasped her necklace and held the trident pendant in her palm. "My wish—"

"Stop." Adriana put up a hand. "Don't squander your wish."

"Then tell me the truth."

"There's nothing to tell," her mom said harshly. "Why must you always be so obstinate?"

"By trident's power, my wish is to know the secret of my heritage." There. She'd said it. No mermaid could deny such a request—or else risk merfolk shunning them for being disrespectful of one of their oldest customs.

The pendant floated three inches above Jet's palm. Mother and daughter watched as it glowed red-hot like lava before disintegrating to ash and drifting down to the hardwood floor.

Adriana slowly sank down on the mattress, eyes on the far wall. "I wish you hadn't done that."

But her words held no power. Jet sat beside her and waited. At last, Adriana faced her with distressed eyes

Jet had never seen before. It was even worse than when Mom had told them that Shelly's parents had died. Jet laid a hand over her mom's. "Whatever it is, I can handle it. It's time."

"I promised never to tell," she whispered. "Forgive me, Waverly."

Jet raised her brows in surprise. Her aunt, Adriana's sister, had died in childbirth before she was ever born and Mom rarely mentioned her name.

"Waverly was your biological mother," Adriana admitted. "My deathbed promise to her was to raise you as my own."

No wonder she never measured up to Lily, the true daughter. "Okay. But why the secrecy all these years? I don't understand."

"Waverly didn't want you to know about your father."

A premonition of what was to come flooded her senses as she remembered Orpheous's blue lips grinning and asking, *Ever suspect you are one of us?* Jet groaned. "He was one of the Blue Merman of Minch, wasn't he?"

Adriana nodded.

Jet crinkled her nose. "How could she fall in love with one of those crude thugs?"

"She didn't."

"Then how—" Jet paused, appalled at the possibilities.

"Pelagia, your biological father, forced his will on her." Adrianna rose and walked to the window. "Waverly sneaked away from our family one evening during the Games and swam alone. Pelagia found her and took advantage of the situation."

Disgust and horror roiled in Jet's stomach. Poor Waverly. "I was unwanted and she died giving birth. I see why you didn't tell me," she said past the sore tightness in her throat.

"There was no reason for you to ever find out." Adriana came back to the bed and sat. "You shouldn't have made me tell you. We kept it secret from everyone."

"Sorry, I'm not doing this to hurt you." Jet bit her lip and pressed on. "Deny it all you want, but other mermaids must know about my parents, too, because I've felt their distance all my life. Ugly secrets have a way of spilling out no matter how you try to hide them." A sudden thought struck Jet. "Is that why we always spent so much time in Bayou La Siryna growing up? You wanted to isolate me in case someone told."

"I wanted to protect you," Adriana corrected. "And honor my sister's deathbed request."

Chill bumps ran along Jet's arms and legs. She'd hoped— She wasn't sure exactly what she'd hoped. Perhaps that her mom would reveal some truth she could understand or correct and make things right with her own kind. But there was no getting past this.

"That's why I have such a temper," Jet muttered. "Why I'm so strong and impatient and untalented and ugly. I'm like my horrible father. The other mermaids will never accept me."

"Stop it." Adriana's crisp retort surprised Jet. "You are who you are. Ever consider the possibility that your prickly personality is to blame? You don't make it easy for others to approach you."

So much for sympathy and understanding. "Wrong. It's my dark looks. They see me and think I'm part of the Blue Clan. Even though we're all merfolk, it's something they can't get past." Little wonder, given that the Blue Clan, particularly the males, were so bloodthirsty and selfish.

"It's more about your treasure hunting than your heritage at this point. You've been reckless and irresponsible about our need for secrecy."

Jet started to deny it, but clamped her mouth shut. They were right. How selfish she'd been, all in a losing effort to try to win Perry's love. Pathetic. If she were one of them, she'd probably feel the same.

She thought of her unknown mother. She'd have to hunt through some old photo albums later and look more closely at the woman she'd always thought of as an aunt. "Who named me?" she asked suddenly.

"Waverly."

A stab of disappointment squeezed her chest. "Why did she pick Jet? It's cheap and common fossil fuel. Not exactly attributes one wants in a name."

Adriana threw her hands up in the air. "Beats me. Waverly did love collecting Victorian jewelry. Jet was quite popular in that era." She rose from the bed and fiddled with the chunk of amethyst bracelets on her right wrist. "I hope you're satisfied with the answer you forced me into giving. I may not be your biological mother, but I did the best I could."

Jet's throat constricted. "You did fine." She could have done a whole lot worse with a different guardian. True, she played second fiddle to Lily, but Adriana—whom she would always consider Mom—cared for her in her own way.

Adriana patted her shoulder. "Glad that's over with. I think I'll go rejoin the party." She went to the door and paused, hand on the knob. "Shelly's filled me in on you and Landry. We're hopeful Perry will leave and never come back."

"Not as much as I do. But I'm worried because he knows our secret. What if he exposes us?"

"No one will believe him. He has no proof mermaids

exist. Just make sure it stays that way. And if the very worst happens, leave the bayou and stay undersea with us."

"Bet the merfolk would love that," Jet muttered.

Adriana left, shutting the door quietly.

Jet opened a nightstand drawer and retrieved an old family photo album. She flipped through until she found Aunt Waverly—*Mom*—standing on a beach with her three sisters, their arms encircling one another's waists.

"I promise I'll try to be a better mermaid," Jet whispered, running a finger over her mother's image.

She was a beauty, as blonde and blue-eyed as her sisters. Jet could find no physical resemblance between them. Her mother's fairness only diluted the dark coloring from the paternal side. At least she could be thankful that the distinctive blue skin was a recessive trait.

She flopped down on the bed and covered her eyes with an arm. Didn't she owe it to her family and to herself to find her place in the world? Shelly had done so. But as a TRAB, Shelly's choices had been more limited. Merfolk acceptance was out of the question, and even if they did welcome Shelly, her cousin wasn't biologically suited for long periods undersea. Shelly's choice had been whether or not to reveal her mermaid side to her true love.

If she could have anything she wanted… Jet pictured living at sea and overcoming the problem of merfolk acceptance there. Adriana seemed so sure it could be resolved despite her Blue Clan paternity. Last night she'd even overheard Mom and the rest of the family discuss what amounted to a campaign for her reputation undersea. They'd inform the merfolk that she'd dumped Perry for good and had donated huge amounts of money to various ocean causes. Lily had insisted that the timing for this to work was now while the merfolk remembered her victory in the Undines' Challenge. Jet had snorted and almost given away her presence. The merfolk hadn't seemed too impressed by the feat that she could tell. If her own kind gave her any chance for hope, it would mainly be because of Lily's popularity and the long-respected Bosarge name.

What about Landry? Bet he wouldn't care about a supposedly tainted heritage. Jet pushed aside the question, unwilling to examine her feelings too closely. She'd trained tirelessly over a year for the Poseidon Games in order to discover why she'd grown up living like an exile. Now that she possessed the truth, she felt unsettled, unmoored, adrift with dashed hopes and purposes.

Landry's fist was raised to knock again on Jet's door when it was suddenly yanked open by a trio of young girls.

"Who are you?" the littlest asked, grinning at him with open curiosity. Another smiled in delight and proclaimed, "You're handsome!" The middle girl giggled and continued licking an orange Popsicle, which was melting and splattered on her yellow sundress.

"Girls," a sharp voice rang out, "I told you to let me get the door." An older lady with arctic-white hair appeared, blinking at him myopically before pulling some kind of old magnifying glasses to her eyes. Enlarged, rainbow-colored irises scrutinized him from head to toe. She let the glasses down. "Are you Landry Fields?"

"Yes, ma'am. And you?"

"Lula Belle Bosarge, great-aunt to your Jet. Come in. I needed to make sure it wasn't that abominable Perry Hammonds come calling again."

Landry stepped into the den, eyes widening at the sight of half a dozen stunning ladies lounging about in light-colored dresses. They looked so much alike with their long, blond hair and graceful figures that he had no doubt they were all intimately related. He searched amid the sea of pastels, honing in on Jet, dark hair and eyes gleaming like a beacon. She gave a bemused smile, as if guessing his thoughts.

He started forward, aware of his audience.

One of the young lovelies arose from the sofa and planted herself in front of him. "I'm Lily, Jet's sister."

He nodded and looked over her shoulder. "A pleasure."

Lily didn't move. "I've heard so much about you." She held out a hand.

He shook her hand quickly and let go. Her voice had a reverberating, musical quality that made him uncomfortable. Despite her bland smile, her eyes had a sly cast. Maybe *sly* was unfair, considering he'd just met her. The kinder word would be...*mysterious*.

"Let him through," Jet said.

Jet's voice, on the other hand, was low, throaty and sexy as hell.

Unexpectedly, Lily began to hum. Was the woman not quite right? She drifted to the piano and idly plucked a few keys, humming louder. A buzzing started at the back of Landry's head, a creeping numbing that felt as if he was being hypnotized. Lily's humming vibrated deep inside, consuming his will so that his only desire was to hear more and...

"Enough, Lily," one of the women cut in sharply.

The buzzing in his brain ceased abruptly and he shook his head. Jet came to his side and introduced him to everyone. He nodded politely, eager to get her alone. "Can we talk somewhere in private?" he murmured in her ear.

She guided him through a dining room and onto a screened-in back porch. They sat next to each other on a metal glider loaded with frilly cushions and pillows. Jet hugged a pink floral pillow to her stomach and leaned forward, eyes closed.

"You might not want to kiss me when I tell you what I've planned," Landry said drily.

Her dark eyes opened and she quirked an eyebrow. "Well?"

Landry stood and paced the long, rectangular room. "That connection I found was between the H-bomb co-pilot's grandson and Sylvester Vargas. We've been after Vargas a long time. He's behind countless illegal operations here and all over the world. The man uses his wealth to bribe and influence others. He and his men have murdered dozens of people over the years. They'll stop at nothing to get what they want. I called my supervisors in Mobile, who agreed that the next step is coaxing information from the low man in the operation."

"I know, and that would be Perry. I told you I'd help."

"Great. We think—"

"—that I can get him talking," Jet supplied. "I'll do it. I want him out of my life as much as the FBI wants to nail Vargas."

He sat down beside her. "Are you sure? I wouldn't put you through it if I didn't think it was the quickest, safest way to resolve the case." Damn Hammonds for drawing Jet into this dangerous situation. He couldn't rest easy until this was over and she was no longer at risk. "Okay, then. Call Perry and set up a time tomorrow to meet in a public place. I'll have you wired and prep you with a list of questions to ask. I promise I won't put you in any danger. I'll be close by."

"Perry doesn't scare me a bit."

"If he doesn't, then Vargas should," Landry warned.

"I'm going to notify the local sheriff what we're doing so that—"

"No! Don't tell Tillman." For the first time, Jet looked alarmed.

"I'm confused. He's practically your family. I thought you liked him."

"I do. It's his deputy that worries me."

"Why?"

Jet sighed deeply. "Because Carl Dismukes is a dirty cop. He blackmailed Perry and me almost the whole time we treasure hunted. Not that we did anything wrong." She squirmed a bit in her seat. "But we didn't want him to bring unwelcome attention to us, either."

His brows drew together. "And Tillman didn't fire him?"

"Tillman doesn't know."

"Then tell him. Or I will. We can't have this Dismukes jeopardize our case."

Jet hesitated. "Let's have Tillman sworn to secrecy. Tell him the feds don't want anyone else local to know about it."

He sighed. "I don't like it. But I suppose that could work." Once this case was over, he'd get to the bottom of why Jet was protecting Dismukes. Right now, he had enough to deal with besides a local crooked cop.

The sound of a piano and singing drifted from inside the house. For some reason, the sound seemed to annoy Jet. "That's Lily," she muttered with a scowl.

"Your sister has a nice voice."

"Nice?" She gave a disbelieving laugh. "*Nice* is for a glass of iced tea in the summer heat. Lily's voice is *spectacular*."

He cocked his head to the side, listening. "She's good, but I prefer a low alto. Like yours."

Her mouth widened in astonishment. "You're kidding, right?"

"Self-confidence issues?" He chuckled. "Never would have thought that of you."

Her lips twisted wryly. "You've seen my family, the golden ones. I'm the drab flotsam floating among pristine, pure waters."

"More like a black diamond glittering in a sandy stretch of blandness." He felt heat rising at the back of his neck. Hell, he wasn't normally one for flowery words.

Jet's mouth dropped open and he was rewarded with a smile that made the embarrassment worth suffering through. "I'm hardly a diamond," she protested. "You know that jet is a kind of coal, right? Lucky me, named after a lump of fossil fuel."

He tenderly ran a finger down her cheek. "When coal is heated and emerges from tribulation, a diamond is born."

The dark eyes lit with a wonder and happiness he hadn't seen on her face before. "I've been through enough heat and tribulation the last couple weeks to last me forever," she said ruefully, deflecting the compliment.

Surely he wasn't the only man to ever comment on her striking appearance. Landry shifted uncomfortably. "You know you're attractive. You must have had men falling over you all your life."

She launched herself at him, kissing him passionately. He chuckled in surprise. How he'd missed her when she'd left, had fantasized about her back in his bed. Landry returned the kiss, pulling her body closer.

A burst of giggles sounded. He broke apart from the kiss to see the little girls pointing and laughing. He sighed and stood up. "We have an audience again."

Jet shooed them away and stood also.

"Come back home with me tonight," he whispered urgently.

"I can't," she groaned. "Our family is having this huge wingding tonight with Tillman and his family. My relatives live far away and might not be able to travel to their wedding later this summer. This dinner is a chance for everyone to get to know each other better."

"Oh, a reunion? So that's why you have a full house."

They drew close together, foreheads touching, their breathing rapid and shallow.

"I'll slip away when I can, but it will be awfully late."

"I'll be waiting for you," he promised.

Chapter 13

Perry lowered the binoculars and kicked the side of the boat. He'd seen the little girls and that dragon-lady great-aunt of Jet's when they had opened the door for Fields. Looked as if the whole damned house was full of folks, and not an extra car in the driveway. He'd bugged Jet for years about where she came and went when shape-shifting at home, but on that subject her lips were sealed.

He stroked the stubble growing on his chin, deep in thought. Likely every one of those mermaid freaks was strong like Jet and possibly armed. Her family had always despised him. But the little kids wouldn't feel that way; and he didn't recall meeting them before, so they wouldn't recognize who he was. If he grabbed one of those little girls, Jet would do anything to save her. He thoughtfully tapped the side of his face, weighing the pros and cons of this new idea.

No, there was too much risk. Kidnapping a kid would bring way too much publicity and attention to himself.

Damnation, he could see no way around the dilemma except to go with the plan that involved help from Vargas's henchmen. One way or the other, he had to deliver Jet to Vargas. If only she'd cooperated from the beginning, none of this would have been necessary. They could have been rich together, but no, she'd evidently developed a conscience while he was away and preferred another man over him.

That rubbed him wrong most of all. He'd never—*ever*—been dumped. He was the one who called it quits in a relationship. He didn't love Jet, never had, but it still wasn't right. She deserved everything coming to her.

But the real pisser of it all was that now he might get scuffed up a bit in drawing Jet to Tybee Island. Bitch would pay dearly for that.

Time was up. Vargas had drawn a line in the sand about getting her immediately. Jet hadn't been at The Pirate's Chest for several days, but no matter. Most days Shelly and Seth were in there putting up inventory and preparing for the grand opening. All he had to do was make sure one of them witnessed his fake abduction.

"You're gonna get it now, you freaky bitch," he muttered, hands fisting at his sides. "Nobody dumps Perry Hammonds. Nobody. Especially a damn fish."

Jet sang loudly and off-key in the privacy of her truck, the only place she ever sang. By water nymph's beauty, she wouldn't expose her voice to ridicule at home, not even in the shower. Fingers tapping to the radio, she sped through the bayou darkness. She had hesitated driving over to Landry's; it was so late, she wasn't sure if he'd still be up. But she'd said she would. She'd go to his cottage and if there was a light on, she'd knock on his door. If not, she'd leave him a text message.

The dinner had run late. Anxious as she was to escape and be with Landry, Jet had stayed close to her family, savoring their time together before they again returned to the sea. Although once Landry arrested Perry, she'd be free to join them, if she chose. Easy enough to hire a manager for The Pirate's Chest after it opened for business. She could begin to try to work her way into merfolk acceptance by banking on her victory over Orpheous at the Games.

The thought didn't produce the customary jolt of hope and excitement it usually did.

Jet pulled her truck behind Landry's BMW, shut off the engine and took a deep breath. She would have to make a decision. Land or sea? Could Landry be the man for her?

All men are not like Perry. Some can actually be trusted. She closed her eyes and remembered the sweetness of their lovemaking and his compliments earlier in the day. And especially the way he had claimed to prefer her alto voice over Lily's. He might possibly be the only man on the planet who would do so.

A sharp rap on the passenger-side window made Jet jump. "Oh, it's you," she said in relief as she unlocked the door and Landry slid in beside her.

Up close, the half-moon shadows under his eyes betrayed a weary exhaustion. "Why are you up so late?"

He yawned and rubbed his hand over his face. "Because I was waiting on you. Besides, Seth didn't get home until thirty minutes ago."

"Is he okay?"

"Yeah. He's been having fun with Jimmy and his new friends."

"He should have called you."

"He did. But I couldn't sleep until he came in."

"You're going to miss him when he leaves."

He snickered. "Miss the kid? My house will be free of his mess and loud music. I'll sleep in peace again."

She didn't believe him for a minute. "Shouldn't we be discussing Perry and the questions you want me to ask him?"

"I'd rather not be talking at all." Landry slid back the satin folds of her dress and placed a large palm on her thigh. "I've never seen you in a dress. It suits you." His hand slid farther up her leg. "Not to mention, it's so convenient."

The contact sent heat shivers into her core. "Got dressed up for the big dinner," she said, gasping. She moaned and arched against his hand as it cupped the curve of her womanhood.

"You're so hot, so damn sexy. The most beautiful woman I've ever seen."

"Really?" Jet's insides bubbled and fizzed with wonder. He'd seen the mesmerizing Lily and the rest of her astoundingly stunning relatives yet thought she more than equaled them in beauty. He saw something special in her that her own family did not.

"Really." Landry ground out the word as he slipped a finger past her swollen folds.

Fire. Heat enveloped her senses until her entire world centered on the hard knot of tension where Landry probed. It was bliss, but still not enough. Never enough. It could never be enough with Landry.

The realization only heightened her desire. Jet whimpered, needing more. Landry slipped in a second finger, gently stretching her insides. She moaned even louder, until he covered her mouth and explored it with his tongue. The intimacy of his tongue and fingers made her wild with need. Her body convulsed and she wrapped her arms around Landry's broad back, holding on. He was a steady anchor while she drowned in waves of passion. She never, ever wanted it to end.

But her body had other ideas. The quivering muscles relaxed, leaving Jet in a euphoric lethargy. She ran a hand through the slightly curling ends of Landry's hair. "Wow," she whispered in his ear. Could he sense she was starting to fall in love? Her emotions ran as deep and strong as an ocean current. How could he not know?

Landry chuckled and fell back against the car seat. "Been a long time since I shared a passionate moment in a vehicle."

"But what about you?" She squeezed his hand, wanting to please him like he had her, wanting to demonstrate with her touch what she was afraid to voice aloud. "Shall we continue this inside?"

He put an arm over his forehead and groaned. "Seth's still up."

The tender moment was shattered. Jet hastily tugged down her dress. "I hadn't thought about that. Damn."

"Soon," Landry promised. He heaved a resigned sigh and abruptly pulled open the passenger door. "Let's go inside and I'll fix some coffee. We'll go over how to proceed with Hammonds."

"Whatever you say," she said lightly. She trusted Landry.

Chapter 14

"What time is your mom picking you up today?" Jet asked Seth. She fidgeted with an old charm bracelet, finding comfort in the smooth, cool texture of the glass beads. It was only ten o'clock in the morning. At this rate, she'd be a wreck before her lunch date with Perry. Landry and Tillman would have wasted their time with the wire setup.

Seth kept unpacking a box filled with conch shells and other nautical knickknacks. "Supposedly she'll get here by three," he answered, not looking up from his task.

He'd been working steadily for the past couple of hours and showed no signs of fatigue. The many perks of youth, Jet decided. Her days of staying up all night and working eight hours the next were over. While he was completely absorbed in his task, she pulled out a gift-wrapped package from under the counter.

"For you," she said, holding it out.

"Huh?" His eyes clouded in confusion. "What's this?"

"A little something to thank you for helping me set up shop. Figured your brother probably strong-armed you into working here, but I appreciate all you've done."

Seth opened it cautiously, as if he expected a snake to pop out of a can. Clearly, he wasn't used to surprise gifts. Jet grinned when he opened the box and his mouth dropped open. He lifted the brass dagger out of its case and cradled it in his palm.

"You're *giving* me this?"

"Somehow I knew you'd like it," Jet teased. It was the same dagger Seth had admired the first day on the job and almost shoplifted.

"Wow. I, um, don't know what to say. Thanks, man."

Jet turned away and busied herself with the computer. "You're welcome." She was probably as embarrassed as he at emotional displays.

They continued working in companionable silence until Seth let out a disgruntled snort. "I can't believe this dude has the nerve to show up after what he did!"

Jet whipped around to see Perry getting out of his Mustang. He was two hours early. She'd called Perry last night, saying she'd meet him at noon by the mermaid statue downtown, that she had reconsidered the job at Tybee Island.

She wasn't ready for this encounter yet, emotionally or otherwise. The microphone Landry had given her this morning was still in her pocketbook, and Landry and Tillman wouldn't be listening in so early even if she put it on.

Perry Hammonds was never early for anything. Either he was suspicious of her sudden change of heart, or he was so desperate for money that he wanted to leave immediately. She hoped it was the latter.

"Don't worry, I'll get rid of him for you," Seth said at her dismayed expression.

"No, don't do that. We were meeting for lunch today. He's just way early."

Seth narrowed his eyes. "Does Landry know about this?"

Does he ever, Jet wanted to say. She leaped off the stool and grabbed her pocketbook. "Tell him I'll be out in a few minutes." At Seth's closed arms and downturned mouth, she added, "Landry knows about lunch. It's okay." Last thing she needed was for Seth to run Perry off before she could get answers.

Jet raced to the bathroom. Maybe it was better this way. She'd get it over with a little earlier than planned. She pulled out the microphone clip and pinned it to her bra strap, hands shaking so badly it took four tries before she was satisfied she'd done it right. She texted Landry about the early change of events and dumped the phone back in her purse.

Jet took several deep breaths and surveyed her image in the mirror, checking to ensure the microphone was hidden. Her button-down shirt had been selected because she figured it would cover a lump better than a smooth T-shirt could. She touched the empty spot in her cleavage where the trident pendant had rested for only two weeks. Damn, she could use it about now. Jet tilted her head to the side and tapped a finger to her lips. No, she'd done the right thing using the one wish to discover her true heritage. Perry was manageable, or at least he had been in the past.

Jet nodded grimly at her reflection and stiffened her spine. She had a job to do and she wouldn't disappoint Landry. One last check of her cell phone—no message yet from Landry—and Jet sailed back into the store.

Perry and Seth were silent, regarding one another with wary hostility.

"Why so early?" she asked. "Did you miss breakfast this morning?"

"I couldn't wait any longer to see you. I was so glad you called me last night." Perry gave his easy, signature grin, stuffing his hands into a pair of expensive black trousers. His silk shirt was a vivid shade of salmon, a color most men couldn't pull off. But Perry's confidence and bohemian style suited almost any look. His teeth flashed a brilliant white against his olive skin. He'd evidently been working on a tan the past few days. That seemed to be the only job he was interested in pursuing, besides the Tybee Island expedition. Even so, Perry's role had always been nominal during their treasure hunts.

Could this man she once thought she loved really be involved in such an unsavory deal with a man like Vargas? Perhaps he didn't realize the true treasure off the Georgia coast was something altogether different than their shipwreck-salvage ventures. And if he knew the truth, did Perry care? Despite the check she'd written, he appeared desperate for this last deal.

"You're looking hot today," he said, giving her a sensual once-over scan from toes to scalp.

If Perry thought he could win her over with his lame come-ons, he wasn't as bright as she remembered.

"That's what my half brother always says," Seth piped up from behind the front counter. "And Jet's probably not hungry at all. They ate a huge breakfast at our cottage this morning."

Some of Perry's insouciant smile dimmed. "She's with me now."

"Excuse me," Jet butted in crisply. "I'm game for an early lunch."

"You always did have a huge appetite." Perry gave Seth a significant look. "After all these years, I know my girl."

"I'm not your— Oh, never mind. Let's go." She pushed past Perry and exited the front door. The Alabama heat hit her like a wall of fire. "I'm not even walking two blocks. Let's take your car."

"Um, sure."

The subtle hesitation in his voice drew her up in surprise. Jet spun around and caught him looking up and down both sides of the street as if afraid of an unknown danger lurking in the small-town streets of Bayou La Siryna.

"What's wrong?"

"Nothing." He pasted on a smile that didn't reach his eyes. "The Sea Basket diner, right?" He placed a hand on the small of her back and guided her to the Mustang. "Where you'll order your usual shrimp platter." He opened the door and pointed at the car's interior with a flourish. "Your carriage awaits, princess."

Jet placed one foot inside the Mustang and hesitated. He wouldn't do something as foolish as kidnap her, would he? And even if he did, she was wired. Jet settled into the seat and waited for Perry to shut the door before discreetly turning the microphone on and checking her cell phone. Still no word from Landry. Damn.

The loud noise of grinding brakes startled Jet and she dropped the phone back into her purse. A black SUV stopped in the middle of traffic and two unsmiling, muscle-bound men jumped out of the driver and passenger doors. Both wore black polo shirts and were nearly identical but for the ornate sleeve tattoos covering one's arms. They left the doors ajar and headed straight to Perry.

Jet put a hand on her chest, her mind racing with pos-

sibilities. Bill collectors? No, these men were too forceful
for that. Repo men? Maybe they were going to wrestle
away Perry's car keys and take it for nonpayment.

If Perry hadn't paid his bills, he totally deserved to
have it repossessed. But Jet knew how much he loved the
Mustang—which was probably more than any affection
he carried for a real person. Still, she could work out a
deal with these men. It wasn't as if she didn't have a ton
of money. She'd try to negotiate with Perry—if she paid
off his car, he'd give up the Tybee Island deal. That way,
maybe Perry could escape from the whole dangerous
mess he'd gotten into and walk away unscathed.

The men surrounded Perry and grabbed his arms. A
flash of metal glimmered from the exposed waist of one
of the men.

A gun? Really? Jet's hand froze on the door handle.
These men might work for Vargas. Perry must have
angered them somehow and now he was in deep shit.
Jet broke out of her paralysis and opened the car door.
"Leave him alone," she yelled, charging forward.

Neither man spared her a glance. The one closest to
Jet pumped his meaty fist into Perry's stomach with a
casual violence that stunned her. She watched, appalled
as Perry doubled over and stumbled. The oaf on the other
side fisted Perry under his chin and he straightened, wob-
bling from the blow. Perry surely would have fallen if the
two goons weren't gripping his arms. Bright red blood
gushed from a cut under his chin and sprinkled the silk
coral shirt. *At least he's not wearing his white Don Johnson suit today,* Jet thought, shaking her head to clear the
hysterical rambling of her brain.

Reaching one of the men, she wrapped both her hands
around the steel band on the biceps of his free arm,

yanked as hard as she could and pulled him off Perry. At last she had his attention.

"What the hell?" he sputtered, bushy eyebrows knitting together. "How did you—"

She ignored him, intent on freeing Perry from the other man. Perry's eyes rolled, so that three-quarters of his eyes were white, the chocolate-brown irises hidden behind his upper eyelids. She heard shouts of "police" and car doors slammed as traffic came to a halt. A crowd gathered.

Her hands wrapped around the other goon's arm and pulled, but it was no use. The unmistakable feel of a gun indented the bottom of her back where spine met tailbone. "There's a crowd. Let's move it," said a guttural voice from behind, the Yankee accent clearly out of place in the bayou. Definitely not local repo men, a tiny part of her brain noted.

The gun was removed from her back and the world tilted as Jet was thrown to the ground. Hot asphalt scraped her knees raw. Bleeding and stunned, she watched the two shove Perry into the backseat of the black SUV. She couldn't see Perry's face through the dark tinted window. The men moved surprisingly fast considering their Atlas-size bodies, maneuvering into the SUV and slamming the doors shut behind them. The vehicle lurched forward, scattering the gaping spectators. It sped off like a mechanical demon returning to the furies of hell.

No license plates, of course.

"Are you okay?" Seth crouched in front of her field of vision, waving a cell phone. "I already called my brother."

A surge of relief flooded her body. "First time you haven't called Landry your half brother," she said, rising to her feet.

Seth raised his brows, an expression so similar to

Landry's it made Jet smile. "After what happened, that's all you've got to say?" he asked incredulously.

"Landry will find Perry."

"How can you be so sure?"

"Because he knows where to start the hunt." Jet scooped up the microphone, which had fallen to the pavement during the scuffle. At least the brazen kidnapping would bring down the full attention of state and federal forces like nothing else could have done.

Seth shook his head. "I still don't like the guy but I feel sorry for him. He got sucker punched something awful."

Pain. So much pain. Those assholes didn't have to rough him up that much to make the kidnapping convincing. They did it for the sheer pleasure of torturing another person. Perry cradled his stomach and wondered if he'd sustained permanent internal injury. Hopefully, it was nothing more than a bruised kidney or spleen or something unimportant like that. At first, he'd thought his jaw was broken, too, but that pain had subsided after a few hours and he was able to swig beer and talk without too much discomfort. His expensive shirt and trousers, however, were ruined beyond repair.

Perry scowled, finally consoling himself that once the job was finished, he could walk into any upscale men's clothier and order a closetful of shirts and suits.

"I don't see why we didn't just take her instead of *him*," the big goon said to Vargas, nodding at Perry. "She would have offered more resistance. That woman is a spitfire."

"She shrugged you off like you weren't nothin' but a seventh-grade science geek," the other guy laughed.

Vargas held up a hand. "Jet Bosarge would attract too much attention. Better to draw her in so she comes voluntarily. Her damn brother-in-law is a sheriff and her new boyfriend's an FBI agent."

"What?" Perry's mouth hung open. "I thought Fields was an IRS auditor."

Vargas puffed a stinky cigar he claimed was Cuban and cost over a hundred of dollars. "Wrong. Let's hope your old girlfriend has some tender feelings left for you. Enough to follow you here to Tybee Island." His eyes narrowed so much they glittered like snake slits. "The deal was for you to deliver the girl."

Perry swallowed an angry retort. "Jet will come," he answered with more confidence than he felt. "We have a history."

Vargas exhaled a plume of smoke into Perry's face. "If she doesn't, I'm throwing you to the sharks, so to speak."

His two hoodlums grinned inanely and one of them cracked his knuckles, evidently anticipating a longer session of fun mutilating his body. What the hell had he gotten himself into? Frissons of ice traveled his spine. For the first time, he felt the chill of fear. He was in over his head. This Tybee Island thing was Big Time, and if he made promises he couldn't deliver, they would kill him. At the very least, he'd end up with the beating of a lifetime. And growing up with a mean, drunk father like his, that was saying a lot.

Vargas leaned across the table, his face mere inches away. Perry smelled garlic from the man's shrimp scampi at dinner. "Jet's mere presence isn't enough. She has to find that bomb. You think you got troubles? I've got buyers from several countries bidding on that baby." He jabbed a finger into Perry's chest. "Don't disappoint me."

Perry's stomach roiled. He needed fresh air; the small dining room belowdecks stank and he was claustrophobic. Perry rose. Pain radiated from his gut but he refused to let them enjoy his suffering. "I'm going up top for a bit."

Vargas nodded at one of his hulking bodyguards and the big man placed a rough hand on Perry's shoulder, pushing him back into his seat.

"Not yet. We need to make a call first, let your ex know where to find you. I don't care what you have to say or do, but you get Bosarge here—alone. Am I clear?"

A computer monitor was placed before him and he saw his reflection, swollen jaw, unkempt hair and all. Perry ran his fingers through his messy hair but it was no use. Probably all for the best anyway; Jet would totally believe he'd been taken by force when she saw him.

And by God, his pain was nothing compared to what that bitch was gonna get. If she'd come along at first like he'd told her, he wouldn't be in this position now.

You wait, Jet Bosarge. Your time is coming. And I'll bring your whole race down with you if I need to.

Landry lounged against the wall, unimpressed with Hammonds's pathetic act. Nothing the man said rang true. The light from the computer monitor glowed eerily beneath the darkened window. A single moonbeam shone on the monitor, like a stage light at the theater.

"Help me, Jet. Please," Perry begged. "And come alone. They know Landry Fields is an FBI agent."

A tattooed arm came into view and it delivered a punch to Perry's jaw. A paper was placed in front of Perry. He wiped away a trickle of blood from the side of his mouth as he read it. "There's a plane ticket for you in a plain envelope in your mailbox."

"I'm not flying," Jet said adamantly. "I'll drive all night and be there by morning."

Perry nodded. "Just come. Please. If you don't…well, the rest of your family is in danger."

Quite a convincing performance, Landry had to admit. The punch added a nice touch of authenticity. But he speculated the whole thing was a setup to draw Jet to Tybee Island.

With those last, pleading words, the screen went black. Jet stared at the dead blankness, no doubt imagining Perry suffering at the hands of his captors. "I have to go," she whispered. "I can't put my family in jeopardy."

"Absolutely not." Landry's jaw clenched. "It's way too dangerous."

"If I don't go, they'll kill him," she said flatly. "And then they'll come after me and my loved ones."

Did Jet still have some shred of affection for Hammonds? The thought made his stomach churn. "Better him than you."

"Look, as of right now you don't have enough proof to nail Vargas on anything. I'll go and you can wire me up. I'll meet with Perry like we originally intended."

She was right. He had nothing. All he had so far was hearsay on the bomb excavation. Damn, they needed to nail that bastard before he compromised national security. This time, they had to get Vargas in custody and stop him for good. "I won't wire you up again. Vargas is too smart for that. He'd have you strip-searched at once."

Jet paced the cottage den. "Let's leave right now. We can be there in a few hours and get this over with. Thank God your mom picked up Seth today like she promised."

Yeah, after numerous phone calls to her all week. In the end, he threatened to cut his monthly check unless she came. But there was another, more pressing matter to take care of. He folded his arms. "We can't leave right this minute."

"Why not?"

"First, I have to call my boss, apprise him of the latest news, and then he'll have to run everything by the brass to get backup in place. Everything will probably have to be coordinated with Homeland Security, as well. And second, we're not leaving here until you tell me how you find things undersea that no one else can."

Jet abruptly stopped pacing. "What does that matter?"

"I need to know why you're essential to this operation. My job is on the line with this and I need the full story."

"Can't you trust me to handle this on my own?"

He had to know the truth about Jet. He would need to at least know everything Hammonds and Vargas knew before he set foot on Tybee Island. "Let me turn that question around on you. Why don't *you* trust *me* with your secret?"

"I'm—intuitive. Let's leave it at that."

A mewling like the hounds of hell erupted.

"Saved by the cat's meow," Jet muttered.

Damn that cat; it was as if it had a sixth sense on how to be disruptive. He'd never gotten around to dropping it off at the shelter like he meant to do. That feline better not be having her litter now. Landry beat Jet to the utility room and yanked open the door. Baby Girl, his temporary name for the tabby, stood in the middle of the cramped space and blinked at them. Over the past few days, he'd earned a semblance of trust from her and in return he'd let her roam the house soon. Little steps.

They regarded Baby Girl as she calmly began grooming her derriere.

"She's been making that awful noise a lot lately. She's close to her due date."

"Why haven't you taken her to the shelter yet?"

Good question. Landry shifted uncomfortably. "I

haven't had time," he mumbled, knowing it was a lie. The cat had grown on him.

Jet bent down and held out her fingers for Baby Girl to sniff. All she got for her efforts was a hiss.

"She doesn't like you very much," Landry noted. "She doesn't hiss at me anymore."

"You should have let Seth stay to watch over her. We need to hit the road." Jet sighed and whipped out her cell phone. "I'll have Shelly or Lily check on your cat while we're at Tybee."

"There's no need for that. I'm sure this isn't her first litter. She'll be fine." Jet ignored him and tried to persuade one of her kin to cat-watch. Evidently, they weren't into felines, either.

Landry called his supervisor and, as he expected, was informed to stay put until he was granted the green light to proceed to Tybee Island. He slipped outside to the deck and leaned against the railing. The sea was calm tonight but his mind was far from peaceful. He closed his eyes and remembered the young girl/sea creature with long white hair that swirled against the blue-black waters. Her thin, pale arms guided the small boat as she swam below the water's surface. Once he'd reached the shallows, close enough to the shore to walk on land, she had let go of the boat and turned, diving deeper.

And that was when he'd seen it. Where her legs should have been was a long fishtail that glittered like an explosion of crushed mica. It flashed but an instant, but Landry would never forget it, much as he tried to logically dismiss the image from his mind over the years.

April had made sure he could never again simply ignore the supernatural.

He put his head in his hands, recalling again the set of scars along Jet's neck. What if Jet's treasure-finding ability stemmed from her biology, because she was the same kind of creature as that other one? He couldn't deny the facts staring him in the face.

Chills ran down his spine. If, if, *if*. If it was true, he would find out.

Open your mind and heart to love and magic. He wasn't sure he could make that leap yet.

It was a no-go on finding a cat-sitter. Jet laid her phone down and went onto the deck, where Landry stood, head in his hands. The trick was how to rush him. They needed to get Perry.

"Ready to go?" she asked brightly.

"I'm waiting for my boss to call back with clearance. Why are you so worried about Perry? I didn't realize you cared that much for him."

"It's not that," she said quickly. "I just want to protect my family and get this over with."

"You sure that's all there is to it?"

Jet pulled his head down to hers and pressed her lips against his. To hell with words, she'd prove it with her touch. She licked his bottom lip, tasted the slight saltiness from the ocean breeze and that indefinable something that was unique to him. An aching tenderness welled inside her. If he discovered her secret at Tybee, this could be their last night alone.

Perry could wait. The whole world could wait. This moment belonged to them. He sensed it, too; she could tell from the way he pressed her body against his, letting her feel his swelling manhood as it ground into her pelvis.

Jet moaned. She wanted Landry in her. Now. Wanted to be joined with him as they explored and reached that shattering intensity and release together.

Landry pulled back and cupped her face in his strong,

rough palms. The lightness of his eyes lit a tenderness inside her that brought tears to her eyes. The things he could do to her with a single look. He ran a finger down her cheek and neck, every nerve of his body in tune with her longing, with her love.

Should she tell him? Jet swallowed away a hard lump of fear and parted her lips to speak. But Landry's index finger, which hovered around the hollow of her throat, rose back up and landed across her lips in a hushing motion. He knew. Somehow Landry always seemed to know her innermost thoughts. Jet's lips trembled slightly. She felt raw, exposed.

"There should be no secrets between us," he said. His voice was gruff. "What are you hiding from me?"

"You don't want to know. Please, can't you let it go, just for now?"

He ran a hand down the back of her scalp, in a gesture so tender she wanted to bury her head against his chest and blurt out the truth. His lips brushed against the top of her head and her resolve slipped. "Later," Jet promised. "Right now I want you to make love to me." When he didn't move, she added, "Please."

Wordlessly, Landry took her by the hand and led her inside. She followed him past his grandmother's knick-knacks in the den, the pitter-pat of Baby Girl in the utility room and the now-barren, tidy room where Seth had stayed. Inside his bedroom, Landry flipped on the light.

Jet turned it off. She hated to keep lying to him about the gill marks on her neck. No way she could relax if he noticed them. And Landry noticed everything.

Landry flipped the light switch back on and rested a palm against it. "The light stays on this time," he said in a voice that brooked no argument.

"But," Jet gulped "but I have some scars—"

"Right here." Landry reached out and drew lines down the sides of her neck. "I know. I've already seen them."

She should have remembered she'd told him about them. "Oh, okay, then." Jet sat on his bed and patted the mattress. A diversion was in order immediately before he asked how she got them.

"We'll talk about all that later," he said, shooting her a look that promised no compromise. "In the meantime—" Landry pulled off his T-shirt and stepped a foot away from where she sat. He picked up her hand and placed it on his right side. "Check out this nasty bugger. Appendectomy from age nine." Her fingers traced the raised, bumpy surgical scar. How painful and scary it must have been for Landry as a child going through that operation.

The crisp clank of metal rang out like a shot as he undid the clasp of his leather belt. Jet licked her lips as Landry's jeans slid to the floor. He pushed her hand down to the inside of his left thigh. "This scar is the result of a junior-high shop-class accident."

Jet leaned into the warm, hard muscles of his thigh. "I don't see anything," she said, her breath exhaling against the soft blond hair on his legs.

"Here," he bit out in a strangled voice.

She narrowed her eyes and saw the faint curve of a white scar. She darted out her tongue and flicked it against the tiny line.

"I'm sure there are many more if you care to look."

Jet smiled at him. "I do care. Take off all your clothes and lie down."

"Bossy woman," he said, stepping out of his jeans. Landry peeled off his boxers without a shred of embarrassment and lay beside her. "Examine all you want."

Jet marveled at his confident ease. She stripped off her own clothes and then started with his chest, where beige hair curled around his rib cage. She took in the outline of muscled biceps and triceps before switching her gaze to his flat abs. Her eyes went lower and stilled. Desire rekindled, hot and as blistering as asphalt in the Alabama sun. How she loved every single detail about this man. She longed to tell him, but she couldn't get the words out.

"Your turn." In one quick move, Landry flipped her onto her back and drank in the sight of her naked body. She tried not to flinch when he touched the sides of her neck. Her ready explanation fled out the window. How could she explain them?

"We'll talk later," he said. "Like you promised."

Relief washed through her agitated mind. For now, she would enjoy making love with a man she truly loved. He trailed kisses down her neck and stopped at her breasts, circling each nipple with his tongue. And then he went lower still, and his tongue grazed her belly button before finding her swollen folds.

Jet arched into the warm haven of his mouth, utterly wanton. She cried out with pleasure and Landry replaced his mouth with his shaft. Waves of ecstasy crashed and swirled in every cell. She held on to Landry, tight, and moaned with pleasure as he came with her.

Afterward, Jet cuddled against his lean body, her head resting on his sturdy shoulders. One of his large hands rested on the curve of her hip. She'd never felt so safe, so secure.

"It's time," he said, the rumble of his voice vibrating against her cheek.

Jet languidly stretched against the cotton linens. "Time for what?"

"Tell me your secret."

Chapter 15

Jet followed Landry down to the shore, careful to avoid the lapping water. "I don't know why you had to drag me out here to talk," she grumbled, kicking sand. "We should be on our way to Georgia."

"Not until my boss has followed all the proper protocol and not until we get a few things cleared." Landry stopped abruptly and Jet stumbled against him. "How do you find sea treasure?" he asked. The blue of his eyes was as implacable as an arctic glacier.

Jet took a deep breath, inhaling the bayou's ever-present scent of brine mixed with pine-tree sap. Her skin went clammy as the salt air settled on her arms and legs. She'd promised him the truth in a moment of weakness, a delaying tactic while she tried to think of some probable explanation. She thought fast. "You know how some people have a great nose—their olfactory senses can pick up scents other people can't? Or people who have lost one sense like eyesight and then develop a hypersensitive ear as compensation?"

Landry raised a brow and she realized he wasn't buying the direction she was leading. Jet threw up her hands. "I don't know how to explain it. This feeling comes over me when I'm swimming in the vicinity of old shipwreck ruins. Maybe old coins and jewelry emit a subtle smell or there's some minute kinetic shift in the waters I pick up on. I don't know."

Her feet were suddenly snatched from underneath and she gasped as Landry's strong arms cradled her back and behind her knees. She instinctively wrapped her arms around his neck.

"What are you doing?' she asked, dumbfounded as he waded into the ocean. If a wave broke close to shore and the spray hit her legs— Jet pushed her arms against his chest, frantic to escape. "Put me down," she ordered. This was a fine dilemma. If she got wet, the jig was up, and if she used her strength to outmuscle him, that would be another issue to explain.

He kept walking, the water halfway to his shins.

"Don't make me hurt you," she warned. "I'm stronger than you."

"Maybe. But you won't make any move for fear I'll drop you."

"Don't let go of me!" Jet clung to him like a barnacle to a ship's underbelly. She couldn't bear to see the disgust in his eyes if her legs disappeared and her tail emerged.

"Your secret."

The moonlight emphasized the hard planes of his cheekbones and jaw. Yet his eyes held a soft glimmer of tenderness that he couldn't hide. Not from her.

"You wouldn't dare," she whispered in soft challenge.

Landry abruptly pulled an arm in, leaving one of her

legs unsupported. She let out a cry and clung harder around his neck, staring down into the black water, mere inches from the tips of her bare toes. "Okay," she gasped. "You win." Better to tell Landry than have him witness the truth. If she was lucky, he'd laugh and call her a liar.

"Is it so hard for you to trust me?" he asked gently. "I already know the truth, Jet."

She snorted. "You have no idea."

"You're a mermaid."

Her mouth dropped open. Had she really heard him right? The world seemed to tilt, spinning crazily. *He knows. Landry knows my secret.* "It's true," she whispered. Jet stared into his eyes, looking to find disgust. Instead, she found a flicker of hurt.

"I wasn't really going to drop you in the water," he admitted. "I wanted you to tell me yourself." He stared past her shoulder at the wide expanse of sea. "I would have believed you. I told you what I saw when I was twelve. Plus, you know about April's ghost."

Landry turned and waded back to shore, still carrying her in his arms.

"But you weren't sure what you saw. Remember? You said you were a scared kid."

Landry set her down onshore and kept walking, his back to her. Jet scrambled to keep up with him. Of all the ways she'd envisioned him discovering she was a mermaid, never once did she consider he would guess it on his own. "Talk to me. Please." Her voice crumpled at the end and Landry slowly made his way over.

"Don't cry. I hate that." He wrapped his arms around her and she nuzzled into the solid warmth of his body.

"Wasn't going to cry," she lied. Why did she do this? She always had to prove she was strong, that she didn't need anybody or anything. Another whopping lie. She needed and wanted Landry and couldn't imagine life without him. Plain and simple: she loved him. Loved his strong moral compass for justice, loved his loyalty and the way he made her feel safe and treasured. Real treasure wasn't the trinkets and baubles she had hunted, nor was it the golden trident she'd trained so hard for and won, and it certainly wasn't the missing H-bomb lying in the dark depths of an obscure salt marsh.

Here. Right here was the real treasure. More valuable than any pirate's cache of gold.

"Sure sounded like you were about to cry." Landry stroked her back. "Look, I'm sorry. I was an ass just now. I shouldn't have threatened to drop you in the ocean. You can't force someone to trust you."

"But I *do* trust you." The words were muffled against his wide chest.

"Not really. Sure, you realize I'm an improvement over that lying bastard Hammonds. But you could hardly do worse than your ex-boyfriend."

Jet pulled away from his chest and faced him. "Don't even mention your name and his in the same sentence. You're wonderful.... I...I..." She swallowed past the lump in her throat. Damn her misplaced pride. Saying *I love you* was too scary. She wasn't lovable. Even with her own mom—er, aunt—she came in second place to the lovely Lily. He'd come to view her as a freak of nature one day, same as Perry. "How did you guess I'm a mermaid? That's never happened to any of us."

Landry lifted his hands and ran his fingers down both sides of her neck. "The same markings I saw on the other mermaid. I should have guessed earlier but it took a visit with Tia to really open my eyes."

"What did she say?" Jet bit her lip. "Does Tia know I'm a mermaid?" If Tia Henrietta guessed the truth, that meant others might have done the same. With each dirt dweller who knew their secret, the risk of exposure grew exponentially for her and her kin—and for all merfolk.

"She didn't mention you. Tia just cautioned me to be open to the possibility of magic and—" He paused.

"And what?"

"Never mind." Landry dropped his hands to his sides and took a step back. "But between Tia and April, I was forced to acknowledge every inexplicable detail in a new light. Besides the neck markings, there was your eerie ability to find sea treasure, your own admission that you had out-of-the-ordinary means in locating treasure. Combine all that with your abnormal physical strength and night vision, and it wasn't hard to add it up."

Just her luck. An FBI agent who noticed every detail, put it all together and didn't discount the supernatural factor. If only they'd had more time together, she might have been able to break the news to him gently. Gradually have gotten him used to the idea of mermaids. And, most of all, had the time to make Landry fall so madly in love with her that he wouldn't care if she turned into a toad on every full moon.

Everything was ruined now. She'd spare them both a lot of pain and end their relationship at once. Jet couldn't bear to watch him struggle to find a kind way to say goodbye. She gave a short laugh and clapped her hands. "Bravo. Well-done, Mr. Federal-Agent-Man. Welcome to the freak show. Before you dump me, I beg you not to tell anyone about my family. Bosarge women have lived in Bayou La Siryna for generations. I don't want to be the one who screws that up."

"Of course I won't—what makes you think I'm dumping you?"

Suddenly, she was crushed against the long, solid width of his body.

"Don't ever say the word *freak* again," Landry said harshly, his breath hot and sweet on the top of her scalp. "Like I said before, you're the most beautiful woman I've ever seen."

Deluded man. Jet squeezed him back, her heart tripping with the small hope they had a chance to make this thing work. Landry hadn't run away yet. "I thought you were mad at me for not being up front tonight," she mumbled against his chest.

He tipped her chin up, forcing her to meet his eyes. "I was hurt you couldn't tell me the truth," he corrected. "I went about it all wrong trying to force you to tell me. Forgive me."

He still cares. He knows what I am and it doesn't matter—unless he only wants to use me like Perry. No, she wouldn't compare the two. Landry was ambitious and hardworking but he also actually had some morals. "If that's the worse you ever do to me, we're good," she said with a shaky laugh. "You wanted to know all the facts before we left for Tybee Island."

Jet relaxed in his embrace as the sound of the waves lulled her fears.

Landry sighed. "Speaking of which…we should pack and be prepared to leave as soon as the call comes in from my boss."

She reluctantly stepped out of his arms. "Agreed."

They strode quickly back to the cottage. Worry settled back in Jet's stomach. "If the FBI sends out a bunch of people, Vargas might find out and kill Perry."

"Hammonds isn't important. Your safety comes before everything. I don't want you involved in their bomb scheme."

That wasn't her biggest fear. "What scares me is that Perry may have told these people about the merworld. Although, I don't know how he could convince them we exist without any proof."

"They would think he was nuts. Your past success in locating treasure is reason enough for Vargas to use you, no matter what kind of story Hammonds may have told them."

✦ They hurried up the cottage stairs to pack.

Landry tossed some toiletries in an overnight bag. "I hope you don't have a problem with airplanes. The Bureau might provide one to get us there quickly."

"No way!" Jet shook her head emphatically. "The high altitude messes with my body chemistry. Mermaids aren't built for it." Too much time in the air caused systemic edema, and the swelling and inflammation could be quite painful. To counteract the edema, it was necessary to return undersea for a long period of recuperation. She didn't have the time or inclination now for weeks undersea.

"Good to know." Landry picked up his cell phone. "I'm calling Sheriff Angier. We might need his help in keeping your—your—mermaid nature a secret."

The early-morning sun cracked through the clouds in a blistering haze of red as Jet drove through streets of rainbow-colored cottages dotting the Atlantic shoreline. She scanned the street names constantly until she found the diner Perry had instructed her to stop at when he'd called five minutes ago. Only sheer adrenaline had kept her awake during the six-hundred-mile journey from Bayou La Siryna and she hoped it stayed kicked in until this ordeal was resolved. She glanced in the rearview mirror and although she couldn't see Landry's face through the tinted windshield, it was a relief knowing he and Tillman were close behind in a government-issued sedan.

Behind the lead car, her family tagged along. Mom, Shelly and Lily had filed into a van and hit the road, much to the consternation of Landry and Tillman. Jet managed a wan smile remembering the heated arguments that ensued when Tillman told Shelly to stay home while he joined the Tybee Island rendezvous. Shelly had immediately gathered the family together, and each insisted they might be of help in some way, especially if the kidnappers held Perry on board a ship. Landry was appalled and Tillman resigned. The men sternly warned the trio of blonde beauties to stay out of the way and out of contact with Jet until the situation was under control. They nodded and gave vague smiles, sweetly agreeing to the conditions. Jet couldn't imagine how they might be of service, but knowing they were along for the ride helped quell her nerves.

At last she spotted the Starlight Diner and turned her truck into the parking lot. Jet staggered, stiff-legged, out of the truck and made her way inside. Her stomach grumbled at the smell of fresh-baked doughnuts. Might as well knock back a couple; who knew when or if she'd get a real meal today? But first, she went to the ladies' room and relieved the sharp tug on her bladder. She freshened up and grimaced at her reflection in the grimy bathroom mirror. Dark circles had formed, and her skin looked dry and parched. She needed to return to the sea and rehydrate. First thing when she returned home, she'd slip down the Bosarge hidden portal for a long, cool swim.

Even the thought of swimming refreshed her and Jet opened the bathroom door with a renewed determination to help Landry catch Vargas and save Perry from himself.

A buzzing vibration in her back pocket made her

jump. "Probably Landry again," Jet muttered, digging out the cell phone from her purse. He checked in at least every thirty minutes even though he was following her.

Instead of Landry, it was Perry's number on the screen. The phone buzzed again like an angry hornet.

Jet hit the reply button with shaking fingers. "Perry?"

"It's me."

Jet frowned down at the phone in her hand. The connection was so clear it sounded as if—

The firm, warm weight of a man's palm encircled her arm, right above the elbow. Jet gasped and instinctively pulled away.

"It's me." Perry's breath was hot and fervent in her ear as he drew her outside the back door. "They're watching us. Just come with me."

"What? How?" Jet stumbled beside him but had enough wits to stuff the cell phone deep into her back pocket. A family sat at one of the picnic tables, children licking their fingers from the sticky glaze of doughnuts. Seagulls squawked nearby scavenging food near an overflowing garbage can, while a few cars passed on the main road.

It was happening too fast, nothing like what they had planned. Before she could protest, Perry had ushered her into the passenger seat of a waiting car, and she heard the door lock with a click. Jet grasped the door handle.

Only there was no handle. Her fingers grazed the smooth expanse of metal overlaid with vinyl. Son of a bitch. Anger sent her synapses snapping with energy and she lurched toward the driver's side. Cool metal poked the sweaty nape of her neck and the deadly click of a cocked trigger exploded in the sealed vehicle.

"You're not going anywhere this time, Jet Bosarge" came a gravelly voice from behind.

In the rearview mirror she saw the burly man who had tried to snatch her with Perry yesterday. He bore a distinctive tattoo on his arm, a skull with a lightning bolt through it. The dude who'd led Perry away was sitting beside him, smirking.

The hell if she'd give them the satisfaction of seeing her panic. "Three-on-one to capture a woman?" she asked with fake nonchalance. "And you even thought it necessary to bring along firepower. Impressive."

Perry slid in beside her. "Already charming them with your sunny personality?" The wide grin did nothing to dispel a feral gleam in his brown eyes, almost as dark as her own. The stench of Aqua de Nausea was suffocating in the cramped quarters. How had she ever found it appealing?

Jet turned her lips upward in angry reciprocation as she rebuked him with her eyes. "You were never kidnapped. You've been in on the whole thing."

"Were you worried about me, sweetheart?"

One of the men in the back grabbed her arms and pinned them down to each side of her seat. Perry snatched up her T-shirt and shoved his hands down the front of her bra. He squeezed her breasts and ran both hands over her back and inside the waistband of her jeans.

"No wire," he declared, then drove down a dirt road so fast that every pothole made her insides feel as if they were being scrambled.

Did Landry have any idea they'd slipped her away? "Let go of me!" she screamed, trying to twist to see if the government sedan was on their tail.

The man let go of her arms and grabbed the purse off her lap. "Got a phone in there?" He dumped the contents out onto the backseat.

My phone. A frisson of hope shot up her spine. She felt the outline of it crushed against her ass.

"I dropped it when Perry grabbed me," she lied, praying Landry wouldn't call. It had been at least twenty minutes since his last check-in. Somehow, she had to turn it off or press his number without anyone seeing. Jet eased onto her left hip, facing Perry.

"How did you get mixed up with this crowd?" she asked.

"Got lucky."

Jet casually tucked her T-shirt into the waistband of her shorts, inserting a finger into her back pocket. Feeling along the phone's edges, she found the button and switched on vibration mode. Success! She put her face up to the rearview mirror and faked surprise. "I think someone's followed us." All three men spun their heads to face the back windshield. Jet seized the moment to slip the phone out of her pocket and place it under her right thigh.

"I don't see nuthin'," the tattooed man grunted. "We plucked you away from the police right under their damn noses. We knew they were following you to the island."

"My bad, then," Jet said with a shrug. "Where are we going?"

"To the boat." Perry slid a sideways glance at her. "Guess your boyfriend, Mr. FBI Agent, told you all about the missing hydrogen bomb."

"He did. If you're smart, Perry, you'll let me out of here now before you get in so much trouble you stay locked up forever."

"I'd rather die." His fingers tightened on the steering wheel. "Bitch," he added.

Jet kept an eye on the passing road names and landmarks. Landry had put a trace on her phone, but she didn't know how well it would work on this rural road. No telling how far they were from a GPS satellite. "Have you always been such an asshole or did prison bring out the worst in you?" she asked Perry, hoping to keep him focused on their conversation.

"Shut up," he growled, raising his hand as if to smack her. "When we get to the boat and meet Vargas, you better show him some respect."

She placed a hand over her stomach and grimaced.

"What's the matter with you?" he asked, eyes flashing in annoyance.

"Something I ate on the road made me sick." She searched for a button to roll down the side window, but there wasn't one. "Are we almost there yet?" Jet retched, deep heaves that shook her upper torso.

Perry wrinkled his nose and leaned into the driver's side door. "Don't you dare throw up."

"How much longer?" she grated out in between heaves. The pretty beach houses were long gone, the landscape fading to stretches of wild salt marshes.

"Almost there. We turn at the next road. Do I need to pull over?"

"No!" one of the men in back roared. "No stopping. I don't care if she vomits all over herself. She'll be getting in the water shortly."

Jet laid her head on the window and groaned as Perry turned right on the corner of Lullwater and Dixie streets.

Now or never.

She doubled over and retched again, spitting on the floor seat. With Perry's attention momentarily diverted, she turned her back to him, flipped on the cell phone and began texting the location to Landry.

"Damn it, what the hell are you doing?" The tattooed man grabbed her right arm and Jet cried out as her shoulder muscles were pulled from their socket. The cell phone dropped and he picked it up. The Send Message had about three-quarters filled the bar when he rolled down his back window and tossed it onto a sand dune.

His partner beside him punched the tattooed man's arm. "Idiot! You should have turned it off, not thrown it out the window."

She prayed the tracer was functioning. Jet couldn't be sure the message had gone through. If it hadn't, how the hell would Landry ever find her?

He will. That certainty radiated from her gut to every inch of her body, instantly as calming as a shot of Demerol. Landry would work tirelessly to find her. Maybe they would find her phone. Or maybe Landry was following now. Perry slowed the sedan and pulled over to the side of the road. "No more tricks, Jet," he said, pocketing the car keys. "The sooner you find what Vargas wants, the sooner you can go home."

"Liar. I'll never be free of you. There will always be new treasure or a new adventure."

He opened his mouth as if to deny it, then smiled, baring a mouthful of brilliant white teeth. "You know me too well." He leaned over and whispered in her ear, "Your secret alone could be worth a fortune."

Jet didn't doubt he'd sell her out like a damned circus act, putting the entire merfolk race at risk. Humans would hunt mermaids down to extinction, much the way of buffalos on the American plains. She'd kill herself before she let that happen.

"Hey, cut out that whispering," said one of the men behind them. "Let's get a move on."

The all exited the vehicle and she waited until the tattooed man jerked open her door. Jet stumbled out, searching for another human or a car passing by on the main road, but there was only sea and sand to witness their march from the car to the shore, where a small boat waited.

She dug her heels into the sand at the sight of the boat. If salt water splashed on her legs, she'd shape-shift in front of these buffoons. Although she could outmuscle them, and probably outrun them if she made a break for it now, she wasn't as fast or strong as a bullet.

Perry scooped her up and waded to the boat. She started to thank him, but Perry did nothing out of kindness. There must be some selfish reason he didn't want these men to see her in mermaid form. He sat her roughly in the boat.

Jet's heart quickened as she stared into the sea. *Jump!* Every instinct urged her to dive overboard. Everyone would see her fishtail, but she could outswim any human. Who would believe these guys even if they swore up and down they'd seen a mermaid?

She scrambled to the side of the boat but the tats man grabbed her shoulders and flung her to the floorboards.

"You ain't going *nowhere*," he said, punctuating the words with a vicious kick to her legs.

Jet instinctively curled into a fetal position, protecting her head and rib cage.

"Stop kicking her," Perry said. "Vargas wants to put Jet to work right away. She can't do that hurt." He knelt beside her and she regarded him cautiously. He firmly removed her hands from her face. "No one wants to mistreat you. For once, do what you're told, okay?"

She rubbed her right thigh, already swollen from the kick, and offered no resistance as the two goons placed her between them on the boat seats. Perry started the engine and they lurched forward.

They motored out only a few minutes before Perry

pulled alongside a larger craft, though not nearly as impressive as she'd expected.

"This is a scout vessel," Perry explained, guessing her thoughts. "Once you locate the bomb, Vargas will bring in the big guns for excavation."

Jet wordlessly followed her captors onto the larger boat, a gun pressed against her back. Several men stood on deck watching as Perry escorted her to a diminutive man with slick dark hair and haughty eyes.

He briefly inclined his head in her direction. "We meet at last, Miss Jet Bosarge."

His accent was thick, but Jet couldn't determine his native tongue. Spanish? Greek? She said nothing.

"Perry tells me you have a unique ability to find sea treasure." At her continued silence, he went on, "He's even claimed you are a mermaid."

Jet folded her arms. "Ridiculous." Once they sent her diving, they would only see the flash of her tail fin as she swam her ass off.

"Nevertheless, I've observed your outstanding luck over the years in finding sea salvage. I've no doubt you'll find our hydrogen bomb. We'll equip you with a Geiger counter and the latest and greatest underwater metal detector. Those tools—combined with your luck or special ability—will make this venture successful."

"What makes you so sure it's here? It could be anywhere in a fifty-mile radius for all anybody knows."

A tall, thin man wearing a gray windbreaker stepped forward. "It's here," he said, pushing wire-rimmed glasses up the bridge of his nose. "The government's been looking in the wrong area all these years."

Vargas extended his hand, palm up toward the stranger. "This is Jim Tindol. His grandfather was co-pilot of the B-47 that jettisoned the bomb. According to his grandfather, the bomb was ejected in this area, not where the navy divers originally searched."

"Granddaddy told them to search where the Savannah River empties into the Atlantic. But they only listened to the pilot, not him."

"Why would the pilot lie?" Jet asked.

"Because he thought everyone was safer if the bomb was never recovered," Jim said. "As long as he lied about where it ejected, he figured everyone would give up the search eventually and the bomb would lie harmless forever."

Jet shook her head. "After five decades, that bomb is probably buried several feet under silt. Why did you get involved after all these years? Oh, wait, let me guess—you've been paid for this information."

"We all stand to profit from this venture," Vargas cut in smoothly. "Even you, Miss Bosarge."

"And what if I can't find it?"

"You will."

She raised her eyebrows. "How can you be so sure?"

Vargas pointed behind her. Jet swung around and saw a man-size shark cage.

"Because every day you'll be placed in that cage and lowered undersea until you find it. I'll drag you around underwater for months if that's what it takes."

Perry pointed a thumb at his chest. "My idea," he bragged.

Jet stared at the cage, rigid with horror. Caged like an animal? This was even worse than poor Dolly trapped in a small swimming pool. She found Perry standing with the others and frowned at him. This was her worst nightmare and he knew it.

Had used it against her.

In that dream, she'd been caged like a hapless manatee and put on display in a glass tank as mobs of people pressed their faces to the wall. An aquarium's newest freak show.

"Doesn't sound like much fun, does it?" Vargas's full lips curled in a humorless smile. "I reckon a few weeks of this and you'll be damn eager to show me where the bomb lies hidden."

Chapter 16

Landry's grip on the steering wheel tightened as he tried to steady the storm of fear and fury waging within. *Like April all over again.* One minute here, the next minute…

Focus. He would find her. Even now, Sheriff Angier was questioning employers and customers in the diner. Damn Perry Hammonds. If he, or anyone in Vargas's group, hurt Jet, they would pay dearly for that transgression. As a child, he'd been helpless at his sister's disappearance, but this time he could stop a tragedy.

His head snapped up at the sound of a vehicle turning in. Landry groaned inwardly as the three blondes exited.

Lily yawned and stretched. "So it's time for breakfast? I'm starving."

"Where's Jet?" Adriana Bosarge asked, squinting her cobalt-blue eyes at Jet's empty truck.

Before he could answer, Shelly spoke. "Something's

wrong." Her gaze was focused on Tillman as he hurried to them.

"Have you lost my daughter?" Adriana's sharp voice cut through the morning air like a machete through butter.

Landry inwardly winced at the accusatory words. He had enough guilt without anyone else piling it on. "She's been abducted but we know where to look and she's close by."

Jet's mother lost her ever-serene composure. Shock and grief momentarily contorted her beautiful features until she snapped her fingers. "Girls. Get in the van. Jet's gone."

"Stay here," Landry said, sliding back into the sedan. "You'll only be in our way."

All three ignored him.

He didn't have time to argue. According to the GPS, they were only .89 miles from the intersection of Lullwater and Dixie. Jet's text had been sent at 7:16 a.m. It was now 7:24 a.m. Only eight minutes had passed since she'd been abducted and placed in serious danger. He should never have agreed to let Jet come along. Screw the case against Vargas.

Tillman slid in beside him. "Someone saw a man fitting Perry's description escort Jet out a back door." Before Tillman even closed his door, Landry hit the accelerator.

Tillman craned his neck backward at the van, which was merely a few feet from their rear bumper. "Stubborn fools," he said in a resigned voice. A swelling of blue from sky and ocean flew by until the disembodied GPS voice announced they'd reached their final destination. Ahead, the road appeared to dead-end, so he pulled over in a spray of beige sand.

They both jumped out of the car and simultaneously discovered a recent set of footprints in the otherwise pristine landscape of sand. They followed until the prints stopped at the edge of a salt marsh, where they disappeared into the water. Landry shielded his eyes with his hands and gazed at the horizon. A lone boat bobbed in the waves—too far away to see who was on board.

"Hold on." Tillman rushed to the sedan and retrieved a pair of binoculars. "Try these."

Landry raised them to his eyes. She was there! The tight contraction in his chest eased a fraction as he observed someone holding out various instruments and scuba gear. He took in the sight of Vargas, puffing one of his ridiculous cigars, and several other men he couldn't identify. He returned his attention to Jet, too far away to see the expression on her face, but the slight slump of her shoulders hit him in the solar plexus, the hunched-over position a sign she was feeling overwhelmed and vulnerable.

"Give me that," snapped Adriana, yanking the binoculars away.

Irritating woman.

"What are they doing?" she asked.

Landry walked away, so Tillman answered for him. "They're showing her how to search for the bomb."

Landry whirled to face Tillman. "Notify everyone that Jet's been kidnapped."

"Why bother? There she is. Go get her," Adriana demanded.

Tillman pulled out his phone. "I'm on it."

"Wait." Shelly placed a hand on Tillman's arm. "If we handle this ourselves, it will be faster and there'll be less risk that Jet will be exposed as a mermaid."

"No!" Landry shook his head at Tillman and faced

Shelly. "I don't give a damn about your secrets," Landry said. "My only concern is to get Jet away from them."

"We'll have the element of surprise," Shelly quietly insisted.

Landry rolled his eyes. "What do you think you're going to do? Swim out there and demand her release? These men have guns, for God's sake."

"So we're supposed to stand by and do nothing?" Adriana's eyes flashed. "I thought you were concerned about my daughter's safety."

He swore under his breath. Recklessness must be a family trait. Tillman paused, cell phone in hand as Landry tried to reason with Jet's family. "That's why I'm not rushing out there," he explained through gritted teeth. "I can work out a plan with the coast guard and have the FBI make an arrest."

"I think you're more interested in your career than you are in rescuing my daughter," Adriana said.

The accusation stung like falling naked into a patch of nettles.

"That's not true."

They all stared at Lily, who had remained silent while the rest of them argued, her musical voice defusing the agitation.

"Landry loves Jet," she continued. "Let's all work together."

Love?

He gazed out at the faraway boat, a small, vulnerable speck in the vast Atlantic. His heart clinched. Jet was alone out there with a team of ruthless men, desperate for treasure. *I have to save her.* Pushing aside his emotions, he thought of the best way to rescue Jet.

He could no longer deny that having a troupe of mermaids in his camp gave him a tactical advantage he'd be a fool to waste. Vargas would see any boat that advanced, but not mermaids. Talk about your "element of surprise." "Maybe y'all *can* help," he admitted. "How quick can we rent a boat?"

Jet followed Perry down the boat's narrow steps until they were alone belowdecks. In the damp, dark quarters, he thrust the dive suit at her. "Squeeze into this and then I'll show you how the air mask works."

"Really? A mermaid in a wet suit?" she asked, snatching it from his hands.

"That compression of neoprene is all that stands between you and your tail fin being exposed. Now get dressed."

"So? You already told them I'm a mermaid." Nevertheless, Jet kicked off her shoes and squeezed into the bathroom stall, which had no door for privacy.

Perry shrugged. "They don't believe me."

She narrowed her eyes at his calm demeanor. "You've been quiet since we came aboard. What's your game?"

"If this doesn't work out with Vargas, you're still my golden goose." His white smile gleamed in the dark, cramped area.

Bastard. "Turn around so I can get this damn thing on."

To her surprise, he did. The metal crackling of a zipper being undone stopped her movements. "What are you doing?"

"Changing into a wet suit, too. Vargas will send me after you if you don't follow the grid he laid out or if you trigger the alarm on the cage lock."

Vargas and his team had thought of everything. The cable wire connecting the shark cage to the crane would be maneuvered in a grid pattern designed to determine where the H-bomb lay hidden.

She leaned against the wall, shaking. Her nightmare was minutes away. *One thing at a time.*

"Explain how you think I'd bring you more money. I won't go on any more expeditions with you." She quickly shimmied out of her shorts and panties and struggled to get her legs through the wet suit.

"You're worth more to me as a circus act than as a treasure hunter."

Jet bit her lip to keep from gasping at his casual cruelty. She wouldn't let Perry see how much he'd hurt her. "Never," she managed to say in a composed voice as she got out of her T-shirt and bra and put her arms through the suit. She zipped it up and exited the bathroom, intending to ignore Perry and return upstairs.

A flash of pain sliced through the right sleeve of the suit. She looked down at Perry's fingers wrapped tightly around her right biceps. "Don't screw this up for me," he snarled. "I promised Vargas you'd find that bomb."

Jet easily shook herself free, partly because she knew it pissed Perry off that she could outmuscle him one-on-one. She walked up the creaky stairs to the blinding sunlight. All the men—Vargas, Jim Tindol, tats man and his fellow goon, and a couple of others she didn't know but assumed were aboard for technical support and machine operations—lined the boat's side. The open cage awaited.

"Find it," Vargas said unsmilingly.

The tattooed man pointed to the shark cage.

She approached slowly, mind desperately searching for an escape route. But Perry was so close at her back she felt his heat through the suit. His hand lay heavy on her shoulder, guiding her to face him. She watched, like a condemned prisoner getting electrically wired, as Perry set a bubbled hood over her face and strapped a heavy oxygen tank on her back. He curtly motioned for her to sit on the bench. Awkwardly, feeling cumbersome, she complied. Perry expertly fitted scuba fins on her feet, avoiding eye contact, as if she were some thing and not a real person.

The muscled goons each grabbed one of her arms and hoisted her up from the bench. Jet jerked her arms free and walked alone into her nightmare.

By high noon, the sun's glare off the water was like broken glass piercing Landry's eyes. The light penetrated through his brain to the back of his skull, burning like a migraine. Their vessel, an eighteen-foot Glastron bass and ski boat, lapped gently on the waves. The Bosarge women must have paid a fortune to nab it at the last minute.

Waiting was a bitch.

"My turn," Shelly said, a palm extended to Adriana.

Her aunt sighed and handed the binoculars over. "They're still showing her how to operate some tools."

Landry frowned. "Stay behind the canopy," he warned. "If they're keeping an eye out on the area with binoculars, they might see you."

Lily gathered a handful of blond hair and raised it over her neck. "It's hot under that heavy fabric. Reckon I'll go for a little swim."

"Don't go anywhere near their boat," Landry said. "If you—"

"I'm not going over there," Lily said. "Yet."

Adriana pursed her lips at her youngest daughter. "Don't you dare do anything until Jet goes underwater."

Tillman leaned down and whispered in Shelly's ear. "Keep an eye on her," Landry overheard him say.

So he didn't trust Lily, either. Smart guy. The two of them had started out rocky after Seth's premature disclosure that his brother was with the FBI. But they were so alike that an easy truce had formed between them out of respect and appreciation of the jobs they performed.

Adriana rose, graceful as a cat. He wondered briefly if the orange tabby monster had had her litter yet. "Guess I'll cool off a bit, too," Adriana said.

Landry ran his fingers through his hair and heaved a frustrated sigh, certain these women were going to do more harm than good. He squinted at Adriana. "Why couldn't you have just swum here instead of following us on land?"

"Didn't they teach you geography in high school? To swim from south Alabama to the Georgia coastline would entail swimming the entire length of Florida. We'd never have got here in time." She waved a bejeweled hand in his direction. "You gentlemen don't look while we undress."

Tillman and Landry each glued their eyes on the far-off boat until they heard the sound of three splashes.

"So you're marrying into all this—this—" Landry raised an arm into the air, at a loss for words.

"This weirdness?" Tillman supplied. "Yeah. Shelly's great. My future in-laws I'm not so sure about at times. But you get used to it. I know how much you FBI types love your protocol but you'll learn to bend a bit if you decide to hang around Bayou La Siryna. There is no contingency on the books that outlines correct mermaid protocol."

Landry gave a rueful smile and picked up the abandoned binoculars, needing to see Jet, even if he couldn't talk to her, couldn't touch her. Couldn't do anything but keep watch from afar.

She wasn't on deck. His gut clenched. Where was

she? He scanned the entire deck, counting Vargas's men. Perry was also missing. "Hell," he cursed. "Jet's gone, along with Perry."

Tillman scrambled forward on the boat. "Let's drive in a little closer." He pulled a baseball cap low over his forehead. "Keep your face covered, in case they're on the lookout," he warned as he started the engine.

"What about the women? Can they find us if we change location?"

Tillman turned the key and the boat engine purred. "Can they find us?" he grinned sardonically. "You have a lot to learn about mermaids."

Landry let out his breath as Jet and Perry emerged from belowdecks, both clad in scuba gear. Fine, once in the water, Jet could swim away from Perry and her family could guide them to this boat. He would call his boss to finalize arrangements and in minutes the coast guard could capture Vargas and seize his ship for evidence. All his hired guns would turn on him soon enough under harsh interrogation. He'd seen it hundreds of times over in his career.

The wind lifted the hair on Landry's neck and adrenaline spiked through him. Finally. After hours of waiting, taking action felt great. Soon, he would have Jet in his arms.

Landry frowned. What the hell was going on? She was being led into some kind of metal contraption. A shark cage, perhaps. His spirits sank as quickly as they had lifted. Vargas had taken out a key and locked Jet inside. As he stepped back, he nodded to one of the men. A winch lifted the cage up a few feet, swung it away from the boat and then descended.

Jet was being lowered into the sea in what resembled a coffin.

Anguish stabbed him. He should have insisted she stay home in Bayou La Siryna. At the very least, he should have demanded she ride in the car to Tybee with him and Tillman, consequences be damned if Vargas found out or the FBI thought he had jeopardized the case.

Screw the agency and his career. Jet came first. A career couldn't fulfill him now that he'd had a taste of true happiness. Landry pictured what his life would have become without meeting her—and it wasn't pretty. It would be an empty existence of working long hours and joylessly shouldering of family duties solely out of a sense of responsibility. He could never go back to that again, could never settle for a life without love or magic. What kind of screwed-up universe would introduce him to a woman like Jet Bosarge and then take her away so quickly?

Landry would never wipe away that moment when Jet didn't answer his phone call or when they found her truck at the shop—empty. He'd never forget that devastation. Not in a million years.

But as much as that hurt, this moment was even worse. Worse because this time he had to stand on the sidelines and watch as she was lowered, entombed and helpless. What would happen when she hit water? Would she shape-shift to mermaid form? And if she did…her family and all merfolk would be exposed when the cage later ascended. Her kind would be hunted down and driven to entrapment like Dolly at that run-down water park.

The cage hit water and Jet disappeared. He watched while the circular eddies from the cage widened and flattened until the water was smooth as glass, leaving no trace of what lay beneath.

They were so desperate to locate the hydrogen bomb they didn't care if Jet was harmed in the mission. To Vargas, everyone was expendable. They would keep her alive only while she served a purpose.

And then?

Landry wouldn't allow his mind to consider the possibility of murder and death. He took out his rifle, prepared to shoot Vargas on deck. Her best chance for escape was undersea, especially with her family nearby.

He couldn't let that cage emerge. If Vargas and his crew saw Jet in merform, she and her entire race were in danger. They would be mercilessly hunted until extinction. And Vargas would be quick to realize that the price of a captured mermaid was more valuable than the missing hydrogen bomb. Jet would fetch a high price for someone seeking the ultimate prize in a rare, precious-oddities kind of collection.

Pain ripped through him, blinding and spectacular as lightning on a Kansas prairie night, until he couldn't deny the truth.

He loved Jet. Loved her dark beauty and deep, unplumbed depths. Loved the hidden softness beneath her muscled body and even her prickly shell. Loved the woman who sported diamond earrings while driving a battered pickup truck.

And she might die not knowing any of that.

He remembered the first time he met her and encountered those flashing dark eyes. She'd been all brambly and defensive, yet sparkling with such energy he'd been fascinated—but had immediately decided she wasn't his type. Wrong. Day by day Jet had worn down his resistance and fear to love again.

Tia's warning rang through his brain. *Your heart and mind are closed to love and magic. You got a mighty big test comin' up. You either pass it or you're doomed to go through life lonely and empty-feelin'.*

He had failed the test last night when he forced Jet to reveal herself, failed in the most important part of the equation. The magic part, he'd passed. He had opened his mind and accepted Jet's shape-shifting mermaid nature. April's spirit had made sure he got that much right. But he hadn't crossed over into love territory. Instead, he'd hovered, unwilling to fully commit. Was he doomed now as Tia had warned—forever lonely and empty inside?

Landry fought to regain control of his wits; he'd need every ounce of control over his emotions to save Jet. He flung the binoculars onto the floorboards and signaled Tillman to stop the boat. "I'll give Jet's family ten minutes to free her. If they haven't resurfaced by then, we'll make our way onto Vargas's boat."

No!

They lowered the shark cage toward the marsh waters. She was suffocating in the rubbery diving suit. Jet clung to the metal bars and looked up at Perry, the man she once trusted. He gazed down with detached curiosity… a stranger. He knew her deepest secret and her deepest fear and used both to send her straight to hell.

She'd forfeit all her treasure for one last glimpse of Landry. If only she had met him before Perry. If only, if only, if *only* she could go back in time and erase all her mistakes.

She was trapped like a dolphin in a tuna net. Poor Dolly. Who would save her and her unborn calf now?

The faces above disappeared in a splash. Blue sky faded to murky water. Bubbles blew out from the air mask.

Compression from the diving suit insulated her skin, preventing her from shape-shifting. Jet flailed the man-made fins on her feet. Awkward. Like a baby taking experimental steps.

The mask reduced her undersea vision, although it was still vastly greater than that of humans.

Black. She was trapped in a deep black void, powerless. No wonder the damned bomb had never been found in this inky water. Her fingers fumbled with the cage, finding the Geiger counter and metal detector attached to a bar. In the darkness, her fingers groped the cage door, struggling to trip the lock and break free.

She couldn't breathe. Jet sucked oxygen through the mouthpiece tube with rapid, shallow breaths, but the quicker she inhaled, the more her lungs ached and the less oxygen entered her bloodstream.

For the first time in her life, she wanted to give up.

Chapter 17

Today the sea held no comfort. Jet gripped the bars and closed her eyes. The neoprene compression cut her off from sensation and she imagined the result was similar to those isolation tanks she'd read about where people in them too long hallucinated and lost their grounding.

Today the sea held no camaraderie. No usual kinship with aquatic life, since she was swaddled like a human dirt dweller. No playing with the dolphins or swimming with shoals of white trout.

Today, instead, the sea was a capricious bitch and she was frightened and alone and powerless.

Black water churned and bits of sand and broken shells noiselessly popped against her scuba mask. The cage hit bottom and Jet was thrown to the ground. Huge puffs of gray sediment exploded around the bars like a mushroom cloud. It felt like being buried alive.

Jet reached her hands outside of the bars and fiddled

with the locking mechanism, to no avail. It wouldn't budge. If only she had her knife, she might be able to pick it open. Normally, at sea she carried one inside the sporran belted at her waist. Always useful in case of a chance meeting with a shark. A thin steel blade was all that stood between her and freedom. Once that lock was popped, she'd tear off the wet suit and swim far, far away.

Ever so slowly the sediment drifted down like snow in a child's snow globe.

With an effort, Jet shrugged off the alienation and panic and set to work. With clumsy, enshrouded fingers, she unhooked the Geiger counter from a bar and switched it on. No sound cut through the liquid, tomblike water pressure on her ears, but rhythmic, pulsating vibrations traveled from her hands and up her arms as the instrument calculated radiation levels. The ocean held natural radiation, but Vargas had instructed how a higher concentration would result in spiked counter readings combined with a higher rate of clicking vibrations.

The cage was mechanically lifted a couple feet from the ground and Jet sensed a slow movement as the attached wire guided it along a predetermined grid.

They're jerking me around like a dog on a leash. Resentfully, Jet activated the underwater metal detector and gripped it in one hand, Geiger counter in the other. If she didn't turn on their stupid devices, they would probably jerk her back up and—beat her? She wouldn't be surprised. Greedy men would do whatever necessary to feed their inner money monster.

Jet couldn't say how long she drifted in the void, scarcely paying attention to the high-tech tools she held. If one of them indicated a promising lead, she'd promptly switch it off and tell her captors it malfunctioned. No way was she helping Perry and his gang uncover a deadly bomb.

Would they really keep sending her down day after day, hours at a time, if the instruments found nothing? Spring and summer stretched before her, an unbroken misery chain.

Landry will find me. He knows Vargas and Perry are behind this.

Time passed—Jet couldn't say how much—and the rhythmic tumbling of the waves lulled her fears. The initial panic subsided, leaving her oddly drained and listless. Eye flutters lengthened to increasingly long eye blinks and her hands holding the instruments slightly slackened. She drifted in a womb of dark isolation in an alien undersea universe.

A sudden jarring jostled her to full alertness. Something was wrong.

Jet turned in a circle and faced a pair of luminescent eyes, mere inches from her own. Yellow ribbons from its head pillowed out in the darkness like jellyfish tendrils. Jet's heart raced double-time for a fraction of a second, until she realized this creature was friend, not foe.

"Shelly," she breathed into the mask. "You found me." Praise Poseidon, help had arrived. Shelly was the most welcome sight ever. And when Lily also swam into view, Jet thought her sister resembled an avenging angel from the old days of Atlantis when mermaids ruled the seven seas.

Shelly mouthed words she couldn't understand. Jet lifted her shoulders, dropped the counter and metal detector and raised her hands, palms out, indicating she couldn't hear. Shelly raised her arms and mimed removing the scuba mask.

Jet obligingly ripped off the headgear. As water blasted her face, her legs tightened and swelled twice their size.

Before she could shrug off the air tank, the bottom half of the wet suit burst into pieces and her mermaid tail fin sea-swished in glorious freedom, a blue-and-purple glitter explosion. Jet reveled at the touch of water, tingled all over in a delightful cacophony of awakening sensation.

Shelly pulled at the cage door and frowned when it refused to yield.

"How did you get here so fast?" Jet gave her a quick hug through the bars, then laughed at Shelly's startled expression. Jet had never been the huggy type. "Never mind, we need to scram. Let me have your knife," she said quickly, suddenly desperate to get out.

Shelly opened her sporran and handed one over. Jet inserted the blade into the locking mechanism and expertly jiggled it around. Many a time before, she'd opened pirates' chests and underwater locked luggage from shipwrecks. She could do this.

Damn, nothing gave. Jet pulled off the gloves and tried again. This time she was rewarded with a distinct *ker-plop* as the lock released its hold.

A roaring, screeching vibration sent bubbles cascading upward like a miniature cyclone.

Shelly clamped her hands over her ears. "What the hell?"

The alarm. She'd forgotten all about it in her haste. They'd send Perry after her immediately.

"Go!" Jet screamed. "Get out of here. I'll be behind you shortly." She struggled to release the air tank. "Go on, I can swim faster than y'all." Not to mention, she was an awful lot stronger, too. "They'll be after me now," she added. "I can handle them. You can't." Shelly was sensitive about her TRAB status, which prevented her from staying underwater as long as a full-blooded mermaid. But now was no time for niceties to spare her feelings.

Shelly nodded. "Okay. We'll be ahead in a small boat. Tillman and Landry are on it."

Lily stayed put. "Silly Jet," she chided. "You forget I can sing and make anyone forget their own name, much less why they dived undersea to start with."

Jet tugged at the neoprene sleeves. "Dumbass," she said with a laugh, shaking her head. "He won't be able to hear you through the scuba mask."

Lily's perfectly formed lips puckered to a surprised O shape. "Didn't think about that. If you're sure—"

"Go." Jet waved a hand, relieved when Lily swam off. A few more seconds and she'd be completely out of the damned wet suit. It felt as if she was wrestling out of a prison straitjacket. She forced her mind to slow and relax. Otherwise, she'd be a panicked kitty, too excited to think straight and make her escape. In seconds, Jet stripped down to nothing and took one last look back at her nightmare. The opened cage swayed harmlessly in the gentle undertow.

Freedom! She grinned and fist-pumped triumphantly.

Overhead, something, or someone, approached. A long, black object trailing bubbles shot downward—straight at her. Her mouth dropped open as the human in scuba gear approached. Through the mask, she saw the familiar brown eyes of her enemy rimmed in topaz; they glittered with the intensity of a hunter determined to capture his prey.

By his side, Perry carried an air-powered speargun. Her heartbeat slowed and her mind froze as he lifted the gun, centered his scope and took aim.

The first shot missed.

Shit. He'd been so close. That left him with just one

more spear. He'd get her with the next one. That bitch needed to be brought in line once and for all.

Perry felt the imprint in his upper arms where Vargas's muscled men had grabbed him and unceremoniously dumped him off the side of the boat the second the alarm rang. Vargas had forced him to sit by the side of the boat, completely clad in the wet suit and at the ready in case Jet tried to escape. "Get her," Vargas had growled at him, thrusting a speargun into his hands. "Injure her if you must, but don't kill her. I need her to locate that bomb."

After that terse instruction, he'd barely had time to seal his air mask before he hit water.

Get her he would. She'd made him look like a fool in front of the man he needed to impress, at least until this venture was successfully completed. Why did Jet have to make this so difficult? What the hell was the big deal about helping him out this time? They'd worked together for years and now Jet acted as if she was too good for him. She'd actually tried to pay him off with a check and, worse, had rejected him in front of Landry Fields. As if he was some low-life, unimportant *nobody*. Perry's blood exploded like hot lava from a volcano, and a blistering heat raged through him, fueling his hunt in the dark waters.

Perry let go of the wire he'd followed into the sea. The wire had led him to the empty cage, its door ajar. Jet was a clever freak; he had to give her that. And strong as any man, stronger than he was. Perry's fingers twitched on the gun. But she wasn't stronger than a damned spear, even if she thought she was hot shit. This little baby would teach her a lesson, by God.

He forged on, swimming in the disgusting, muddy waters. He was too good for this shit. A man with his looks and smarts should be sipping high-priced bourbons on a private island with half a dozen whores attending to his every need.

Once Jet found the missing bomb, he'd be set for life and she'd be even richer. She was already filthy rich but even the wealthy always wanted more money. Money held power, provided the freedom to live life on your own terms, not beholden to a boss, social convention or, in his case, a former lover. The selfish thing—as long as Jet had money, what did she care if he had to toil all his life like some pathetic, mediocre nobody? To hell with her.

But Jet's worst sin, the unforgivable one, was that with all that money, she had let him rot in prison. She could have bought off the corrections officials in South America, but she didn't; Vargas did. So it was her own damned fault they were in this mess together.

Where was she? He had to find her down here. He shuddered to imagine what Vargas would do if he returned to the boat alone.

A sparkle of—*something*—caught his eye. Perry swam closer and an entire cluster of blue, purple, pink, green and gold appeared, shimmering and twitching like jewels against black velvet. An outline emerged as the rainbow colors morphed into a pattern. A huge tail fin. He raised his eyes, saw where fish scale merged into pale skin at the hip, saw the naked torso and rosy nipples, and continued upward to the angular jaw and dark, blazing eyes, so like his own.

Jet.

Jet Bosarge in mermaid form. He'd seen it a few times in their past, but avoided it as much as possible, uncomfortable knowing he made love to a freak fish. Perry raised the speargun again. He wouldn't kill her, otherwise Vargas would be furious. And she was worth so much more to him alive. There were treasures yet to be found and a world of people to amaze when he exposed her to the public. He could set his own price for paying customers to gawk at the mutated thing, could build an empire.

As quick as she'd appeared, Jet disappeared into the darkness. Damn it. She might escape.

Another flash of sparkles glittered; Jet was still in range.

Perry knew the spot to hurt and humble Miss High-and-Mighty. He leveled his gun at the freaky fishtail and took aim.

Landry glanced at his wristwatch, surprised to find only six minutes had passed. They'd stopped their boat about a hundred yards from Vargas's vessel. He and Tillman held fishing rods, as if they were merely out for a few bites. Their firearms were on the floorboards, hidden but loaded and at the ready when needed.

It felt as if hours had passed since Lily, Adriana and Shelly went under. Waiting here and knowing that somewhere beneath the sea's calm facade Jet was trapped and her family was down there—doing God knew what.

He glanced at Tillman, curious about his relationship with his fiancée. If Shelly and Jet were cousins, Shelly was a mermaid, as well. He'd read all about the serial killer Sheriff Angier had captured last summer, who had been caught after trying to abduct Shelly.

The sheriff's close tie to Jet's family had kept Landry from contacting him when he first arrived in the bayou. But Tillman's actions with Seth had won Landry's respect. He'd handled everything fairly. Tillman was obviously an intelligent, decent man.

But one question niggled at Landry. "Why do you keep your corrupt deputy around?" he asked.

Tillman's gray eyes narrowed. "Carl? Corrupt? What makes you say that?"

"According to Jet, Dismukes took a cut for years to keep quiet about her and Perry's more unethical treasure sales."

"Son of a bitch," Tillman spat out.

"Worse, he keeps threatening that if Jet goes back in business, he expects a share of the profits again." At the thunderstorm in his eyes, Landry felt for the guy. "What about Jet's family? Are they trustworthy?"

"Adriana Bosarge is fine when she warms up to you a bit. Now, Lily." Tillman shook his head. "Guess you have to make allowances seeing as she's a special siren."

"I thought they were all the same."

"Shelly explained that Lily's a *phonic* siren. Like in those old books where sirens entranced men with their voices and made sailors shipwreck."

Landry's palms tingled. A magical voice? "But Jet's not one of those phonic sirens," he ventured. "Right? I mean, she's drop-dead hot and has a great voice..." He stopped at Tillman's expression of amused astonishment.

"Beautiful? Jet's, er, arresting, unusual. I'll give you that."

Was the man blind? He was like Seth, unable to see what was before him. Shelly was a pretty girl—in a bland, sweet, vanilla sort of way. But Jet was a complex, surprising woman full of contrasts. Fair skin with blue-black hair, athletic and feminine, powerful and vulnerable. He couldn't get enough of her. The more she let him into her world, the more fascinated he was and the more he wanted.

A loud thump rocked the bottom of their boat. Landry jumped up, dropping the fishing pole. "What was that?"

"One of them is back," Tillman answered calmly.

"How can you tell?"

"It's a signal. At least one of them wants aboard. Let's stand together and shield them from view as they get back under the canopy, in case anyone's watching on Vargas's boat."

They moved alongside one another, examining a fishing lure Tillman held in his hand, as if they were swapping fish stories. A loud swoosh arose from the water and the boat rocked slightly. Landry had an unmistakable urge to peek. The only time he'd seen a mermaid was over two decades ago. He'd been so young, and the day so dark and long ago, that over the years he had stored the memory of that strange underwater glimpse in the attic of his mind in a locked trunk marked Do Not Open.

Thump. The boat careened side to side as a mermaid dropped onto the floorboards. Chills clawed his skin but he kept his face turned away.

"The girls found Jet." Adriana's voice was slightly breathless. "We need to go—" her words were muffled, so Landry knew she was pulling clothing over her head "—north, at least fifty yards or so."

"Is she okay?" he asked anxiously.

"I'm not sure." She tapped Tillman's shoulder. "I'm dressed. Start the boat."

Landry faced her. Jet's mother was the same handsome woman as before jumping ship, only now her long hair was dripping wet and her dress damp. Would he ever get used to this family? Landry shoved aside the wayward musing. "Tell us what's going on down there."

"Shelly and Lily are younger and faster swimmers than me. They sped ahead and by the time I saw them again, they had found Jet and were freeing her from a shark cage."

Jet was free. Landry's heart swelled with relief and

he looked down into the water, expecting the blue-and-black water to shift and form a pattern, an outline of a mermaid. Jet would burst through any moment. First thing after he saw she was fine, he'd give her hell for veering off to that doughnut shop without checking in first. Stubborn woman.

Tillman accelerated the boat. "This is almost over," he growled out. Landry knew by his tense manner he'd been as worried about Shelly's welfare as he was about Jet's.

"There's bad news," Adriana warned. "Someone in a wet suit was after Jet. I rushed back here to get y'all closer to them."

Perry Hammonds? Tension and dread slammed back into his chest and squeezed. "But Shelly and Lily are with her. Three against one are good odds. Plus, they're in their element. The diver isn't."

Tense silence greeted this remark. Hell, he didn't believe his own words. He surveyed the larger vessel and saw the men on board had finally noticed the small craft headed directly their way at top speed. Sons of bitches, all of them. Men with no morals or heart, willing to sell their own country short for a price.

Landry radioed his boss and reported their location. "Send in the coast guard or Homeland Security or whatever is closest. Vargas knows something's up and we have every reason to believe he and his men are armed and dangerous."

His boss started hammering questions, but Landry turned the radio off. He'd face his boss's ire and internal investigations when this was over. Details and explanations could wait. For now, all he cared about was saving Jet.

If he wasn't too late.

Chapter 18

He meant to kill her.

Jet whipped her tail fin and swam. Swam with all the speed and strength she'd honed from months of daily training for the Poseidon Games. She had been so close to a clean escape. She prayed Shelly and Lily were long gone and out of danger. *If anyone dies, let it be me.* All this was her fault; she'd brought this on herself and her family when she'd told Perry her secret and let him use her for his own selfish gains. Stupid, stupid, stupid.

Thrum-ripple. A spear whizzed less than three inches from her right ear. Had he aimed at her head or was it a bad shot on his part? The two-foot-long metal rod shot past and then lost velocity and fell harmlessly downward. If Perry tried to retrieve it and reload the gun, the party was over. He'd never catch up to her. She glanced back, dismayed to find Perry hadn't wasted time with the discharged spear, but swam toward her like a full-speed torpedo.

Ten feet ahead, Lily beckoned from underneath a boat, one graceful hand pointed at the aluminum hull. Almost home free! Jet surged ahead, racing. It was the only race that truly mattered. The Undines' Challenge at the Poseidon Games had been a mere dress rehearsal for this moment. The past hurt and injustices from the merfolk, her insecurity and worry about her heritage… none of it mattered.

Above water, Landry awaited. He was the world to her. In time, he'd see that she was worthy of his love. She would never, ever desert him like everyone else had in the past. All she needed was one more chance. Just one.

"Go away!" she screamed at Lily. "He's right behind me."

Instead of retreating, Lily surged toward her, eyes fixated at a point to Jet's right. Jet turned and saw another diver, armed with a speargun, had entered the fray. Vargas evidently didn't trust Perry to handle this job on his own.

Magical singing burst through every water molecule, a captivating cadence so lovely it lit the murky water like a street lantern enshrouded in fog. For a second, Lily was illuminated, the angelic wide eyes, flowing blond hair streaked with pink and lavender, Cupid's-bow lips and unblemished, alabaster skin that morphed at her hips into a glittering tail fin. The knife's blade in her right hand reflected particles of light, a beacon of justice.

The diver's eyes widened behind the mask and at last he raised the gun. His helmet had provided enough of a sound barrier that Lily's siren voice had neither immobilized nor enchanted him for long. A spear sped through the water, but Lily dodged it.

She had to help her sister. This whole mess was her fault; she'd put her family in danger. If they were harmed or killed, Jet could never forgive her foolish self. But before Jet caught up, Lily had swum up behind the diver and used the knife to saw through the diver's air hose. Bubbles exploded as the freed hose whipped and jerked like a furious eel. Her sister had the diver under control.

"Go!" Lily shouted. "Another diver's on your tail."

Jet swam upward, close to the water's surface. Small bubbling swirls from the boat's idling engine ceased. They must have spotted her and didn't want to chance the propellers getting in her way.

Another five feet and her fingertips could touch the boat. Landry's face came into view. His jaw was set in grim lines and his frosty blue eyes lasered in on her. Through rippling water, his face shifted and blurred, but always the blue of his eyes pierced through the muddy sediment like a homing beacon, calling her home.

Two feet away. Landry leaned overboard, strong arms extended, ready to pull her to safety. She could almost feel his strong, hot skin against her body, smell his clean, masculine scent as she nuzzled her nose into the curve between his neck and shoulder.

The world suddenly faded to black.

Firm pressure around the bottom of her tail fin pulled her down, away from the light. Jet twisted, propelling her arms up and away. The pressure released, but Perry emerged only an arm's distance away, exploding into her view like a sea monster from the deepest depths.

The rims of his brown irises glittered like burned topaz. Perry raised an arm, wielding a rubber-handled diving knife. It was long, hooked, lethally sharp—a fish-gutting dagger. A bluff? He'd never harmed her before but she'd never crossed him before, either. And he'd al-

ready come damned near to shooting her brains out with
the speargun. For a split-second, her brain processed the
danger and tried to plan an escape.

That was all the time Perry needed to lower the knife.
Jet jerked back, but she knew she had reacted too late as
her eyes tracked the blade's descent. She braced herself
for the inevitable pain.

It never came.

A body dropped between the exposed skin of her bare
shoulder and the knife's path. The weight knocked her
down and backward. Lily? No.

Her mouth dropped open at the sight of light brown
hair with the slight curling tips that brushed the wide
nape of his neck. No, Landry shouldn't be here. The sea
was her world.

The two men struggled, sinking lower as they pushed
and wrestled. One bone-shattering snap later, and the
knife spun out of Perry's hand. Jet watched, mesmerized,
as it twirled down, innocent as a majorette's minibaton
flipped skyward, glinting in the sun at a Saturday-morn-
ing football game. Falling, falling, right into Lily's out-
stretched hand.

Her sister, free of her attacker, had swum this way,
about a dozen yards beneath them.

Jet jerked her gaze back to Landry. Despite the un-
natural bend in Perry's right arm, Landry was losing the
fight. His large body was slumped, sinking under a bar-
rage of hits from Perry's one good hand.

He can't swim! Belatedly, Jet remembered Landry's
shamed admission. No wonder Perry was besting him.
It was an unfair fight.

Jet rushed over and thwacked her tail fin with all her
might, connecting with Perry's upper back. The oxygen tank ripped away from its moorings and sank. Perry

thrashed about, futilely trying to grab his fast-sinking lifeline.

She hadn't intentionally knocked off the air tank, but Perry was an excellent swimmer and they weren't deep. He could survive as long as he didn't panic and grow mentally confused. Jet spared Perry only a second; she firmly grasped his chin, making sure he made eye contact with her, and pointed upward. All the while, she kept her attention on Landry. He was the one in the greatest peril, and he was the one she loved. Landry's eyes bulged and he gulped copious amounts of water while uselessly flaying his arms and legs to stay afloat.

Jet shot past Perry and swam to him. She hooked an arm across Landry's waist, scooping him up and hurtling to the sea's surface with the speed of a dolphin. She breached the water and lifted his head out to take in oxygen. His face was gray, lips blue, eyes closed.

"Over here, quick!"

Jet wildly sought out the location of her mother's voice. Adriana waved from a small vessel. They were all there—Tillman, Shelly, Mom—but no Lily. Jet couldn't spare her sister another thought as she dragged Landry to the boat. Lily could take care of herself, always had.

Tillman grabbed underneath Landry's arms and heaved him on board while Mom and Shelly hovered over her as she climbed in. Shelly darted nervous glances over her shoulder.

"There's a nearby boat," she explained. "Can't let them see us in merform."

Vargas and his men. But Jet didn't worry about it. All her attention focused on Landry's inert body. Tillman rolled Landry onto his side and seawater spewed out his mouth. Jet sank to her knees, only vaguely aware of her mom's hands, dressing her as if she were a little child.

"There, there. I'm sure he's going to be fine," she whispered in a low, soothing tone. A cotton robe slipped against her skin. Her mom wiped clumps of wet hair from her face with a towel, then gently rubbed her scalp, drying the dripping hair.

Live. Damn it, live. Jet wrapped her arms around her waist and shivered violently. Shelly patted a knee, offering unspoken sympathy. Tillman administered CPR, alternately breathing into Landry's mouth and pumping his chest. Jet closed her eyes, unable to bear watching the trickle of brackish water run down the corners of Landry's mouth. Despite the midday sun, her chilled body shook uncontrollably.

Her mother, in a rare show of tenderness, engulfed Jet in her arms and rocked her like a baby. Jet clung to her, savoring her mom's strength. When she most needed them, her family had rallied behind her in their own special way.

"Where's Lily?" Shelly asked.

"Sh-she was fine when I saw her," Jet said between chattering teeth. "She was out of harm's w-way and Perry was—"

A large, hacking cough rent the air. Jet's eyes flew open. Landry lay propped on an elbow on one side, wheezing huge gulps of air into his lungs. Jet found it the most beautiful sound she'd ever heard, far lovelier than any siren's song. She crawled to him at once and ran her fingers down his unnaturally pale cheeks flecked with golden, morning stubble.

Landry's blue eyes opened at last, zeroing in on her. "You okay?" He frowned, looking over her body as if checking for wounds.

His voice was rough as sandpaper. The second most beautiful sound she'd ever heard in her life. The trembling and cold whooshed away in a warm wave of joyful release. "I'm fine, you fool." She sobbed and laughed at the same time. "What do you mean jumping in the ocean when you can't swim?"

"I saw Perry raise the knife and I had to stop him. I knew…" A large round of coughing racked his lungs before he continued, "I knew you'd save me."

Landry trusted her. That was a start, something she could work with. She'd prove to him every morning that she would stay for as long as he wished.

"Where's Perry?" Tillman cut in, looking in all directions.

The only answer was a faint lapping of waves licking the boat's hull. They all leaned over the side of the boat but the smooth, dark surface yielded no answer.

"Maybe I should go look for him," Jet said reluctantly.

A chorus of "No" greeted the lukewarm offer, along with a "Hell, no" from Landry, who gripped her arm. "Lily's down there," he said. "She can save him if he needs rescuing."

If Landry noticed an odd silence, or a furtive exchange of glances between the Bosarge women, he let it pass without comment.

A bullhorn sounded from around the bend, rousing everyone to action.

"The coast guard can search for Perry," Landry said, standing up. His legs were surprisingly wobbly but nothing would stop him from finishing this case.

Help had finally arrived and Landry smiled in grim satisfaction. He would take great pleasure in arresting Vargas. Their boat was close enough now he could see the panic of the men on board as they gathered on deck and gestured wildly with their hands. Vargas must be stunned that Jet had escaped and Perry was unaccounted for. Someone had pulled up the wire cable and the shark cage hung swaying and dripping in the breeze.

Empty.

"Time for me to get out of here and check on Lily," Adriana said. "You coming with us, Shell?"

Shelly placed a hand on Tillman's forearm. "We rented the boat in my name, so I better stick around or they'll ask questions about it later."

Landry's brows drew together. "Where are you going?"

"Swimming home, of course," Adriana answered matter-of-factly, then turned to address Shelly. "Good idea. Plus you'll have to return the rental car, as well."

"Home?" Landry repeated incredulously. "As in... swim all the way back to Bayou La Siryna?"

Adriana nodded. "Watch over Jet." She dived overboard in a perfect arch, leaving only the tiniest of splashes in her wake. Seconds later, her yellow cotton sundress bobbed on the mucky salt marsh like a happy daisy in a mud field.

"You'll get used to their ways," Tillman said drily. "Sort of."

The horn blew again, shaking Landry out of his mermaid musings. Time for that later. Now he needed to focus on his job. After years of tracking Vargas, the FBI needed a charge that would stick. They couldn't get him for illegal salvaging; he'd bet anything they had all the proper licenses and permissions in place. There was the kidnapping charge against Jet. But he'd rather leave her out of this matter, if possible. Jet and her family needed their anonymity to guard their secret race.

With all the men trapped on board, one of them was bound to talk and rat out Vargas's involvement in trying to get the bomb. But Vargas could always claim that if he found it, it was his intention all along to offer it to the United States government for a small reward.

How ironic if the only charge that stuck on Vargas turned out to be a murder or manslaughter charge on the missing Perry Hammonds. He radioed his boss. "Tell the coast guard we have a man-overboard situation."

Landry surveyed the muddy, salty water half expecting Hammonds to pop up like a monster creature from the black lagoon. Too much time had passed for a rescue, unless Lily or Adriana had taken pity on Perry and reattached his oxygen tank.

He rather hoped they hadn't.

Chapter 19

"So what happened to the bad dude?" Seth asked with wide eyes. "Did y'all ever find him?"

"Navy divers found Hammonds two days later, along with another one of Vargas's men," Landry reported with satisfaction. "Both drowned. One evidently had some equipment malfunction with his tank's air hose. Hammonds had been in a struggle and had a broken arm and a huge bruise on his upper back."

"Must have got in a fight on the ship and one of the other guys threw him overboard."

"That's the official theory on the final report." That report had tied him up for five days in Atlanta, days he'd much rather have spent with Jet.

"What about the bomb?"

Now, *that* was the million-dollar question. Homeland Security sent a letter to the FBI stating that Jim Tindol's claims were unsubstantiated, although in Landry's mind, all the government agencies involved had given up rather quickly on the search.

Officially, that was.

"Nothing found," he said. "But at least Vargas is in custody and charged with kidnapping and manslaughter. His international crime ring will be easier to dismantle with their boss put away."

Seth frowned. "Don't see why they had to take Jet."

Landry stole a sideways glance at his puzzled face. Would he and Jet be able to guard her secret around one very curious, constantly underfoot teenager?

"She and Perry used to be partners and he convinced everyone that Jet's underwater skills could prove useful." Underwater skills…understatement of the millennium.

"Jet's cool. I hope she's okay."

Bubbles of uncertainty skittered in his gut. During their brief late-night calls over the past few days, there had been some emotional undertone, some nuance in Jet's voice he couldn't quite decipher. "Says she's all right when we talk on the phone."

"But you don't believe it."

"Jet's the strongest woman I've ever met, but she went through major trauma. And it doesn't help she's alone right now."

Seth straightened. "Where are Lily and Shelly?" he asked with way too much interest.

"Shelly's off with Tillman and Lily…" Landry strummed his fingers on the steering wheel. "Lily went on a long trip with her mother."

Seth leaned back in his seat, clearly disappointed.

Landry wondered, yet again, what the hell had happened at the bottom of that Tybee Island salt marsh. Had Lily killed Perry? Or perhaps she had merely let him drown, watching the oxygen bubbles from Perry's lips slowly trickle to nothing while she held the oxygen tank with that blank, serene gaze and slight upturn of her lush lips. And what had happened to the other dead diver? Malfunctioned diver equipment, his ass.

He shifted uncomfortably in his seat. Maybe he judged Lily unfairly. Truth was, he didn't want or need to know what happened down there. Jet and Lily had been under attack while undersea—it was their world, a mermaid realm. *Not my jurisdiction,* he thought wryly. All that mattered was that they were alive and safe.

Landry whipped the BMW into a used-car lot on the outskirts of Bayou La Siryna.

"Why are we stopping here?" Seth asked. "Thought you were in a hurry to get home."

"If you're coming to stay with me for good, we need another set of wheels."

Twenty minutes later, Landry signed the papers on a slightly rusted pickup truck that was over ten years old. Outside the dealership, he tossed a set of keys to his brother. "It's all yours."

Seth gave a tentative smile. "I'll pay you back one day." He took a few steps toward the truck, then turned back to Landry. "Wait. Wrong keys."

"Truck's mine," Landry said. "If I'm going to become a local here, this truck's more practical."

"So, you're going to let *me* drive your car?"

"It's not mine anymore. I'm giving you the BMW. When we get home, sign it and the car's officially yours."

Seth stood immobile, frowning. Hardly the reaction Landry had expected.

"Why are you doing this for me?" his brother asked suspiciously. "What do you want?"

Patience. The kid hasn't had much experience with kindness. Landry put his hands on his hips. "I want you to be honest with me, attend classes next fall and stay out of trouble."

"That's it?"

"Yep."

Seth nodded, serious. "I can do that." He walked to him and extended his right hand. "Thanks, bro."

Seth didn't make the usual "half brother" reference. Landry clasped his hand. "Get out of here," he grinned. "And no speeding. I know the sheriff here, but he doesn't cut me any deals."

Seth got in the car and carefully backed up in the gravel parking lot. Landry motioned for him to let down the window. "Do me a favor. Run by Jet's shop and see if she needs help with anything. Tell her I'll be along in a bit."

Seth gave a mock salute. "Okay, then I'm going to see Jimmy. Wait until he gets a load of my wheels."

"Tell his grandma thanks for keeping an eye on the kittens." Baby Girl had delivered a litter of six while he was away at the FBI office in Atlanta. He owed her big-time.

Landry waved and headed for his new-to-him truck. Maybe the big-brother-role-model thing wouldn't be as hard as he feared. After all—

The screech of tires peeling onto blacktop brought Landry up short and he spun in time to see gray gravel spitting on the road. Over four-hundred horsepower of German engineering roared off.

On second thought, coaching Seth through another year of high school might be the most difficult job he'd ever tackled.

After years of driving a smooth, sleek sports car, the truck would take some getting used to. He felt every bump in the road on the way to Bayou La Siryna Water Park. Landry navigated through the numerous potholes, parked by the entrance, and followed a group of chattering middle-school kids and their chaperones as they skipped inside. Before he spoke to the owner, he wanted to see Dolly. He waited patiently in line to pay, listening to the kids' chatter. The dolphin was quite the draw; no wonder Andrew Morgan kept it around.

He took in the cracked pavement, sinking pool liners and faded umbrellas. The park was tidy and clean, but old and in need of repairs. Ticket paid, he followed the kids again to the saltwater pool. A man in bathing trunks and a Bayou La Siryna Water Park T-shirt was at the side of the pool with buckets of fish.

"Welcome," he bellowed. "Y'all ready to feed Dolly?"

The kids scrambled for the buckets. In the far right corner, taking up nearly a third of the pool space, a large silver blob lolled underwater. Even to his untrained eye, Landry could see the pool was too small and inadequate. No wonder Jet worried about the dolphin.

As minnows were thrown in, Dolly ambled toward the kids.

"Don't throw out all the fish at once," the trainer said. "Let's see if we can get Dolly to perform some tricks first." He waited until Dolly gobbled up the fish already thrown in, then held up a bright red hula hoop.

Dolly ignored him.

One eager red-haired boy sank to his knees and leaned out so far over the pool, a whisper of wind could knock him over. "Can we go for a dolphin ride?"

The other kids squealed and clapped.

"Oh, I don't know about that," one of the teachers said, frowning. "Could be dangerous."

The trainer rushed to reassure her. "We don't have insurance in place yet for rides, but we're working on it."

The teacher's face smoothed. "Not today, kids," she announced.

Amid a chorus of boos, Landry left. He was doing the right thing today. Before seeking Andrew's office, he went back to the park entrance and scanned the parking lot. A large van marked Aquatic Rescue Operations pulled in. An entourage of three more vans and trucks snaked in behind it.

Landry hurried to the manager's office and rapped sharply on the door before entering. A bearded, lean guy, in his mid-fifties or so, glanced up from a pile of paperwork. Landry automatically reached in his back pocket for his FBI badge, only to realize before his hand hit his pocket that it wasn't there. Old habits would take a while to break.

"I'm here to transport your dolphin to a wildlife refuge." He put an authoritative command into his voice, born of over a decade in law-enforcement training.

"Wh-what?" The man jumped to his feet. "You can't do that. Who do you think you are?"

"I'm the new deputy sheriff in Bayou La Siryna." Or at least he would be as soon as he got to Tillman's office and filled out the paperwork.

"I ain't broke no laws." Andrew looked more scared than angry, despite the bluster.

"I'm sure you haven't." Landry paused for effect. "Not knowingly."

"What do you mean?"

"I mean that there've been several complaints about the dolphin's housing." Landry glanced out the window. A crew of over a dozen muscular men exited parked vehicles and made their way to the entrance. "You've violated a host of marine-mammal protection laws."

"I—I didn't mean to," Andrew said. "I took her in after she was injured and beached. I'd never hurt her."

The man's eyes were huge. Landry read a flash of guilt in them along with a huge dose of nervousness. He lowered his voice, tinged it with understanding. "I'm sure you never meant to," he agreed. "But over the winter season, Dolly became a tourist draw, a way of bringing in needed money at a time when you normally don't have business. Now with warmer weather arriving, you see the potential profits she can bring your park."

Andrew folded his arms. "I take good care of her."

"No. No, you don't."

"Who says I don't? Bring—"

"Did you know she was pregnant?' Landry cut in.

The man's mouth dropped open. "How would you know?"

"Didn't think you did." Landry pointed to the men approaching the entry. "These men are going to transport Dolly to a safe home in Florida." He leaned over Andrew's desk. "You're a decent man, Andrew. You want what's best for her and this is it."

Andrew hung his head and sighed deeply.

Landry straightened. "Look at it this way. Let these trained professionals rescue Dolly and not only have you done the right thing, but you'll also save yourself from huge fines and a ton of bad publicity."

Andrew nodded slowly. "Yeah, guess you're right."

Landry went to the door and motioned the crew leader inside the office. "The owner will sign off on any paperwork you need."

Outside, most of the schoolkids had already tired of the lethargic Dolly and headed for the bathrooms to change into their bathing suits for a swim. The rescue workers expertly carried over a huge nylon sling. Landry knew from his research that Dolly would be hoisted to a saltwater vat and placed in a padded fiberglass transport unit to make the nine-hour trip. The mammal would be stressed by the journey, but after today, she and her unborn calf would be healthier and happier.

They'd better be. A huge portion of his savings had been donated to the Florida Aquatic Wildlife Center to make it happen.

Three days without Landry felt like three years. Jet listlessly ran a dust rag over a shelf. The morning had been filled with easy, mindless tasks, mere final touches before The Pirate's Chest's grand opening. Yet she was tired, drained, as if her body still hadn't recovered from the arduous return home after the stress at Tybee Island.

The front doorbell chimed. Jet laid down the rag and turned. "We're not open—" She stopped speaking as the wall of fury came her way. It took a moment to recognize him in street clothes. She couldn't recall ever seeing him dressed in anything except the Englazia County sheriff's uniform.

Carl Dismukes got within three feet and stopped, waving a gnarled finger in her face. Jet blankly took in the nicked fingers from years of whittling, and other fine, white scars at the base of his fingers—scars from plastic surgery to correct a congenital disorder. Like so many other bayou residents, he was born with webbed fingers and the soft tissue between the digits had been removed. Unlike most of the other bayou residents, Carl knew the webbing came from mermaid ancestry.

"This is all your fault," he growled. "What did you tell Tillman about me?"

Jet slapped his hand away with enough force to show she was no pushover. "It was bound to come out one day. You're lucky you got away with blackmail all these years."

"Lucky?" His face reddened. "There was no *lucky* to it. I'm a hell of a lot smarter than that dumbass sheriff and his dead daddy that held the job before Tillman took over."

"Shut up, Carl. Tillman's almost family."

"Did you tell your new boyfriend about me?"

"Not about your mermaid heritage. Only that you're a corrupt, untrustworthy, backstabbing crook."

He angrily ran a hand through his silver, short-cropped hair.

Jet lifted her chin. She was finally free. "You don't have anything on me anymore. Now get out of my store."

His face reddened even more, hands fisted at his sides. Carl lowered his voice to a growl. "Better watch your back from now on, bitch." He backed away with one last sneer and left.

She let him have the last word, ready for the confrontation to end. As the chimes announced his retreat, Jet sank into a chair. The air compressed in on her and she took a deep breath to counteract the swimming lightness in her body. What the hell was wrong with her today? She wiped tears off her cheeks with a rough fist. This was stupid. Resolutely, she went to the restroom and splashed water on her face. A few more details to take care of and she'd close shop.

When she reentered the store, Seth was at the counter, eyeing the antique swords. He looked up with a grin that washed away as he studied her face. "Have you been *crying?*" he asked with such a look of horror that she laughed, her spirits lifted.

"I'm fine," she answered, waving a hand dismissively. "I've been alone at the house too much." She looked past him and spotted the BMW parked across the street. Her heart lightened and beat faster. "Where's your brother?"

"He had a couple errands to run." Seth followed her gaze. "Oh, that's my car now."

"Really?" Landry was so proud of that car.

"He bought a used truck. Said it was more practical."

After all the cracks he made about her old beater? She grinned.

"He wanted me to stop by and see if you needed me for anything."

Seth's animated face was so different from the first time she met him. Landry had told her his brother was moving in. No doubt Seth was happy with the arrangement. "No, go enjoy your car."

Relief washed across his face. Really, teenagers could be so comically transparent. "I'm going to Jimmy's now," he said. "Got a big weekend planned."

Jet stood. "I'm going to start my weekend early, too, and head home."

She grabbed her purse, locked up and got into her truck. The day was sunshiny and held a humidity that hinted at the coming summer meltdown, which lasted from June until practically Christmas.

She went past the downtown mermaid statue, its eternally perfect face staring out to sea. The smooth stone, steel and copper facade, as familiar to her as the sight of her own home, hit her with an unforeseen poignancy that had her eyes watering—again. Hell, this wasn't like her. She was happy, damn it. By tonight, she'd see Landry, be able to hold him in her arms and not just hear his deep, sexy voice on the phone. Jet put in a Lynyrd Skynyrd CD. The upbeat Southern anthem of "Sweet Home Alabama" always lifted her spirits.

Tapping her fingers on the steering wheel, Jet drove

mindlessly out of town and into the rural landscape of lush live oaks draped with Spanish moss like long, dangling earrings. She unrolled her window, letting in the tang of brine that wafted in the breeze, a scent as familiar and deep-rooted as soap and baby powder. Birds and bullfrogs and crickets played background to Skynyrd's melody.

An unseen force guided her hands and she drove past Perry's old cottage rental. In the driveway, the red Mustang sat like an abandoned orphan. She'd been in touch with Perry's mother. His body had been shipped home to Pennsylvania and Mrs. Hammonds would arrive next week to take care of what little remained of Perry's last worldly possessions.

A memory tugged like an undertow, pulling her down into the past. Perry, dark hair whipping in the wind, grinning and waving at her on the dock, the first time she laid eyes on him. The promise of fun and adventure in his wide smile that had beckoned her.

She swallowed past the painful sting in her throat, emotions churning chaotically. At one time, he'd had some goodness, and that was what she'd try to remember—the laughter in his eyes on day one, not the flashing hatred in those same eyes on his last day on earth.

Jet reached home, even more exhausted from memories of Perry. She unlocked the door and entered the too-quiet house. Rebel finally roused from somewhere and ran to her, barking. He launched himself at her feet and lay on his back, exposing a hairless, extremely freckled tummy. She rubbed him while he made high-pitched moans of delight. He'd been good company while the family was gone.

The thing to do was take a little nap, get refreshed before seeing Landry tonight. The promise and anticipation of the night lifted her spirits. As lonely as the house had been with everyone away, the good news was that she and Landry would have privacy. She finally reached her bedroom, stripped down to a pair of panties and threw on an oversize T-shirt. At last, she sank into the mattress, curling into herself like a child under the cool cotton sheets. Rebel lay at the foot of the bed, immediately settling into snoring slumber. Delightful lethargy descended and she relaxed into a dream.

Water surrounded her body and she drifted—content to let the tide take her in any direction. Bits of seaweed brushed against her arms like the touch of a friend in greeting. Fish swished past, paying her no attention in their endless hunt for food. Jet wiggled her tail fin, admiring the shimmering colors against the turquoise waters. She surrendered to the sea's surge, the constant to-and-fro of the tide, the pull of the moon, the mysteries of the deep. Her belly distended and she placed one arm under her lower tummy and the other across the top in a loving, protective, gesture borne by women down the ages as they cradled...

Jet came to with a startled intake of breath. No. It couldn't be. Could it? She rubbed a hand over her flat, muscular abs. Of course it was possible. TRABs like Shelly weren't uncommon. Jet winced at even thinking the slur name for halflings. She never considered them "traitor babies" unlike so many of her kind.

"It's a dream," she said aloud. "I am *not* pregnant." Even she could hear the fear underlying the denial. She flung off the sheets and went to the window, surprised that twilight approached. She'd slept for hours. And wasn't *that* telling. She crossed her arms and rubbed them. No need for panic until she knew something for sure. She'd get dressed, run to the drugstore and....

A loud knock at the door made her jump. It had to be Landry. Rebel's ears perked and he ran downstairs, barking and growling. She glanced in the mirror, running hands through her mussed hair. She frowned at the reflection, at the fear and worry banked in her eyes. That wouldn't do. The last thing she needed was Landry pestering her to tell him what was wrong. No need to bother him until she knew for sure one way or another. Jet gave a mechanical smile at the mirror, but it only marginally improved the effect. It would have to do.

She raced downstairs and stood at the door. "Who is it?" she called out.

"It's me. Landry."

Just the sound of his voice sent eager tingles from her toes to her scalp. The past few days had been a lonely hell without him. "Stay," she ordered Rebel before flinging the door open.

His tall, lean body filled the doorframe. In one hand he carried a mass of red roses.

"For me?" she squeaked. No one had ever brought her flowers. *Ever.* Her vision blurred with dumb tears. Until this moment, she hadn't realized that such a quaint, romantic gesture could reduce her to a quivering mush of joy, that it was something she'd love.

Damn, she loved this man.

Jet took one of his arms and drew him inside. Landry bent and offered his hand to the growling Rebel.

"We've met before, ole boy," he said softly. "Remember?"

Rebel sniffed and poked his malformed face into Landry's palm. Even Reb, leery of strangers, apparently loved this guy.

She had to tell him. Jet took a deep breath. Why was this so hard to do? She couldn't ever remember telling anyone she loved them, except maybe her mom when she was little. "I—I, um…"

He waited, roses in hand.

"You know that I…" Again, the words failed to come.

His jaw clenched and his blue eyes darkened with intensity. "You love me."

She gulped and nodded. Landry had figured it out, just as he'd been able to deduce she was a mermaid without her saying a word. "Do you—"

"Yes. Hell, yes."

Jet threw her arms around his neck. "I love you, too," she mumbled, burying her face in his broad chest.

Oh, the things she wanted to do with him and for him. She inhaled his clean, masculine scent, which intermingled with the roses. She tightened her arms around his lower back and hugged him fiercely. He kissed the top of her head, his warm breath heating her scalp, a previously undiscovered erogenous zone. One hand raked through her hair, the other pressed against her lower back.

Rebel jumped on their legs and pawed. Jet didn't let go of Landry as she pushed open the screen door with a leg. "Go outside."

Reb shot through the opening and she closed it behind him. She pressed against Landry hard enough that his back crushed the door.

He chuckled. "I take it you missed me, too," he said.

The rumble of his voice vibrated deep in his chest, and she pictured the amused smile on the face that was buried in her hair.

"Not a bit," she denied. "I didn't miss these cute curls—" her fingers played with the ends of his hair "—or these lips—" she traced his mouth with a fingertip and a chaste kiss "—or, you know, this hot body of yours." She ran her hands down his chest and gave him a once-over stare.

"Liar." He held out the flowers. "But you still get roses."

Jet accepted them and closed her eyes as she inhaled their bouquet. "Thank you. They're beautiful."

"Not half as beautiful as you." There was no trace of a smile on his face.

"Oh," she breathed. He was truly at least a little in love to think so. If she was in a beauty contest with Lily, Shelly and other mermaids, well, she couldn't even win Miss Congeniality with her acerbic personality. Now that Landry was staying permanently in Bayou La Siryna, maybe in time she could prove to him that he could count on her forever. She wouldn't disappoint him like so many others in his past. That was, if he didn't bolt at the *p* word.

"Something wrong?" he asked.

Jet shook her head, appalled he could read her emotions so easily.

"You've been through so much, it's perfectly understandable." His mouth tightened. "Perry's death must be hard to deal with."

"No. There was nothing between us for years. I do feel sorry for his mother, though. She doted on him."

"You sure?"

Landry's hesitation and vulnerability undid her. "I'm sure," she said huskily. And she would make him understand that, would love him like no one else. Jet kissed him; her tongue probed the warm slickness of his mouth. The contact sent flaming arrows down to her core and dampness pooled in her panties. She whimpered, a needy sound from the back of her throat.

His hands cupped her ass and he groaned. "You're so damn hot," he muttered.

Jet wasn't sure she could make it all the way upstairs to the bedroom. She wanted him now. She jerked away and took his hand. "This way." She dragged him into the living room and shoved a mound of sea-treasure books to the floor. She carefully placed the roses on the coffee table and lay on the soft cushions, arms reaching upward for Landry.

He slowly lowered his body on top of hers, bearing most of his weight on his elbows. Jet arched her hips against him and felt his body's hard response to her own. She kissed him eagerly, her hands at the back of his neck, urging him deeper as their tongues collided.

"I missed you," he said in a ragged breath. One hand traveled up her rib cage and cupped her breast. "Missed this." He squeezed a nipple between his thumb and index finger, making her insides clench. His mouth replaced his fingers and he suckled her, dampening the cotton fabric of her T-shirt.

More. She wanted so much more. Landry switched his attention to her other nipple and she groaned. She tugged at the waistband of his jeans.

He stood and unfastened his belt, eyes riveted on her. It was the sexiest thing she'd ever seen. With no trace of embarrassment, he pulled off his jeans and boxers at the same time, then removed his shirt.

"Your turn," he said succinctly.

There was no more need for pretense or subterfuge. He knew all her secrets. Except, she corrected herself, perhaps one teeny, tiny secret. Jet immediately thrust it from her mind. Time to sort all that out later. Right now, her body was on fire for Landry. Jet pulled the T-shirt over her head and wiggled out of the panties.

A warm, slightly callused hand stroked the gill markings on the side of her neck. "Do these bother you?" he asked matter-of-factly.

She searched his face closely, looking for any sign of distaste. "No. Do they bother you?"

"Of course not." He leaned over and brushed a gentle kiss on the scars.

Jet's stiff spine relaxed under the caress. And again, she was caught off guard at the tightness in her throat and the tears pooling in her eyes.

"Are you sure nothing's wrong?" he asked again.

She stroked the inside of his thigh, working her way up until she cupped him. "You talk too much," she whispered.

"Yessss," he hissed. "God, it feels so good."

Jet explored his long shaft with a featherlight touch. Landry placed his hands over hers and squeezed. "Harder."

His face scrunched in an agony of pleasure that turned her on as much as his caresses. The last time they'd been intimate, they'd been in the cramped car and he had pleasured her. Now it was her turn. Jet placed her mouth where her hands had been and her tongue fondled his manhood.

Landry pulled away and leaned his face down by her belly button. "I want to taste you." His hot breath fanned her stomach as he traced light kisses downward. When he reached her core, Jet shuddered with anticipation. His tongue found her wetness and she was lost. The center of her world, all that mattered, was the desperate fury for release. His finger entered her and she bucked.

"Now," she commanded. "I want you in me."

Landry grabbed his jeans and pulled out a condom. "We weren't careful the first time."

No shit. What would he say if she was pregnant?

He ripped the foil and quickly put it on. The moment he entered her, Jet's worry dissolved into a storm of need. He drove into her hard, fast, and it was even better than the first time. Landry matched her passion. Watching his face tighten with need fed her own desire until the unbearable tension released into a climax.

Jet held Landry close as his body immediately found its own release. Afterward, they lay entwined and she lazily rubbed the insole of one foot up and down one of his muscled calves. Landry lazily surveyed the living room. "Everything's so shiny in this room."

"You mean like...clean?" she asked, puzzled.

"No." He rubbed his jaw. "Must be all the mirrors."

It was true. Mirrored tiles banked a large part of the back wall and silver lay scattered everywhere—from the large antique tea-serving set to silver-handled brushes and combs. Funny, she'd never noticed before. Small wonder her family loved this room. They could sit and surreptitiously preen for hours at their lovely reflections.

Unfair? Perhaps in Shelly's case. But not for the full-blooded mermaid Bosarges, especially Lily. Not even the teeniest drop of jealousy trickled through her mind. Let them have their vanity. Jet ran a hand down Landry's hip. As long as he thought she was gorgeous, it didn't matter how she stacked up against other mermaids.

And even with their vanity and somewhat privileged airs, her family had come through for her in the end when her life was in danger. If not for Lily, she'd never have escaped that dark salt marsh alive. They loved her in their own way.

A high-pitched whining accompanied a scratching at the front door. Jet reluctantly got up and pulled the crumpled T-shirt over her head. "Guess I better let Rebel in. He won't shut up until I do."

Landry stretched out on the sofa, hands behind his head. Jet sucked in her breath. The sight of him stretched out buck-naked in her living room made her insides tighten with desire all over again.

"Aren't you getting the door?" he asked, amusement lacing his voice. He knew damned well the effect he had on her.

Jet let in Rebel, who rushed past her to his food bowl in the kitchen. The mutt was always hungry. Hell, so was she. Starving, actually. "How about I fry us some shrimp?" she asked Landry, who was up and dressing.

"We can grab a bite on the way out."

"Out where?"

"I've got a surprise for you." He buckled his belt and sat down to put on shoes. "Thought it would be fun to take a little vacation after the craziness of last week." He held up a hand, as if to forestall any objection she might have. "Only a couple of days. You'll be back in time for your store opening."

It sounded like a lot of bother. "But we could hang out here all weekend. I've got the house to myself."

"I've made the arrangements already," he argued. "C'mon. It'll be fun. I promise."

"If you have your heart set on it," she said, trying to muster some enthusiasm. She'd rather have spent the weekend in bed, just the two of them. Her family came and went at unpredictable times and now that Seth would be staying with Landry, it might be hard to have privacy. "Where are we going?"

"Florida." He glanced at his watch. "Pack light, nothing fancy. I've got a room reserved."

Jet stifled a sigh. "Give me a minute to pack." She

started up the stairs and then paused. "Besides grabbing some gas-station fried chicken on the way, I need to stop at the drugstore."

Epilogue

Moonlight flickered like fairy dust on the gentle sea swells. A few small boats were tethered to a wooden pier along the small harbor.

"Why are we stopping here? It's—" Jet checked the radio on the truck's dashboard "—almost one o'clock in the freaking morning." They'd driven for hours yesterday, spent the night at a motel and hit the road again this morning, leisurely stopping in scenic coastal towns to eat or shop.

"There's an envelope in the glove box. Hand it to me." His voice sounded tight with either worry or excitement, she couldn't determine which.

She found it and handed it over. "What gives?"

"Got a little surprise for you," he said, ripping it open and pulling out a set of keys. "Let's go."

She followed him out of the truck. "We're going on

a boat ride? Now?" This made no sense. They both had boats at home. No novelty there.

"Trust me." He grabbed her hand and pulled her onto the dock, surveying the boats until he found the one he wanted. "Here it is." They climbed aboard the small craft, Landry dutifully putting on a life jacket.

"I'll have to teach you to swim. It might be the only perk of having a mermaid girlfriend."

He grinned, obviously enjoying some secret surprise. She'd play along.

Landry started the engine and they shot forward. Jet closed her eyes, enjoying the rush of salty air. Only minutes later, Landry shut off the motor. "This should be the place, as far as I can tell anyway."

"Okay. What gives? Did you bring me out here to secretly kill me?" she teased. "'Cause if you did, drowning a mermaid isn't the brightest idea for a former FBI man. I expected better."

"Especially since you're stronger than I, and I can't swim," he agreed. Landry took her hands in his. "I know how much you worry about Dolly."

Jet didn't know what she had expected, but Dolly hadn't entered her mind. "And?"

"She's here."

Jet jumped up and spun in a circle, looking for Dolly to breach the water. "Really?" Seeing nothing, she faced Landry. "Explain, please."

"This is an aquatic-wildlife refuge. They take injured or mistreated sea lions and dolphins and provide a home and safe care for them."

She wanted to believe him. "But how?"

"There's over ninety thousand square feet of seawater lagoons here with low fences that separate them from the open waters of the gulf. They're protected from predators, but the fence still lets in fish and other marine life they need for food. A natural tidal wash flushes the lagoons daily. A lot more hygienic than Andrew Morgan's setup at home."

Her mouth dropped open. She'd never heard of such a place. "Will they take care of her forever?"

"That's up to Dolly. They've already examined her and found she's a bit malnourished and weak, but she should recover quickly. After her calf is born, they'll open the fence and give her the option of returning to the open sea to find a maternity pod that will accept them, or she can stay here."

"I want to see her."

Landry gestured at the sea. "Go ahead. We should be near the fence."

She hastily stripped, leaned over and kissed his mouth. "I love you," she said. It felt wonderful to say the words out loud, not hard at all. "I love you, love you, love you," she repeated for good measure.

"I know." He tapped her lightly on the ass. "Go say hello to your friend. She's probably stressed after the move."

Jet eagerly poised on the edge of the boat to dive.

"Have fun and take your time," she heard Landry say before she dived in and the water enveloped her. Legs instantly morphed to tail fin and the nictitating membrane covered her eyes. She adjusted to the low light and spied the fence, only a few yards away.

"Dolly," she called out, swimming over the fence. "It's me, Jet." She swam close to the ground. The lagoon pools were blasted out of coral and were fairly shallow, anywhere from a few feet deep to about twenty feet deep.

Water vibrated with the approach of several dolphins, clicking away in their undersea language. Jet had no idea what they were saying, but knew curiosity drove them to check out this new addition to their world. "I come in peace," she said. They wouldn't understand her words any better than she did theirs, but her calm voice would show she bore no ill will. "I'm looking for my friend. She's new here." Jet rubbed her belly. "She's pregnant, too."

One of the dolphins, missing a dorsal fin, gestured with its beak for her to follow. Could he have possibly understood? She would never bet against a dolphin's intelligence. She swam in its wake, repeatedly calling out Dolly's name.

A faint, warbling cry arose from one of the deepest lagoons and Jet swam to it.

A large gray shape came into view. She'd recognize Dolly anywhere. Jet let out a gasp of delight. "It's me, Dolly. Are you okay?" She went closer, extending a hand. Dolly perked up and pushed her beak into Jet's palm. "It's okay, baby. You're going to be fine." Jet stroked her smooth head. Minutes passed as Jet tried to convey to Dolly that all would be well.

Clickclickclickclickclickclick.

Several dolphins came their way, gently brushing against Dolly's side. The one with the missing dorsal fin blew bubble rings at Dolly's face.

"See?" said Jet. "He wants to play and be your friend."

After much coaxing, Dolly responded to the other dolphins' gestures of acceptance.

Time for her to leave. Jet slowly backed away. Although relieved to see Dolly in her natural environment, she would miss her. Jet waited until she caught Dolly's eye, then waved goodbye with a forced smile. She abruptly turned and headed toward the fence. As she breached the fence and reached the boat, Dolly came up from behind, clicking excitedly.

Jet eyed her, the fence between them. "Go back," she said. "I'll visit you again if you decide to stay."

Dolly regarded her a moment and dipped her head once before turning to rejoin her own kind.

Jet burst out of the sea, startling Landry. She slipped aboard, fins shifting to legs. Her face heated in embarrassment. Landry had seen her naked many times, but never in merform.

"That's amazing. *You* are amazing." He shook his head, looking stunned at the transformation.

He'd get used to it.

"Thank you," she began. "I don't know how you arranged all this, but you're wonderful. No one has ever done anything like this for me before." The niggling doubts about their future were wiped away by this one act.

"Happy?" he asked.

"Extremely. You know what they say. Good things always come in threes."

"What do you mean?"

Jet held up a hand and ticked off her fingers. "First, I discovered Dolly was with calf. Two, you found a cat about to have babies. And three…" She let the night's silence settle over them.

His brows drew together. She watched as understanding dawned. "Do you mean what I think you mean?" he asked cautiously.

"Yep." She went to him and nuzzled her face in the crook of his neck. "You okay with that?"

Landry crushed her in a fierce hug, then abruptly held her at arm's length. "I didn't hurt you, did I?" He looked down at her stomach.

"I couldn't be better. Or happier," she assured him.

Landry sank to one knee. "In that case…marry me, Jet."

Bliss bubbled inside her like an underwater spring. And she'd thought the roses had been the grandest romantic gesture of all time. This was more than she'd ever dared dream. A man who loved her and a child on the way. A real family.

Jet sank to her knees and took his hands in hers, felt the hot strength of him travel through her fingers and palms. "Yes," she said, loud and clear in the dark night.

The boat's engine revved up in three loud, quick bursts. "What the hell?" Landry looked over his shoulder at the dashboard and patted the front pocket of his jeans. "The key's here, not in the ignition," he said slowly.

Jet waved and blew a kiss into the wind. "Then I'm guessing your sister is letting us know she approves of our engagement."

Dolphins splashed nearby, as if sensing her joy. "I love you," she added. Those three words came so easily now. She'd tell Landry that every day, the rest of their lives.

Forever.

* * * * *

MILLS & BOON®

'Tis the season to be daring...

The perfect books for all your glamorous Christmas needs come complete with gorgeous billionaire bad-boy heroes and are overflowing with champagne!

These fantastic 3-in-1s are must-have reads for all Modern™, Desire™ and Modern Tempted™ fans.

**Get your copies today at
www.millsandboon.co.uk/Xmasmod**

MILLS & BOON®

Want to get more from Mills & Boon?

Here's what's available to you if you join the exclusive **Mills & Boon eBook Club** today:

✦ *Convenience – choose your books each month*

✦ *Exclusive – receive your books a month before anywhere else*

✦ *Flexibility – change your subscription at any time*

✦ *Variety – gain access to eBook-only series*

✦ *Value – subscriptions from just £1.99 a month*

So visit **www.millsandboon.co.uk/esubs** today to be a part of this exclusive eBook Club!